IN THE
ORBIT
OF
YOU

also by
Ashley Schumacher

Amelia Unabridged
Full Flight
The Renaissance of Gwen Hathaway

IN THE
ORBIT
OF
YOU

a novel

Ashley
Schumacher

WEDNESDAY BOOKS
NEW YORK

First published in the United States by Wednesday Books, an imprint of St. Martin's Publishing Group

IN THE ORBIT OF YOU. Copyright © 2024 by Ashley Schumacher. All rights reserved. Printed in the United States of America. For information, address St. Martin's Publishing Group, 120 Broadway, New York, NY 10271.

www.wednesdaybooks.com

Designed by Devan Norman

The Library of Congress Cataloging-in-Publication Data is available upon request.

ISBN 978-1-250-88604-0 (hardcover)
ISBN 978-1-250-88605-7 (ebook)

Our books may be purchased in bulk for promotional, educational, or business use. Please contact your local bookseller or the Macmillan Corporate and Premium Sales Department at 1-800-221-7945, extension 5442, or by email at MacmillanSpecialMarkets@macmillan.com.

First Edition: 2024

10 9 8 7 6 5 4 3 2 1

*To my fellow Texans and editorial fairy godmothers,
Vicki Lame and Vanessa Aguirre, with all my
thanks for turning my stories from pumpkins
into the loveliest of carriages.*

*And to the entire team at Wednesday Books—past and
present—for making sure I didn't trip on my dress and
that I knew how to get to the ball on time. You have
made the last five years my most magical yet.*

Thank you.

IN THE
ORBIT
OF
YOU

The Beginning

All stories have lore to them, even the boring, ordinary ones. It's part of the pattern, you see. No story—the fairy tales, the epics, the anecdotes we share across dinner tables and text messages—exists in a void. Everything comes from something.

And this something, this story, came from beneath a giant oak tree. The place doesn't matter. (It might have been Florida or Kentucky or Colorado.) The weather doesn't matter. (It could have been snowing or sunny or completely still.)

What mattered—and matters still—were the two tiny heads crammed together beneath the oak tree, her stick-straight pigtails catching in his little-boy curls as they observed the progress of the town they aptly named Snailopolis.

"Fredrick is missing," the girl said, her voice sad.

"He's not," the boy replied, holding a white shell between dirty fingers. "He's right here."

"That's not Fredrick. Fredrick has a crack on top."

"Does not," the boy said.

"Does too," the girl said.

When the boy leaned forward to put the snail in her hand, a jagged red line peeped out from beneath his sleeve. It made the girl stop worrying about Fredrick the snail. The marks and bruises the boy tried so hard to hide unfailingly made everything else leave her head. There was only room for him.

The girl did what she always did when she noticed the marks: She leaned forward and kissed his palm—the closest thing to this particular line without actually touching it—and whispered, "It goes where it needs to go."

The boy nodded and said what he always said: "It feels better already."

Like most myths and legends, this one is blurry around the edges. There might have been a great many things that happened between the disappearance of Fredrick the snail and the displacement of the boy who named him. Maybe a teacher noticed the boy's marks *and alerted the authorities. Maybe it was the boy's uncle. Maybe it was a combination of things.*

What matters is that one day the boy and girl were the king and queen of Snailopolis; the next, the boy stood beneath the oak tree with his arms folded and looked down at the girl through the hole in the fence and his freshly bruised eye and said, "I have to go."

She scrambled to her feet, forgetting the snails entirely. "But why?"

The boy didn't want to say, but he did anyway. "I'm moving away," he said. "To live with my uncle."

The girl didn't understand—not really—so she did the only thing she knew to do: She cried. And then, crying still, she flung her arms around his neck and cried some more.

Because they were the rulers of Snailopolis. Because they were best friends. Because who would be there to kiss his hand and make him feel better if she wasn't there? Who would find the snails she lost?

"But why do you have to go?" she said, sobbing.

The boy didn't like to see the girl cry, so he did the only thing he knew to do: He made an impossible promise and hugged her back.

"I don't know," he said. "I just do. But we'll always be friends. I promise. When we're big, I'll find you again."

"How big?" the girl sniffled into his neck.

"Probably really big," the boy said. "Like eighteen."

Eighteen seemed like a big, too-far-off, impossible number, but the girl nodded.

"Promise, promise?" she asked.

"Yeah," the boy said. "Promise, promise."

And so they grew up, apart in body but—more often than they would have guessed—together in thought.

For though they aged and changed and became far different people than the ones who ruled Snailopolis, though their planets remained chained to their separate orbits, the little girl never forgot the little boy, and he never forgot her.

Chapter One

Nova

I'm used to the stares, especially at smaller schools like this. And I'm not stupid: I know I'm not getting attention because I'm stunningly pretty or because the resident vampire is about to fall in love with me; I'm just a break in the chain, something different to look at.

Humans are designed to pick up patterns. It's probably how we've survived this long, figuring out that *that* slain woolly mammoth smelled funny or bad. We couldn't identify the *why*, maybe, but it was enough that we didn't eat it.

I'm a temporary pattern disruption, nothing more. And

everyone is trying to figure out if I'm worth eating or if I should be left behind.

But I know *their* patterns, too. I mean, I've been here all of ten minutes, but a school is a school is a school is a school. I've been in too many to count since kindergarten, thanks to Mom's "fixer-upper" accounting job that keeps us moving from place to place, business to business. Mom comes in and annihilates the problem with spreadsheets and projections before putting it all back together again, and then we move on to the next. Since then, the longest we stayed in one place was two years—for some big airline company—and that was when I was so little I hardly remember it.

Hardly.

I'm only a junior, and this is my *sixth* high school. The paperwork is a nightmare, but it turns out that if you have fairly decent grades and a mom who is a whiz at logistical red tape, it's entirely possible to be a teenage vagabond who has sampled nearly two dozen different square school pizzas. (Spoiler alert: They taste *exactly* the same.)

That's part of the pattern; the first thing other kids usually ask when they find out who I am and how long I'm here is *Don't you hate moving around so much?*

I can answer honestly each time: *Absolutely not.*

It's a dream, really. I can be whoever I want with zero consequences because the stakes are *so low*. Miscalculate and make a fool of myself for the six months I join the improv comedy club? No biggie. I'll be forgotten by summer break. Spend an entire semester dressing in cottagecore attire just to find out that I look *awful* in ruffles? Literally doesn't matter. I won't even be here for school picture day. (The cottagecore was a disaster, by the way. Winter in Cincinnati was not the ideal location for an aesthetic that is mostly eyelet shirts and frilly skirts.)

Sure, it would be *nice* to be in one place long enough to make friends who don't disappear a month or two after you move to the next place, the next school, the next group you wrap yourself in like a cocoon before springing forth like a chaotic social butterfly destined to always fly and never land. I've gotten used to it, though. I *like* it sometimes, not worrying so much about how compatible I am with the people around me because they're going to change in a minute anyway. Fewer friends means fewer goodbyes. It's a good thing. Really.

But back to patterns.

I know that everybody staring at me as I walk into the lunchroom—the most high-stakes entrance for a new kid—is sizing me up, but for once I'm not formulating who I want them to see, how I want them to *react*.

I don't want them to react. I don't want to be perceived at all.

Because this is going to be my shortest stint yet, just under two months, and I'm *not* going to try out any new personas. Partly because of he-who-shan't-be-thought-of from my last school, near Seattle. Because I've been too busy pushing the pieces of my broken heart around in my chest to figure out which Nova Evans I want to try on next.

And also—most importantly—because I'm *tired*. I've never tried coasting at school before, just getting through, not making waves, simply . . . being me, whoever she is.

God, that sounds cheesy.

But college is knocking, and if I can't figure out who I want to be, where I want to go, I'm going to continue to be a pattern breaker, but not the good kind.

Mom was a first-generation college student. My grandparents didn't even finish high school, dropping out their senior year. Education has *always* been super big to my mom.

"I don't care where you go," she's always said. "So long as you go, get in, get out with a degree that means something, something that will earn you a secure income."

It's the secure-income thing that is really tripping me up. Because so far, from what I can tell, my only strengths are chameleoning from school to school and knowing how to pack my boxes exactly the same way every time (if I bother unpacking them at all).

How am I supposed to know what will (a) make me happy and (b) make me money when I'm not even sure how to tell the difference between what I *actually* like to do and what I "tried on" or did just to fit in at all my previous schools?

I went to a career day last year where the principal made this speech over the feedback of the cheap microphone. It was hard to make out with the chatter and the mic acting up, but I heard her last line loud and clear: "You might not be able to turn your hobby into a career, but if you can figure out what part of your hobby calls to you most, what part of it makes you tick, you'll have a clearer avenue for what you want to do with the rest of your life."

I'm pulled out of the chaotic jumble of my brain when I feel too many lunchroom eyes burning into the back of my chosen first-day-of-new-school outfit: jeans, a T-shirt from a bookstore I visited once in Michigan, and my super-comfy-but-not-actually-great-for-sports sneakers left over from my athleisure phase three schools ago.

Even though I've resolved to simply exist for the next two months, I still have to find somewhere to sit. What I really need is a corner seat with no one around, but this cafeteria is too small. I can see mismatched chairs pulled up alongside the plastic ones attached to the long skinny tables. It's one of those schools where the infrastructure is stretched to the max to accommodate everyone, which leaves me nowhere to hide and nowhere to sit without making a statement.

I end up on the far side of a table of football players—I hope the only statement I'm making is *trying to not intrude*. Their letterman jackets and general demeanor of being gods of the school are part of another predictable pattern, and these guys are no different. Loud and boisterous, even their lunch trays sound amplified when they thump them on the table. Nobody seems to be paying attention to the noise, though I catch a number of people looking toward them like they can't help but watch the minutia of school celebrities. I swear I see a girl walk closer, like a comet drawn into a planet's orbit, before she corrects her trajectory and walks away.

It's refreshing, actually, that no matter where I go, jocks are king: hockey, basketball, football—it doesn't matter. They're all the same when they sit in groups in cafeterias and have adoring entourages around them at all times.

But at least I can count on them not speaking to me, thank god.

Maybe if I was in my "hot-girl summer" outfit from two schools ago they'd care, but I might as well be invisible for all the attention they pay me.

In a flash, I can see how the next two months will go: I'll sit and read a book or scroll on my phone during lunch. In between classes, I'll say hello to the one or two people who have deemed me interesting enough for small talk, but otherwise I'll float through the day, do my assignments, and go home to . . . I haven't figured out that part yet, but whatever it is, I'll be doing it alone while Mom finishes up her twelve-hour workday.

I can see it so perfectly—and it's a comfort, the whole coasting-while-figuring-out-a-hobby-and-life-direction thing—that I almost don't notice when he sits beside me.

At first, I don't *see* him at all. He's handsome, sure, but lots of boys are handsome. He's not a pattern disruptor. He's stereotypically cute: curly darkish hair, brown eyes, tall, the kind of broad-shouldered that is probably half genetic, half a result of lifting weights.

I'm about to look away when he smiles at something one of the other boys says, and it makes me pause. There's something about the *way* he smiles, a curve of the mouth that makes every cell inside me feel like it has been electrocuted at the same time.

I hardly know this feeling. It's one I almost never have in a life that has been a rootless, patchwork existence of places and people I won't ever see again.

It's recognition.

And just like that, every plan, every persona, every *me* flies out the window and I am dragged—fingers clawing at dirt and hours and grains of sand in an hourglass—across space and time to an old oak tree, a broken wooden fence between his house and mine, and a pit of snails that we named Snailopolis.

Sam Jordan.

When I say I hardly remember the time when I was little, *he* is the hardly, the one big thing I recall from the time before Mom and I traveled from place to place, school to school.

Sam. Sammy. I used to call him Samuel to tease him. I've thought of him over the years. I even asked Mom about him a few months ago, when Seattle Boy broke my heart.

I asked if she remembered the boy from the fence beneath the oak tree one rare morning when we were eating breakfast together. Normally she eats while she works in whatever office space she has carved out for herself, but that morning we stood on opposite sides of our apartment bar eating our respective yogurts with plastic spoons.

"Who?" Mom asked. Her voice was weird when she said it, a little high, but she got like that sometimes.

"Sam," I repeated. "My friend who moved when I was little. The one who lived next door. We would ride bikes and play in the dirt between our houses and stuff, remember?"

"Oh, yes." Mom nodded. She wasn't really paying attention to me, busy scraping the last bit of yogurt from the sides of the cup. "He moved before we did, yeah?"

"Yeah," I said, thinking of our promise, promise. "He did."

But if Mom remembered the cuts and the bruises, she didn't mention it. I could tell she thought nothing of the conversation at all.

She had no way of knowing that I think of Sam every time I see a tree with an impressive canopy or a snail or someone with a bruised eye. How could she? I've forgotten so much, myself.

But to look at him now, sitting feet away from me, is to remember. Looking at him is memory itself, as if I've stepped back in time.

Even now, miles and years away, I can *feel* what it was like. How the moment he stumbled across me poking a stick at the rotted fence wood felt like, *Oh, there you are.*

I don't have words for it, but it felt safe. It felt . . . monumental. Important.

And it's all coming back to me, the emotions from my five-year-old self, and they feel out of place in this seventeen-year-old body.

Finally, like he's drawn by my gaze, Sam looks up. Our eyes meet.

We're inches apart, close enough that I can look straight into his face and superimpose the Sam I remember over the Sam in front of me. He's not a little boy anymore, but the boy I remember is still there in the nose, a bit in the cheekbones, and *definitely* in the eyes.

For a second, something flickers across his face, and I wonder if he recognizes me. I wonder if he is on fire with memories, too.

The smile is slow and pulls at both corners of his mouth. I hold my breath, waiting to see what he remembers. Waiting for the promise, promise.

And then Sam Jordan, king of Snailopolis and someone I still, to this day, consider my closest childhood friend, opens his mouth, grins his football-god smile, and says, "Do you mind moving over a seat so my girlfriend can sit next to me?"

Chapter Two

Sam

The new girl has a weird look on her face, but she pushes her tray to the seat directly across from her and mumbles, "Sure."

I don't have time to think about it. Abigail plops beside me, occupying the vacated seat in an almost seamless choreography.

"Sammy." Abigail smiles.

"Abby." I smile back.

I still haven't found a way to tell her I hate being called Sammy. It reminds me of childhood, of *before*. I don't like to think about it, to be honest. It's too late to bring up the nickname thing now. I'd look like a weirdo if I mentioned it after months of her writing it in social media captions and on notes she passes me in class.

God. It's been *months*.

We've been together since the end of our junior year, when her boyfriend dumped her two days before prom. I felt bad about it and asked her last minute to be my date to prom because I didn't have a date anyway and it seemed like the right thing to do after her jerkwad boyfriend from another school cheated on her.

So I don't want to upset her by complaining about something as small as a pet name. Abigail is a constant, the person I can reliably look toward nearly every class, every football game and *know* she'll be smiling in my direction. It's easy being with Abigail. And I can't stand the thought of being like the jerkwad who dumped her. I have this thing about hurting people: I don't do it. No matter what.

Beside me, she twirls her ponytail around her hand. It's so long, her hair. When she has it piled high in her cheerleader Friday ponytail, the ribbon almost always comes loose before halftime. I've spotted it from the field the last three games.

"So, homecoming," Abigail says, opening her lunch box. It looks like a purse. Why should lunch boxes look like purses? It makes no sense. "What color do you like me best in?"

I blink. "Don't you have to wear your uniform?"

Abigail laughs like this is the funniest thing she's ever heard.

"*Sam.* This is for the *homecoming dance.* I know this is

Texas, but we *can* wear something other than uniforms and jeans, at least occasionally. What color dress should I look for? Mom is taking me shopping after school."

The mere mention of Mrs. Shepherd makes my stomach feel black and sticky like hot tar. I always feel this way when people bring up normal things like after-school shopping or holidays. Which is a total dick move, because, for one thing, Mrs. Shepherd has been nothing but nice to me. She gives me an extra serving of everything when I come over for dinner and is always saying I'm "a gem."

For another thing, the tar makes me feel guilty because Uncle Keith and Aunt Dawn are the best things that ever happened to me. I've called them Mom and Dad for years. Shortly after I moved in with them, I accidentally called Dawn "Mom" on the phone when I needed to be picked up from my new school. I could tell how happy it made her, so I kept doing it. It seemed like the least I could do.

Calling them Mom and Dad instead of Aunt and Uncle is easier, anyway. I don't have to explain to anyone that they're not my real parents if I don't want to. I don't have to explain anything.

Nobody knows about my before. They only know this version of me, the after.

Abigail draws me back to myself, gripping my arm.

"A *limo*," she says. "We'll go with them, right?"

I've missed the entire conversation, but a glance around our table and the way that Fox—my best friend, with either the best or worst football nickname—is looking at me says enough. They're *all* excited about homecoming and I'm . . . not.

Which, again, is a dick move. Abigail *should* be excited to dress up and go to a dance with her boyfriend. I'm the broken one. Not her.

Fox is looking at me in that pointed way again, so I turn to Abigail and smile. I know exactly what I look like when I smile. I used to practice it in the mirror.

"A limo will be awesome," I say.

She squeals again. She's so *cheerful*, so sure and confident in what she wants, she has no trouble expressing it. It used to be cute, the squealing, but lately it makes me feel sad because I've practiced that, too—the exuberant-happiness thing—and no matter how hard I try, it looks fake.

Abigail deserves better.

And I wish I could find a way to tell her that without making her hate me, without being just as bad as her ex. And maybe selfishly find a way to do it without me hating myself.

Which is a theme in my life, the whole swallowing-my-tongue thing. For starters, I actually kind of hate football. Not because I'm not good at it—I'm *very* good at it—but because I do it out of habit, or maybe because everyone *says* I'm so good at it, so I keep playing. I keep nodding and smiling when Dad and my coaches talk about college scouts and scholarships and "my veritable shot at going pro." I smile my good, practiced smile when a recruiter, seeing the picture on the fridge of me and Abigail in our respective football and cheerleader uniforms, says something like, "Colleges love all-American boys, and it doesn't get much more all-American than football boys and cheerleader girls."

I buried the piece of information deep into my heart as they made *a note of it*, my high school relationship, on the all-important form they will use to hold me up next to the other candidates, the other players who could just as easily get an athletic full ride instead of me.

So there's no going back now. Not on Abigail or football or anything. It's not fair to Abigail—all-American thoughts floating in my mind or not—to break up with her before the homecoming dance she's so excited about. *Especially* after what's-his-face broke her heart just before a dance, too. After homecoming there will be winter formal and then Valentine's Day and then, and then, and then . . .

Sometimes she talks about how we'll either go to the same college next year or manage long distance, and, if I'm just going along with my life anyway, I might as well add Abigail to the bargain, especially since she's actually great.

And quitting football is *literally* laughable. I chuckle a little under my breath thinking of how that conversation would go with Mom and Dad or my coaches: *Hey, guys, thanks for spending, like, thousands of dollars all these years getting me the best cleats and pads and private lessons and whatever. And thanks so much for setting up these meetings with college recruitment scouts, but I think I'm going to just not if that's okay with you.*

I'm a jerk for thinking any of this at all.

Because sitting here beside an objectively beautiful girl who writes me love notes and a table full of generally good humans who call me their friend . . . what right do I have to complain?

None.

So I pull myself together. I stop thinking about the sticky feeling in my stomach and remind myself that this life is a good one. A *great* one, even.

When Fox makes a joke about how the pepperoni on his cafeteria pizza looks like our defense coach, my laugh is almost real.

* * *

Nova

The girl at the back of my new Spanish class looks up from her book to smile at me.

"Is this seat taken?" I ask, gesturing to the seat beside her.

"Now it is." She smiles. "You're new?"

"Yeah," I say, bracing myself. She seems friendly, which means she's probably going to ask too many questions and I'll have to answer them all.

But she surprises me by saying, "Cool. Sorry to be rude, but I've only got, like, three pages left and I'm trying to finish before class. That okay?"

"Oh, sure," I say. "Go ahead."

"Thanks." She gives me an awkward little finger wave with the hand not holding the place in her book before returning to her reading, and I decide I like her. I know this is supposed to be the pit stop with no ties and no roots or whatever, but she seems the nicest of shallow roots, someone I can sit by comfortably under the guise of being sociable but really we're both doing our own things.

I just have to find my own thing first.

And that can't happen if my brain keeps doing what it's doing now: forcibly running back the scene from lunch with Sam over and over like a glitchy video.

I *swear* there was a flash of recognition, a brief second where we were both occupying the same in-between space stuck somewhere between the lunchroom and the old oak tree. But then he looked at me like I was . . . a stranger. Nobody. And I guess that's for the best. Because I really, *really* need to figure out who I want to be so I can go to the right college and major in the right thing and not waste my time and Mom's money groping around in the dark trying to figure out something as basic as *who I am*.

Despite my spiraling, class goes by like most classes do, blessedly free of the forced "introduce yourself with a fun fact" bit. I'm practically ignored, which is ideal, except for when my seat neighbor—whose name I learn is Holly—occasionally leans over and whispers the correct vocabulary word or proper phrasing. She finished her book before class and has started to read another one beneath her desk. Mr.

Mesa, the teacher, keeps trying to catch her, but every time he asks her a question, she answers perfectly.

I'm watching her silently flip a page as Mr. Mesa drones on about conjugations when there's a knock at the door.

It's a group of three students. One carries a clipboard, one wheels in a portable charging station for tablets, and the other clutches a pen—his one shred of legitimacy in what is clearly a clever bid to miss class.

"Mr. Mesa, we're the senior student council, and we're here to issue the Crush fundraiser test. It should take less than ten minutes." This from the girl I place as Sam's girlfriend from lunch. She hands a note to the teacher. "This is from the front office. It's to benefit the new agriculture barn?"

Mr. Mesa barely glances at the paper, idly waving them in.

"Sounds good," he says. "I saw the email."

Sam's girlfriend's smile is straight and neat, and even though a small part of me wanted to hate watching her and Sam together at lunch, I didn't. He looked all right, mostly, if not a little faraway at times. He was probably just tired and hungry, but he smiled when she looked at him—even if it didn't quite reach his eyes—and he laughed at her jokes . . . I hope he's happy.

At the front of the room, she claps her hands together once and turns to the class.

"Perfect. If you haven't heard, this is the Crush test. Everyone has to take the personality test for it to work, even if you don't plan on purchasing the results. So you take the test online, and then after school later today you can log on with a code we'll give you to buy access to your personalized results. Crush's algorithm will give you *your* top matches in the school based on the answers to your personality test."

She pauses and waggles her eyebrows as the boy with the cart begins to hand out the school iPads. "Now, I'm *supposed* to tell you that Crush results are just for fun and are about finding who you would be compatible with as friends. A friend crush, kind of." Her smile grows suggestive. "*Butttt*, we can't control what you do with the information if you happen to hit it off with a top match. Don't forget, homecoming is right around the corner, and if you don't have a date for the dance yet, this might be a good chance to find out who you would have the best time with!"

From behind his desk, Mr. Mesa makes a vague sound of disapproval, but Sam's girlfriend presses on.

"So, fill out your test here in class, and then don't forget to log on after school and pay your ten bucks to find out who *you* should be crushing on. It all goes toward the new ag barn, so it's for a good cause. Oh, and don't forget to write down your access number when you're finished with the test. You'll need it to get your results."

Around me, I can hear the blunt tapping of people who begin their tests and know their answers without thinking. They probably see the question *Are you an early bird or a night owl?* and have an instant response. They're not sifting through their past two school personas—one of which included an early-morning running phase and the other a late-night board-gaming habit—and finding themselves conflicted about which one they *actually* identify as their own self.

And that's one of the easier ones. There's lots of *strongly agree, neutral, strongly disagree* statements like, *I value friendship over external successes,* and *People who know me say I'm kind.*

It doesn't help that Sam Jordan's *literal cheerleader goddess* of a girlfriend is standing at the front of the room, watching us in that bland way of someone who is ready to move on to the next task.

She's not even particularly looking at me, and I feel my cheeks heat. Because even if *she* doesn't know who I am, I know who her boyfriend is.

Which is a stupid thought. He clearly didn't recognize me. From what I can tell from the collage of my little-kid photos Mom is always sure to hang in whatever space we're living in, I haven't changed much: Same round cheeks, same round *everything,* as the baby fat turned into teenage fat. My skin is still too pale (except for the freckles) and my eyes are still the same brown they've always been. My hair has stayed its natural blondish-brownish-reddish (depending on the light) except for my brief platinum-blond theater-kid moment, which I quickly rectified because even my theater-kid persona wasn't dedicated enough to keep up with *that* many hair appointments.

My outsides have stuck to their initial pattern way more than my insides.

Did Sam recognize me *at all*, though? Maybe even sub-consciously? Does he *remember* enough to have told his girl-friend I existed?

Of course not. He looked right at me at lunch and said nothing beyond a polite "Please scuttle along so my clearly-more-gorgeous girlfriend can sit next to me." (I might have embellished that last part, but *still*.)

In the end, I answer the Crush test with something be-tween gut instinct and paranoia that I'll be the last one still taking the straightforward personality test. I'm a blur, tap-ping the tablet faster and faster as I fight the panic that I don't know myself at all. I have no hunch, no heading, and, *god*, why does every school either have to be freezing cold or—in this case—burning-hellfire hot?

I wish that instead of matching me to other students, the test would just tell me who I am, what I would be good at, what I should do in my spare time. Something *useful*. But be-fore I can fall into complete despair, I remind myself that *this* is my focus of the next two months.

It's the perfect amount of time to take a break, to self-analyze, to figure out who I am, what I want to do, who I even want to be. God knows I have enough data to sift through from trying so many different activities and versions of "me." I just have to pinpoint it, whittle myself down to a core essence that I can summarize in a paragraph or two for colleges and for my own self.

Maybe it's good that Sam didn't recognize me. It would

only get in the way, and my time is limited. I'm supposed to have everything figured out in time for college.

Seeing Sam again is a fun break in the pattern, I tell myself, but not a pattern changer.

It's no big deal. Just a fluke.

Mr. Mesa is eyeing me when I ask to go to the restroom after I turn in my tablet. I'm not sure why teachers think we're all going to the restroom to be delinquents instead of, like, just *peeing*, but I can see him calculating, trying to decide if I'm going to smoke or Sharpie on the stall doors or something.

He lets me go, thank god. I don't really need to pee, but splashing some water on my hands and moving my legs for a minute might mean I can shake off the mild feeling of panic the quiz has left in its wake.

I make it down two hallways in a daze before I realize that I have *no* idea where the bathrooms are located. Pattern recognition tells me they'll be at the end of one of these stretches of classrooms, but I haven't seen signage and I can't hear the sound of toilets flushing or see water fountains to guide my way.

I'm about to turn back and return to Mr. Mesa's room before I get properly lost when the door beside me opens and I have to leap out of the way to avoid getting smacked. Whoever came out must notice this, lunging toward me—To stop me from falling? To apologize?—but it only makes matters worse.

There's a jumble, the kind that ends up with more bumped elbows and potential bruises than there would have been if we'd just stood still, but we're frantically trying to disentangle ourselves like cartoon characters stuck together by a wad of gum. Physics has taken over, a force neither of us can argue with, and we're about to go down in a heap when the boy anchors his hands firmly on my shoulders, balancing us both, his letterman jacket sleeve cold against my elbow.

"*Sorry,*" he says. "God, I didn't mean to hurt you. I should've looked where I was going, but I didn't think there would be anybody . . ."

His voice, Sam's voice, because of course it's him, trails off, and he looks at me almost exactly like he did in the cafeteria, but I'm not stupid enough to fall for it twice. He's just confused. I'm a pattern breaker, and he's trying to figure out what I am, not who.

He doesn't remember me, and that's *fine.*

"Hey, you were at my lunch table today," he says. "You must be new."

Sam's smile is fool's gold, perfection if you don't know where to look, but I do. His eyes aren't quite right. Guarded. Wary.

It's selfish, my impulse to see if I can make him smile, *really* smile. I should leave him alone, let him go back to his world and his life without trying to throw a wrench in it by reminding him of who I am, who *we* were . . . and everything that came with it.

When Sam and I were a *we,* his life was in shambles. He

was . . . I can't think of the word. But he has every reason in the world to have blocked it out, all of it. Even me. Even Snail-opolis and our tree. If leaving it all behind—if forgetting—has helped him heal, who am I to try to reverse that?

Sam blinks down at me, waiting for an answer from the weird new girl who's been silent for too long.

"Yeah, hi," I say, decision made that *I* won't be the one to remind him. "Just looking for the bathroom."

I swear something in his face changes. *I swear it.* His smile isn't fake because it isn't there anymore, and he's squinting at me like he's trying to focus through a fog, and it reverses my decision as soon as I've made it.

"Are you okay?" I ask. The words are out before I can stop them, and there's nothing to do now but cover up the raw awkwardness of them with "Sorry, I just mean you rushed out of the room, and I probably interrupted your mad dash to the nurse or something."

Sam is still squinting at me.

"Do I know you?"

I'm ice-cold. I'm not sure where all the blood in my body went, but it's certainly not my hands or feet, because they're suddenly freezing.

"I'm new," I say, clenching and unclenching my fists, willing the blood to flow. "Today's my first day."

He's still looking down at me, and now that he *might* recognize me, I'm panicking for some reason.

"Before this," he said. "Where did you live? Where did you come from?"

"Seattle," I say. "Ever been?"

Something changes in his expression again, but it's too quick for me to identify.

"Yeah, actually. Earlier this year I went up there to check out the Huskies."

It's my turn to squint. "Are you, like, a dog enthusiast?"

His laugh is sudden, loud. He immediately stifles it before it can echo any farther down the still-empty hallway.

"It's the football team." He smiles. This time, it *almost* reaches his eyes. "At the University of Washington."

"So *not* a dog enthusiast?" I tease.

It feels good to smile at him.

"Not really."

"Cat person?" I guess.

He's *still* smiling. "I think I'm more of a houseplant kind of person, but I probably shouldn't be trusted with those, either."

I should go. It's *past* time for me to go. Mr. Mesa definitely thinks I'm playing on my phone in the bathroom at this point.

But if this is the last time I'll see Sam . . . I'm already toeing the line of blatantly reminding him of who I am. What's one more inch?

"So you like football?"

He sounds startled, defensive. "What? Why would you ask that?"

I hold up my hands in surrender. "I just meant you went all the way to Seattle to check out a team and"—I gesture at his letterman—"you obviously play, so . . ."

Sam seems to collect himself. It looks like he may be counting in his head.

"I'm good at football," he says in answer. "I'm being scouted."

That last part is said without an ounce of bragging but also with no trace of excitement or pride or . . . anything.

He says it like it's an undeniable fact.

I shuffle my feet, watching them instead of him.

"I hope . . . I hope you're happy," I say. Which, *god*, could I sound any more ominous? He doesn't remember me. I'm just a new girl standing in the middle of the hallway interrupting his day and—

"I mean"—I make myself look up at his face—"I just . . . You seem nice. I hope your life is as nice as you are."

Okay, so I've gone from horror movie to Hallmark card. At least I'm giving him an easy out. I'm *clearly* weird, not someone worth fretting over or thinking too much about, no matter how much he stared at me just now.

"You don't know me," he says, and now he sounds the tiniest bit defensive, like *Who is this girl?*, and he's right.

I shrug and breathe an internal sigh of relief that he seems to be dismissing me.

Good. It's for the best.

"I've met a lot of people," I say, hoping it's explanation enough.

I take a step back toward Mr. Mesa's classroom and where I'm supposed to be. Which is *not here with Sam*.

Sam's step toward me is followed by the dismissal bell. How long have we both been out here?

"Are you *sure* we don't—"

It's all he gets out before the door he burst through opens again, the hallway suddenly engulfed in chatter and backpacks and announcements from the PA system overhead.

We swing apart just as quickly as we came together, like planets passing by.

I should be grateful I got to see him at all, I remind myself. I once read that certain planets only line up in their orbits once every hundred years. How lucky that Sam and I crossed paths twice.

It's enough. It'll have to be.

Chapter Three

Sam

I can't stop thinking about the girl from the hallway.

Even the fifty forties (which is just running to the forty-yard line and back *fifty times*) we had to do as punishment for talking during practice couldn't get her out of my head. By the time I lost count around thirty, I knew I couldn't blame the heat exhaustion. It was *her*.

Whoever she was. Is.

I'm not even sure why I left class to go to the bathroom. I didn't *need* to go, but it's like my legs were suddenly jittery and my hands were tingling in a way that reminded me of the heart attack symptoms we learned about in health class.

Whatever caused the unsettled feeling, I forgot about it when I ran into her.

It just . . . vanished.

Now I'm home from football practice and from school and girls in hallways, and Abigail is beside me. She's cross-legged on my bed as she scrolls through her phone, looking at her matches from that stupid personality quiz they made us all take after lunch today. My hands are starting to tingle again.

"My top match is *Mason Gallagher*," Abigail groans. "Mason. I mean, I feel personally victimized by this algorithm. I still haven't forgiven him for ruining my 'Remember the Alamo' project in fifth grade. And it's a *seventy-eight percent* match, too. That's the highest I've seen, and everyone's posting theirs online, so I've seen *a lot*. Even Dominique and Jason only got fifty-two percent, and they're practically married."

I'm looking at my phone, too, but I'm scrolling absent-mindedly through the photos I took when Mom, Dad, and I went to Seattle. There's a lot of Husky Stadium and the school grounds, but there's also pictures of the interesting bits of architecture in the city and a few I snuck of the huge desk in the head coach's office made of mahogany and oak.

I'm looking at the grain of the desk when Abigail leans into me and peers at my phone.

"Getting excited?" she asks.

"About what?"

She taps my phone.

"*College football*, silly."

"Of course," I say like a trained seal. "It's what I've been working toward."

And like a trained seal that gets excited about a pail of fish, Abigail's smile fills me with relief.

It means she doesn't suspect I'm lying.

"Don't stress about it," she says. "You're a shoo-in wherever you want to go. Now, *please*," she repeats. "*Please* look up your Crush results and tell me you have a match that's higher than me and Mason? So I can sleep tonight?"

It's my turn to groan.

"I'm *not* spending money on some stupid quiz," I tell her. "Does it even matter? If I'm not in your top matches, there's no way you're going to be in mine."

Abigail rolls her eyes. "I *know that*. But still, aren't you the least bit curious?"

I'm not, not really. But ten dollars seems a small price to pay to make Abigail happy with me. I put in the debit card number attached to Mom and Dad's account, silently remind myself to mow the lawn or something extra to pay them back for such a frivolous purchase (even though I know they won't really care), and hit Submit.

In the two seconds it takes the results to load, I just know my top match is going to be Leanne. It's been a running joke forever that we're the same person in different bodies and that's why Fox loves her so much.

"You love me because I remind you of Sam," she says regularly.

It's my job to add, "But you have better hair," and Fox makes finger guns at us both and goes, *"Exactly."*

When I read my top match, though, it's not Leanne.

Abigail is sitting close enough that I have to pretend the chill that makes my arms shiver inside my letterman jacket is normal.

It has nothing to do with recognizing the name of a childhood friend, one that I could have tried to look up online but never did. I guess because she was from the "before"—and to try to find her directly would be like trying to remember that time of my life.

So the chill has nothing to do with the memory of oak trees and palm kisses.

It has nothing to do with a promise, promise.

Nope. Not at all. It must be the air-conditioning Mom always keeps humming at a brisk seventy degrees, even in the summer.

But Abigail notices my shiver. She turns and places a hand on my shoulder, pinching gently.

"Cold? I still can't believe we're not even in each other's top ten, can you?" she says, peering over at my phone screen. "Bummer."

"Yeah," I echo, "bummer."

When I have nothing to say to that, Abigail adds, "You got *new girl* as top match. And *holy shit.* A ninety-nine percent match? That's too weird. I'm surprised they even let her fill one out. Catherine told me they have math together and she told Catherine she's only here for two months."

"Catherine's leaving?" I ask.

My brain isn't focusing—not on Abigail, anyway. It's flashing the name *Nova Evans* over and over in my head like a bright neon sign.

What are the chances it's not her? What are the chances that it *is*?

Abigail sighs through her nose. "*No*, the *new girl* is only here for a couple of months."

When I raise my eyes from the Crush results, I see a very irritated Abigail.

"*Sammy*," she says. "You know it's not the end of the world that we're not in each other's top matches. It's just a stupid test, like you said."

I'm looking back down at my phone, at the bold 99 *percent*, so I almost don't hear Abigail's quiet, nearly inaudible, "*Right?*"

"Of course," I say. "Yeah, it's just a stupid quiz. Like you said."

Maybe I misread her annoyance, because now she looks a little confused, possibly even hurt. I'm not used to Abigail being anything but a ray of sunshine. It's who she is. I've always been jealous of the way her internal mood thermometer autocorrects itself instead of leaping to extremes.

"What is it?" I ask when she doesn't say anything.

"Nothing," she says. "It's nothing."

When I pull her into my arms, it's familiar: Her smell, the feel of her arm muscles built through years of cheer and basketball and softball twitching against my own, the way she settles into my chest with a quiet sigh like I'm *her* safe place.

"It's something," I whisper into her hair.

She's quiet for what feels like a long time but probably isn't.

"I just . . ."

Abigail turns her head into my neck and says something I can't make out.

"What?"

She raises her head with a sigh.

"That's a high percentage, Sam."

"It doesn't matter," I tell her. "Really."

And it doesn't. Even if it *is* the Nova I remember. It doesn't change Abigail and me and our plans.

"You're right," she says. And then, to herself, "You're right."

She springs back quickly, though. She pecks me on the lips and stands up. This time her sigh isn't sad but resigned, like she doesn't want to leave but has to.

"I'm going to see if Catherine wants to go catch a movie. There's a new one out with that one buff guy we both like. You know the one from those vintage Disney movies? *High School Musical*? He's in some wrestler movie."

"The singing guy?" I ask, trying my best to stay tuned in to Abigail.

"Yeah! You can come if you want," she says. "It's sporty, so you'd probably like it."

"Sorry," I say as I stand up from my bed. "I promised Fox I would go to his house after practice. Rain check?"

When Abigail smiles at me, it's like the past five minutes never happened. Normal. Expected. *Safe.*

"Sure," she says. "See you tomorrow, okay?"

I sit back down and wait until I hear Abigail say goodbye to Mom, until I hear her BMW drive away, and count to two hundred slowly. Then I stand up from the bed.

There's not much room for pacing. I cleared a space at the end of my bed to do push-ups and sit-ups on weekend mornings, but that means my wooden trunk is shoved between the bed and dresser, so instead I prowl at the edge of my footboard like a caged lion. The flashing neon is growing brighter, frying any other thought that dares enter my brain.

Nova.

I remember. Of course I remember.

I remember Snailopolis. I remember a girl in the hole in the fence. I remember the way she smiled at me and how it made me feel, how it made me—at least for a while—forget what happened in the house behind me.

Thinking of that house gives me a different kind of chill. Usually when I think of my before-life, the one that I never have to go back to, I run the other way. I think of literally anything else. Because what's the point of going over and over something that hurts so much?

Except . . .

Forgetting *everything* means forgetting Nova, which I clearly haven't.

For the first time in a long, long time, I let myself linger in my favorite memory of us. It's near the beginning, maybe just a week into meeting up every day after school. We were playing in the dirt.

It was our favorite thing—more than riding bikes, even. I think Nova liked it because she got dirt under her nails, which always made her laugh. She said it made her look like she had fancy nail polish. I liked it because sometimes she would put a snail in my palm and then pet the shell with a finger. Even though she was petting the snail, sometimes her fingertip would brush *me*, and it felt nice.

The night before my favorite memory was a particularly bad one. I almost didn't come out to play at all. I could hide the worst of it beneath sleeves and a carefully tucked shirt, but not all of it. There were burns on my hands and my arms, tiny and gruesome and raw. I thought about wearing mittens. I thought about not going out at all, but the desire to sit beside Nova was so great, I told myself I didn't care if she saw.

And she did see. She immediately dropped the white garden snail she was holding and inspected my hands.

"Why?" she asked.

"It's okay," I told her. "It was an accident. It doesn't hurt."

It *did* hurt. But I wanted to play snails. I wanted Nova to call me a king, the king of Snailopolis, and place little bugs and critters in my palms. I wanted to forget the hurt.

Nova seemed to understand. She didn't say anything else about the marks until her mom called her for dinner.

"I've gotta go," she said, standing up and brushing dirt off her knees.

"I know," I said.

"You can come to dinner if you want," she said. "My mom won't mind."

"I can't," I said. "I'm not allowed."

I wasn't allowed to go *anywhere*. In fact, I was sure my parents would be livid if they ever caught me sneaking out to the hole in the fence or to ride bikes. But so far they hadn't.

"Okay." She turned to leave but suddenly stopped, whirling back toward me. "Sammy?"

"Yeah?"

"My mom kisses me when I hurt myself. It makes me feel better."

I didn't know what to say, so I stayed quiet.

"Do you want me to kiss you?" she asked.

I had seen kissing before, of course. On TV, never at home. It seemed a little gross, putting mouths together. That's where the food went and—when you didn't have food to put in there for a long time and your stomach rebelled— where stuff came back out. Why would you want to touch mouths?

But I didn't want to upset Nova, so I said, "Sure."

I closed my eyes and pushed my lips out like I had seen in movies.

My eyes were still closed when I felt her hands on my sleeve, gently pulling up the fabric to reveal the line of three cigarette burns.

I watched as—so gently I almost didn't feel her lips at all— she kissed my palm three times, one for each burn.

"The kisses go where they need to go," she said quietly.

For some reason, I wanted to cry. Maybe it was because she was so scared of hurting me she wouldn't even kiss the burns directly. Or maybe it was because I couldn't remember the last time someone had touched me and meant for it *not* to hurt.

"It helps," I said. "Thank you."

"Okay," Nova said, scrambling to her feet once more. "I've gotta go."

That time she didn't stop.

But that night, when I finally fell asleep in my bed, I swear my hand didn't hurt as badly. She had magic kisses, I remember thinking. My friend was magical, even if my family wasn't.

I shed my letterman jacket as the memory fades and glare down at my arms. If I look really closely, some of the marks are still there, little rivers and potholes of white against my pinkish skin. It's been a while since I've searched for them—why poke the bear of memory if I can avoid its den entirely—because each one I find is evidence of my before-life . . .

But also of Nova.

I'm downstairs before I think about it. In my hurry, I round the corner to the kitchen too quickly and knock my knee against an open cupboard door.

"Um, *ouch*," Mom says, sticking her head up to glare at me. "Son, did you intend to decapitate me? Because there are far more efficient ways than kitchen cabinetry, let me tell you."

"Sorry, sorry," I say. "I didn't see it until it was too late."

Mom hands up a ceramic baking dish that I take while

she stands. She gently closes the cupboard and gives me a wry look.

"I assume you came careening down here because you need something?"

"Yeah," I say. "Yeah, I was supposed to pass this new girl Fox's math notes, and I forgot to do it before school was out. Can you get her address from that parent-portal thingy?"

"It depends if her parents already signed her up," Mom says. "And sharing your address isn't mandatory, so hers might not be listed. Let me go check, but why can't Fox do it?"

"He's got after-school detention for the week," I say, and at least that part is true.

"What for this time?"

I shuffle my feet. "He skipped first period to stand by the bus that was carrying Leanne and the other band kids to their competition."

"Was he cheering them on? That hardly seems punishable with a week's worth of detention, even if he did skip class."

"*Yeah*, but he might have been in only his boxers when he did it."

"Oh god," Mom says. "Don't tell me he made another sign. It's not as bad as the volleyball one, is it?"

"Worse," I said. "This one said, 'I don't undie-stand how to march, but kick ass at your competition!'"

Mom does that thing where she tries not to laugh but she does anyway, so it comes out like a cough. "I'm sure Leanne was *super* thrilled."

I shrug. "She knew what she was getting into when she

agreed to be his girlfriend. I think he drew a really crappy doodle of her clarinet on the corner of the sign, so she probably forgave him for that."

"That boy is one antic away from suspension."

"He's all right. He makes up for it by volunteering for everything and having the best grades," I say.

Mom knows all of this, but the neon sign in my head is flashing, and I'm nervous and rambling.

"Just make sure you don't get tangled up in it," Mom warns. "I doubt he'd get into any serious trouble, but I don't want you missing out on any scholarship opportunities. Your dad and I are so proud of you. We'd hate to see it get thrown away on something silly."

I pause, trying not to let the anxious buzzing in my hands come out in my voice as I try to steer the conversation away from football and back to Nova.

"Mom, can you check for the new girl's address? Her name is Nova Evans."

She straightens. "Nova Evans?"

"Yeah," I say. "That's it."

"Oh," she says, pouring a bunch of raw chicken tenders into the bottom of the pan and smothering them with barbecue sauce. "Sure. Let me get this in the oven and then I'll check my phone, 'kay?"

In the five minutes it takes her to chop onions and carrots and then find her phone, I consider abandoning the mission and not going to find Nova at all. What if the new girl isn't her? What if she *is* and she doesn't remember me? What if she *does* remember me and now that we're older, she knows how screwed up my life was and doesn't want anything to do with me? Or what if she wants to get to know me and realizes how screwed up my life is *now*? That I'm too pathetic to change what's happening around me?

But when Mom gives a dry chuckle after scrolling on her phone for a few seconds, I instantly say, "What? Did you find it?"

"Sure did. Remember the Teegans' old house? The one that management company renovated and turned into a rental?"

My heart is thumping loudly in my ears. I clench my hands into tight balls before dropping them to my side. *No. Freakin'. Way.*

"The house *right behind us*?" I clarify. "*That* house?"

Mom nods. She's got a crooked smile on her face I don't see very often, and I think it means I'm being overeager and she knows it. I try to tamper it down.

"Yep," Mom says. "That's the one. Looks like Nova is our new backyard neighbor. Give me an hour, I can whip up some cookies for you to take as a 'welcome to the neighborhood' for her and her mom."

"I can't," I say, because now that I know she might be *so close*, I can't sit still. "I have to get her these notes. She needs them to review for the test tomorrow."

Mom is half looking at me, half peering through the oven window to eyeball the dish. She burns things a lot, my mom. Watched pots boil faster when she's the one watching.

"Well, let them know we're here if they need anything. And ask if they prefer butterscotch or peanut butter."

"Got it," I say in a rush. "Gotta go."

I'm almost out the door when Mom yells, "Jacket!"

"Don't need it," I say.

"*Notes?*"

Sheepishly, I run upstairs and grab the first paper I can lay hands on before racing out the door.

Chapter Four

Nova

Mom is upstairs in the office wearing her sound-canceling headphones when the doorbell rings, so I go to answer it. Probably just a FedEx or UPS guy. They're constantly needing signatures for Mom's business documents. I've stopped saying, "I'm her daughter," and instead say I'm Mara Evans to save time. I know her signature and everything.

I open the door, not looking at the delivery person as I take a pen from an open box on the entrance table.

"Thank y—" I begin, holding the pen up to sign.

But it's not FedEx or UPS.

It's Sam Jordan, and he looks as stunned as I feel.

"It's *you*," he says.

He means the girl from the hallway, not the girl from Snailopolis, but my heart beats hard and fast and in my throat all the same. He's looking at me like he *knows* me, but I know he doesn't remember because why would he? If he was going to remember, it would have been during our stolen conversation.

My words are stuck, and I tell myself to be cool. I don't know *why* he's here, only that it has nothing to do with the dozens of happy reunions playing out in my head.

My voice thaws enough in my throat for me to say—in an impressively normal tone, I might add—"Oh, hey!"

Sam doesn't answer. He is looking at his feet, face panicked in a way I don't remember seeing when we were kids when he had every reason in the world to be agitated. He always seemed so calm then, which I never understood. I freaked out when I got a papercut, but Sam—*Sammy*—looked as if new scars were nothing, as if the bruises didn't hurt him at all.

Right now, though, he's moving his arms around so frantically it's like he has bugs stuck in his jacket sleeves.

"Yeah, yeah. Um, I brought you these." He shoves a folded-up sheet of paper into my hand. "It's notes for math class."

The paper is a bright card stock, too colorful to be hand-written class notes. When I unfold it, I don't expect to see math symbols and numbers, but I also don't expect to see *Sammy and Abigail* written over and over and decorated with little hearts and stick figures holding hands.

"I think this belongs to you," I say handing it back to him and something like disappointment settles deep in my chest. Is this his idea of a joke? Does he remember me or not? I'm so confused.

He looks down, but it's like he doesn't see the paper. "Oh, yeah. I guess it is."

"Why are you here?" I blurt, disappointment shifting to irritation. *Smooth, Nova. Smooth.* "I mean, how did you find where I lived? And why did you assume I needed math notes?"

"Sorry," Sam says, and he still can't look right at me. "I just . . . I didn't . . ."

"You could have given them to me at lunch," I say. "I sat right next to you." My voice drops in reverence when I add, "Or in the hallway."

It was probably nothing to him, but it was *everything* to me to see Sam Jordan alive and well in a school I had no business calling my own.

Sam looks straight into my eyes, and does that very-boy thing of running a hand through his hair. He looks caught somewhere between impatience and panic. "*Yes,* but I didn't know it was *you.*"

"Me?" I ask, but my heart is thumping too hard for me not to have heard him correctly.

Now he looks frustrated, too. Suddenly, he leans forward and gently grabs my hand from my side, turning it over so my palm is faced toward the sky. I expect him to hand me the paper again, but instead he reaches into his pocket and pulls something out, placing it on my palm with two fingers.

It's a snail.

A tiny, perfectly round, perfectly ordinary snail.

He remembers. And it fills me with a thousand stars.

"You're early," I whisper, still looking at my palm, at the snail.

"What?" And his voice is filled with such hope, I know he heard me.

I look him in the eye. "I'm only seventeen. You said you'd find me when we were eighteen. You're too early."

His answering smile is the kind that people write entire novels about. It's better than I remember from childhood, because it's like he's *actually* happy instead of trying to be.

"I could come back later," he says.

"No," I say quickly. Because even though this is supposed to be my sixty days of self-discovery, and he has a whole life that I'm not a part of, and we were, like, *five* the last time we saw each other, and he didn't recognize me instantly but I did, and, and . . .

I don't know many things about myself, but I know I don't want him to go.

In my head, it was yesterday, the two of us sitting beneath the tree. It's like we went to sleep as kids and woke up today standing on opposite sides of a literal and proverbial open door that I know—I *know*—I should shut. Not slam, but definitely close.

We're too far removed from that old oak tree. Besides, trying to go back to that time is not only impossible, it's *highly ill-advised*. I should be doing the opposite, running toward my unknown future and pointing my flashlight toward *that* instead of shining it backward.

Especially if looking backward is looking at Mr. Popular Jock Jordan.

It's like Sam can read my thoughts. He always could.

"I should go," he says, but he doesn't move.

"You should," I say.

He nods but says, "Yeah . . . but I don't want to."

"But you should."

"But I don't *want to*," he repeats. "Even if Ab—" He cuts himself off. "Even if I know I should."

It feels like we're at a crossroads, but I tell myself we can come right back here, to this doorstep, to this moment, and pretend it never happened. I want to walk a little bit down the path of Sam Jordan. It doesn't have to be forever. Just for now. An hour.

What could it hurt?

"Let's go for a walk," I say, already taking my phone out of my pocket to shoot a text to Mom.

Sam shuffles his feet. "Anywhere in particular?"

I step out to join him on the porch, closing the new heavy wooden door behind me. "I'm not sure. I don't know where anything is."

It's weird to watch Sam think, to stand close to him again and watch as his eyebrows scrunch, his mouth twists.

"I know a place," he says. "But we'll have to drive."

"I don't have a car," I say.

Sam smiles, and his hand twitches toward me like he

means to take mine. He stops short, the backs of our fingers brushing against one another.

"Um, we can take mine. It's . . . not a long walk to my house."

"Oh, where do you live?"

"Let's just say if there was a hole in your backyard fence, it would be much faster, but as is, it'll be three minutes at most."

I blink. "What?"

Sam's laugh is easy and low. "You'll see."

★ ★ ★

"I can't believe we're neighbors again," I say.

We're in the cab of Sam's truck. It's obnoxiously big and white and streaked with dirt and smells like too-strong body spray and exhaust fumes. There's no reason for anyone other than an industrial farmer or a professional mover to have a monstrosity like this as a *personal vehicle*, but he's hardly the only one. We pass at least five others on our way out of the neighborhood.

"Me either," he says. "I freaked out when Mom told me."

My words leave my mouth before any brain cells have a chance to catch up.

"You live with your mom, now?"

The silence that blankets the truck is absolute and lightning fast. The atmosphere plummets.

"She's my aunt," Sam finally says. He turns on his blinker

and keeps his eyes on the road—and off me. "I've called her Mom for years."

"Oh," I say. "That's nice."

Oh, that's nice, I think mockingly to myself. As if Sam didn't casually gloss over years of childhood trauma. I really, *really* hope that my true self I eventually discover has more brain cells than this. Maybe I should add a psychological evaluation to my activities for these six weeks, just to be sure.

"Is it?" Sam asks, wry.

"I'm sure she likes to hear it," I say, desperately trying to find an exit from this conversation. "Do you have siblings? Er, cousins?"

He exhales. "Nope. It's always just me, no matter where I go, I guess."

"Same," I say.

The air between us is still a little off, so I figure I might as well press my luck in case this is the last time we talk.

"When did you realize it was me? You saw me twice and . . . nothing."

"Oh." Sam laughs. "I guess you haven't looked at yours."

"Look at my what?"

He hands me his phone, rattling off his passcode so I can unlock it. "Go to the internet app," he says. "It should still be open."

It takes me too long to realize what I'm looking at, so Sam says, "It's the Crush results. From that personality test they made us take today."

"Oh," I say. "Cool." My eyes are stuck on the long list of

names. None of these people are familiar to me. His number fifteen is someone named Violet, and twenty-two is a Samantha.

"Sam and Sam would be fun," I say.

This Sam pulls into one of two dirt parking spots beside a rickety wooden sign that reads NATURE PRESERVE in white spray paint. He leans over and takes the phone from my hands.

"Scroll to the top, Nova," he says.

I freeze again. Does he realize this is the first time I've heard him say my name since we were kids? I recover quickly, moving the screen with my thumb until I see his top five matches and the "match potential" percentage beside them.

There, at the top, is my name, next to a bold, red 99 *percent*.

"That seems . . . improbably high," I say.

Sam turns a little in his seat to face me. "Yeah," he says, and I can't read his expression or his tone. "How about that walk?"

It's a bit of a drop from the truck cab to the ground, enough that I have to straighten my sweatshirt from the jolt. When I do, I remember the snail I tucked into the front pocket and take it out.

"You better be glad I remember Snailopolis," I tell Sam, holding up the snail. "This would be a really creepy welcome gift if I didn't."

"Everyone loves snails." He smiles.

"We should put it in this nature preserve," I say. "If that's really what this place is."

"It is," Sam says, and then seems to think better of it. "Well, sort of."

"How can a place be *sort of* a nature preserve?" I ask. "Do they only preserve certain species? Is it like, *All of you wild-flowers can stay, but may the odds be ever in your favor to the birds?*"

I might be able to see traces of little Sam's face in the Sam who stands beside me, but not when he laughs. I don't remember his little-kid laugh, actually, but I *know* it didn't sound so deep and rumbly.

"Not like that. There was this old guy who lived here forever," Sam says. "I think his family owned the land since the Civil War. Anyway, when the town started to get bigger and more and more stuff started being built, he kept getting offers to buy his land and turn it into stores and coffee shops. Like, *big* offers. I guess millions?"

We're walking now, close enough to link arms or hold hands, but we don't. Because . . . well, for so many reasons, not least of which is he has a girlfriend and I have a plan. All around us are the sounds of birds, twittering from the canopies above and from the floor of the wooded area surrounding the dirt trail Sam is leading us down.

"But he didn't want to sell?" I ask.

Sam shakes his head and snorts. "*No.* Not at all. Apparently he wanted the land to stay as it was, but he was getting older, and some of his kids were planning to sell after he died. So before they could, he donated it to the city. But nobody has gotten around to doing anything with it yet. There's almost never anybody here."

"Is he still alive? The old man?"

Sam shakes his head. "Died this past summer. His house is still here, though, until the city knocks it down, I guess. We'll pass it here in a little while."

We've completely lost sight of the parking lot and its accompanying handmade sign. If I strain, I can hear the distant sound of highways and vehicles and humanity, but it's dim compared to the low hum of insects and the bright birdsong.

It's a little overwhelming—okay, *very* overwhelming—being here in this blank slate of a place with Sam. It's like time has been wound backward, like there *aren't* any patterns and my world has been reset.

And yet, I'm still here, a product of everything that has come before: Seattle and he-who-must-not-be-mentioned, moving and moving and moving again, every persona I've tried on like a new outfit, the uncomfortable clash of who I am against who I am pretending to be.

I'm not entirely dissimilar from this nature preserve. We're both waiting to see what comes next after years of being one way and now being expected to become another.

I wish it really was a blank slate, this clandestine meeting in a sort-of nature preserve, but it's not. I'm still me. Sam's still . . . whoever he is now.

And he has a girlfriend.

And I need to stick to the plan. I'm only here two months. It's not worth it.

Maybe if I keep telling myself that, it'll be true.

Chapter Five

Sam

Something's changed. I keep looking at Nova, trying to study her face without getting caught, and it's the same as the lunchroom, before I realized who she *was*.

She looks disappointed. She looks . . . resigned.

I mentally run through the past few minutes of conversation, about the pseudo nature preserve and the snails, but nothing stands out. All the same, my heart rate picks up in my chest like I've just run the length of the field in all my football gear. I'm good at hiding it, but my skin prickles at the *thought* of Nova being upset with me.

I went to therapy for a while—a long while—after I came to live with Mom and Dad. The government ordered it, I think, but eventually the weekly sessions drifted to once a month, and then, in junior high, to nothing at all. It was too hard to keep up with both football and the sessions. But also? I just didn't want to go anymore. I didn't see the point.

But something the last doctor said sticks with me.

"Your early years regrettably set you up for a lifetime of seeking dangers and triggers everywhere, including from people who wish you nothing but good," she said. "Humans have emotions, and most of them don't equate to physical danger. You have to reteach yourself how to identify threats in your environment to help with your anxiety episodes."

Basically, my entire body goes into hyperdrive at the smallest hint of conflict.

Because conflict used to mean pain of every kind.

But this is *Nova*, I remind myself. She's the opposite of a threat. No matter what has changed, no matter who she has become in the years since we sat beneath that tree, she's still the queen of Snailopolis. She's still the one who kissed my palm when I couldn't bear to be touched by anyone else.

She's not going to hurt me.

"You okay?" I make myself ask. My words come out a little higher pitched than usual.

Nova jerks her head up toward me. We're still walking along the path. I can almost see the roof of the preserve keeper's house.

"Yeah," she says, her steps not faltering. "Why wouldn't I be?"

My heart rate and the low thumping in my skull want me to leave it alone, but instead I say, "You seem off. Was it . . . was it something I said?"

I see the surprise when it shows up on her face. "Not at all. I was just . . . thinking."

"About what?"

Looking at her, I don't know how I didn't recognize her earlier. I guess because I wasn't expecting to see her again, or maybe because I don't really remember what she looked like when we were little. I don't have pictures, and it was a while ago.

But now that I know, I can piece bits together. Small things. Like how her nails are shaped the same as they were when they were delicately pinching stones and snails and dirt. And her eyes, wide and fringed with long lashes that I remember noticing when I was a kid. They would sometimes brush my arm when she kissed my hand. As for the rest of her . . . Well, I can't think about how great she looks in her T-shirt that has VAL'S BOOKSTORE right beneath her collarbones and the jeans that have tears-but-not-holes in the knees.

"I guess I was thinking about how you have a girlfriend," Nova says, like she can hear my conflicted thoughts. "And how great that is."

It's the last thing I expected to hear her say, and it's enough to yank my eyes back to her face from where they have accidentally drifted to her hips.

"Great?" I echo.

Nova nods. "Isn't that, like, one of the points of being a human? Loving other humans? It's cool you have that."

I choke on spit from the back of my throat for what feels like a whole minute before I manage to say, "Um, I don't know about *love*."

Safety, certainty, predictability. As close to love as I'll get, I think. *If you don't fuck that up, too,* I tell myself. I push away thoughts of Abigail whispering her fears into my neck. Nova and I aren't even Nova and I. It's just Nova, period. Sam, period. No *and* or *we* to complicate things.

Nova waves her hand in a dismissive way. "Whatever you want to call it. You know what I mean. It's cool that you have a partner."

I make myself count to seven—my jersey number—before I ask, "Do you?"

"Do I what?"

"Have someone you love?"

If I wasn't watching her so closely, I probably wouldn't notice how her laugh sounds a little strained. "Unless you count my mom and cousins and other family, no. Not like that."

I have about a hundred follow-up questions, and literally any one of them would have been better than the first one that comes out of my mouth: "Do you ever wonder what would have happened if I hadn't moved?"

"I'd rather not," she says, her voice quiet. "You weren't safe there. It's good you left."

It's weird, having someone remember the before with me, but I keep talking. "Okay, but if I had and it *had* been safe. Do you think we would have stayed friends?"

Nova snorts. "Snailopolis would have had a better hydraulic infrastructure than just pouring that cracked plastic cup all over it, that's for sure."

We're surrounded by tall grass and taller trees as we walk along a dirt path sprinkled with pebbles, yet this feels like a business meeting. Like we're negotiating everything: what we'll remember, what we'll be going forward.

I want to know who Nova Evans is *now*. I want to know why we matched at 99 percent. I want to know why I don't have to count breaths when I'm around her, why she seems to fit when nothing else in my life does.

So, for once, even though all my conflict-aversion techniques are yelling in my head to change the conversation back to something easy and light, I tell her.

"Ninety-nine percent," I say.

"Huh?"

I take a deep breath. "Aren't you curious? Why we're such a high match?"

Her answer is the last thing I expect.

"Not really."

I count to seven again. "Any particular reason why?"

Nova shrugs. "I don't even know if the answers I gave were true," she says.

"You lied on the test?"

"I didn't *lie*. I just . . . didn't know some of the answers."

I'm about to say the first thing that comes up in my head again—*that's a cop-out, how could you not know*—but then I stop and think about some of the questions. I was mostly happy to have an excuse for a break from SAT prep in English class when Abigail and the others came in to give us the Crush test. But once I started reading the multiple-choice personality questions, some of them made me wonder if I'd rather hear Ms. Latera tell us about "eliminating obvious wrong answers" for the millionth time.

The worst offender was, "Your favorite childhood toy: (a) plush toy (b) action figure (c) bike (d) video game."

Most of the test answers were like that, weirdly specific so that you kind of *had* to fudge your answers if you didn't have something that directly lined up. I answered "plush toy," even though the old pillowcase I called Blanket doesn't really fit the bill.

Thinking of Blanket makes my head pound, so I quickly tell Nova, "I get it. But still, aren't you curious about why we matched like we did? There has to be *something* to it even if the test was stupid, right?"

She stops suddenly, the words out of her mouth before she has completely turned to face me.

"Sam, I'm glad you're happy. And I'm glad we've gotten to see each other grown up, like we promised, but we shouldn't think about the Crush thing again, okay? Maybe we should just enjoy our walk and then . . . be done, you know?"

"Be done . . ." I echo.

She gestures hopelessly toward me, and I have the sudden urge to grab her hand and hold it. I don't, but barely.

"It just doesn't make sense anymore. You're a football player and obviously super popular, and you have a *girlfriend*, who probably wouldn't love if she knew we were hanging out right now, and—"

"She wouldn't care," I interrupt.

And Abigail really wouldn't. She would understand, I know it. *If* I told her everything, which I never will, but that's all beside the point. My allegiance lies with Abigail no matter what. Nova and I can just maybe be what we were before: Friends. Really good friends.

I try to ignore the nagging memory of Abigail's breath on my neck, the unfamiliar insecurity etched on her face like grain on wood, but when I can't, I tell myself a new truth: The right thing to do is not worry Abigail with it. Nova and I aren't going to become anything. This is an investigation into the *past*. And even if it knocks against the present, it's not going to affect the future. Not really.

"Even if that's true," Nova says, interrupting my spiral, "*I* can't. I'm only here for a couple months. Wouldn't it be worse if we started . . . if we found out that we're . . ."

I should save her from the fumbling, but I don't. I want to know what it is she thinks would be worse. If we found out we're still as good of friends as we remember being as kids? If we could be something *different*, now?

But Nova stops talking altogether and looks at me with those wide, wide brown eyes. In this light, they look hazel. Maybe even a touch green.

"I think it's a bad idea," she finally says.

For the first time in a long time, I *want* to argue. I want to press and see what it is Nova *really* thinks, because if she re-members our friendship even half as well as I do, she wouldn't feel this way.

She would be curious about the 99 percent and us and the promise, promise.

But it's not up to me to decide how she feels, even if I dis-agree. (I learned that in therapy, too.) Besides, I don't want to hurt her or ruin whatever memories we *do* have, even if she's saying we aren't going to make any more.

So instead of saying, *I think you're wrong*, or *What if we just give it a try?*, I turn us back toward the direction of the parking lot and say, "Then let's just enjoy our walk."

We're mostly quiet on the ride home. When we get to her house, I open Nova's passenger door because it might be the last thing I can do for her before tomorrow, when I guess everything will go back to the "normal" that existed before I realized we were in the same place again.

But instead of hopping out of the cab like I think she will, Nova gently—*so* gently—leans forward and puts her hand on my arm.

"I'm glad I got to see you again, Samuel Jordan."

With her still sitting in my truck and me standing beside her, we're almost the same height. She's a little taller than me this way, so I get to look up at her. Her smile is tilted and perfect and a little sad and . . . perfect.

"Same," I say.

She's biting the corner of her top lip, twisting her face in thought.

"What is it?" I ask her.

"I'm debating whether to ask if I can kiss you goodbye."

It takes approximately zero seconds for my head to light up with images—of me stepping onto the footboard to press my lips hard against hers, of dragging her down to ground level and tilting her face up toward mine, of getting back into the truck and driving until we run out of gas.

It's a little scary how quickly the pictures come. This isn't *me*. I don't rock the boat. I don't complain because—compared to my before—there's nothing to *complain about*.

But there's something about Nova—then and now—and that makes me feel safe, like she's a life jacket that will keep me afloat me if I cause the boat to capsize.

Abigail *should* be there in my head, too, but she's not. It must be because I'm in shock. Because Nova shouldn't be here but she *is*, and my brain doesn't know how to handle it. It has nothing to do with *not* wanting to be with Abigail. That's it.

So I nod, leaning forward so that I'm close enough for Nova to reach but not so close that I'm too eager, and close my eyes.

I'm still waiting for her lips to meet mine when I feel her take my hand, the visions in my head still clouding my common sense. It takes me an embarrassingly long time to realize that when she turns over my hand, it's to kiss my palm.

And even though the pictures on repeat in my brain are *definitely* still there, this . . . this is better.

Even if it feels like I'm being stabbed from every direction.

"Goodbye, Sam," she says, still not moving from my cab.

I open my eyes. "Goodbye, Nova."

"And . . . we'll go back to the way it was before, right?" she asks.

"Because this is a bad idea," I say, nodding, knowing it's what she wants to hear and what I'm supposed to say.

"Right." She nods back.

"I promise, promise," I whisper, keeping her hand in mine longer than I should under the guise of helping her to the ground.

She straightens at that, and I wonder if she's remembering everything, too.

"Good," she says.

And this time *she's* the one walking away, and I'm left standing in the street wondering if she just did us the world's biggest favor or if this ridiculous attempt to ignore each other has a 99 percent chance of failure.

* * *

Later, as Mom finishes handwashing the last pan after dinner and hands it to me to dry, the doorbell rings.

My heart leaps. My first thought is that it's Nova, but of course it's not.

Fox's and Leanne's voices mingle with Dad's as he lets them in the front door. I gather from their conversation that Fox and Leanne were out on a study date and wanted to stop

by on their way home to give me a mint-and-chip shake from
Susan's, the ice cream parlor down on the corner.

"It's a little soggy." Leanne smiles when she comes into
the kitchen and hands it to me. "*Someone* needs to get his
car's air-conditioning fixed."

This, a pointed remark at Fox, who doesn't even look the
least bit embarrassed to be subjecting anyone who rides in his
car to Texas heat with no air circulation.

"It's inhumane," I agree. "Thank god Mom and Dad got
me the truck. I would have died of heatstroke over the summer if I had to get any more rides from him after the end of
practices."

"Weaklings," Fox mutters. "Where is your sense of adventure?"

"It melted," Leanne deadpans.

It goes like this, the picking and teasing and verbal spar-
ring that is practically Fox's love language. It never scared me,
though, not even directly after the before. Fox is one of those
people that others trust from the get-go. I know I did. Still do.

I remind myself, not for the first time—and not for the
last, either—that this is enough: a friend who is ride-or-die, a
friend's girlfriend who always thinks to bring my favorite des-
sert, and my own girlfriend, who anyone in the world would
find charming and perfect and gorgeous.

It's enough that I have parents who love me, my own bed
to sleep in, my own room, and a football career that stretches
out before me like a shiny yellow brick road.

Don't ask for too much, I remind myself. *You don't want to risk what you already have.*

* * *

The clock on my bedside table says it's two in the morning, but it feels much later. Despite my best efforts, I haven't stopped thinking of Nova's lips on my palm, reimagining it in great detail before banishing the memory—again—from my brain. Only to circle back to the feeling after a few fruitless minutes trying to think of complicated math equations, or famous works of art, or formulating new football plays that play to the strength of our first string.

My thoughts are clouded over with Nova, but I tell myself it's the mint-and-chip shake keeping me from sleep.

I fall asleep reminding myself again and again to not ruin everything, but when I wake up the next morning, eyes crusty from troubled sleep, my palm is tingling.

Chapter Six

Nova

Mom is looking at me like I've lost my mind. And maybe I have.

It's not a desk, really, but something I've become good at over years of living in the already-furnished places we've called home is making what I need from what's in front of me. Sometimes I luck out and our place will have everything I need in my room already: a bed, a nightstand, and a desk. Other times, like now, I get random extra stuff—a tiny makeup vanity that looks like something from an eighties movie, a stack of suitcases that are actually a useless wooden decoration, and a duck statue that I'm pretty sure is supposed to be a lawn ornament—but no desk.

So I fashioned my own desk from the suitcases and the makeup table. I crammed them in the corner nearest the window so that I could have something to look at when orienting myself with another college pamphlet PDF from another school in a long line of schools that promises to have the best of everything but is just like every other place. Patterns. Always with the patterns.

My job is to find which pattern I'm supposed to be a part of, which is all the more challenging since I'm exhausted.

I didn't sleep well last night because . . . Well. Because.

Even though I tried, I didn't dream of him. I had let the little snail go, but I found a stray index card and pen and managed to draw a pretty decent spiral that was snail-like if you squinted. I put it beside my bed, hoping it would crawl into my dreams and bring Sam with it. Because *that* wouldn't count as plan-ruining, surely, to waste my sleep on him. It's not as if I can figure out who I'm supposed to be when I grow up in my sleep, so I might as well spend it doing what I want to do. And what I want to do, even I can admit, is find out more about the 99 percent.

But no, I dreamed of nothing. When I finally managed to nod off, it was that kind of blackout sleep that makes you wonder if you slept at all when your alarm goes off.

But I'm not thinking about it—about him—today. *I'm not.*

And as punishment for wasting so much time doing just that, I've set my alarm an hour earlier than usual to look at the offerings from—I check the open tab—the University of Chicago.

That's not what is making Mom lean against my open door with a look of concern on her face, though.

No, that's because I was mumbling to the duck statue when she came in.

"Good chat?" she asks.

She's my mom, and she's caught me doing many a stupider thing before, but my face still heats.

"Yeah," I say. I decide to play into it and reach up to pet the statue's head. "Duck here thinks Chicago looks cold."

Mom walks into my room, her running clothes damp with sweat. She must have already been up for an hour or two. She always goes for long runs after we get to a new place because it helps her settle in.

"Duck is right," Mom says, looking over my shoulder. "You'd need another parka, for sure." She pauses, her eyes scanning my screen. "I didn't know you were interested in social sciences."

How would you know? I want to ask. *I don't even know what I'm interested in.*

"It's one of their top majors," I say instead.

I expect the conversation I've been dodging to happen, here, now, beside this duck statue and before I have to go back to school and possibly, *definitely*, see Sam and go back to . . . nothing. Mom is going to ask point-blank what I want to do, who I want to be, and I'm going to disappoint her and all our ancestors in one fell swoop by saying, *I have no idea.*

But she doesn't ask. Instead, she hands me a granola bar and a cheese stick.

"For school," she says. "To eat on the bus."

After she leaves, my heart is still pumping too fast on adrenaline, but the kind that runs on dread.

Every time Mom asks what I'm going to do, if I've "narrowed down" my list of interests—as if I have one—I mumble something about how business seems versatile and she doesn't tend to ask much after that. Probably she can't guess how much I'm waffling, how freaked out I am that I have to *choose*. I've done a pretty good job of hiding it. It's like my one directive in life, the one nobody told me about but the one I've clung to since I can remember: Don't make life any harder for the mom who loves me and is doing this all on her own. She's got enough to worry about without me adding to it.

I tell myself it's fine. *Tonight*, I'll start really figuring out what I want to do. *Tonight*, I'll make a list of majors and mark them off one by one.

I can do this.

With that solved, my heart eases but my stomach begins to feel like it's stuck in someone's fist, and whoever that someone is, they are squeezing. Hard.

For the first time in what feels like forever, I panic about what I'm going to wear to school. There's no template, no persona, and—even though I won't fully admit it, even in the privacy of my own thoughts—there's the fact that Sam will *see* me today.

My outfit won't change anything. It won't suddenly make me decide this plan to return to normal is a bad one and that Sam and I should give it a go at friendship. It won't cause me to second-guess my plan of self-discovery, but *knowing* Sam will see me makes me feel seasick and on edge. Like there's a right answer and I'm missing it.

After nearly making myself late, the panic takes over and I go with a nearly identical re-creation of yesterday's outfit. I figure no matter who you are, you can't go wrong with jeans and a T-shirt. Despite my anxiety, I forget all about my outfit when I step through the side doors of the school, their heavy metal *thud* sealing me into the stream of hallway madness.

I pretend I'm not looking for Sam. I pretend I'm not hoping he'll ignore what we said yesterday—what *I* made him promise yesterday—and he'll come up to me, smile, and say, "Oh, there you are. I was looking for you, too."

I do see him, standing beside Abigail and her open locker, leaning down in that way boys do when they're either outright flirting or thinking about it. Curved spine, downturned head, gentle smile. I've seen it in dozens of hallways. Been on the receiving end a few times, too, so I recognize it.

Which is good. Great, even. This is *exactly* what I wanted: for Sam and me to go back to normal, to pretend like we don't know each other. To leave Snailopolis in the past, where it belongs.

The fist around my stomach clenches again as I watch them. It must be because I didn't have time to eat my granola bar breakfast.

It's only day two of my time at Tyler High, and I'm already seeing flaws in my plan to lay low and be as unobtrusive as possible. It's boring as hell, for one. No friends means there's nobody to greet in the morning or to compare homework answers with.

But it's fine. *This is fine.* All of this—Sam ignoring me, no friends, no extracurricular commitments—is what I wanted, what I've been telling myself for weeks is the best plan.

I'm so committed to killing time by rearranging the nonexistent books in my locker—Why do we even *have* lockers anymore when we only use e-books?—that I don't sense Sam come stand beside me, Abigail noticeably absent.

"Hey," he says.

I jump out of my skin, somehow knocking my hand against the open locker door, which stings.

"Um, *ouch.*"

"I don't remember you being this jumpy." Sam laughs, and he's much too tall and much too close for me to discern if he's leaning to be flirtatious, or if he's just doing it because otherwise, I would have to shout for him to hear my response.

"You don't remember *anything* because we haven't met before, right?"

He rolls his eyes. "Literally no one is paying attention to us."

I close my locker and fiddle with the strap of my backpack so I don't have to look at him.

"We talked about this," I whisper. "It's for the best that—"

"Ninety-nine percent," Sam interrupts.

"I know, but—"

"It's all I thought about last night," he says. "Don't tell me you weren't thinking about it, too."

My face must give something away, because he gives me a smirk that instantly takes me back to races with broken Hot Wheels in the dirt where his cars *conveniently* always won.

"We agreed," I try, but even I can hear my voice softening. "You promise, promised."

"Yeah," he says, "but that doesn't cancel out the first promise, promise, so really the second one is invalid, right?"

"The first promise, promise was to find me when we were older," I say, and my voice is not so much a whisper as a plea. What if his girlfriend comes up? What if *anyone* comes up and we have to explain ourselves and then I'm drowned in social obligations and . . .

"And you found me," I say. "So, yes, yesterday's promise, promise is also perfectly valid."

"You know it didn't only mean *finding* you," he says. "What would be the point of that? Like it was just a really long game of tag?"

"Well, then, what did it mean?" I ask.

The bells—the old mechanical kind that I didn't think existed anymore—shrill their two notes down the hallway.

Sam smiles. Were his teeth this straight and white when we were kids?

"It meant I would find you," he said, "and we'd pick up where we left off."

"That's impossible," I say. And because we're already late for class and my cheeks are warm and the hand fisted around my insides has relaxed enough so I can breathe, I add, "We're not little kids anymore."

Sam's expression doesn't change, exactly, but something in his eyes shifts. "Maybe not."

He leaves after that. He gives me an awkward bow of the head like we're in one of those British society TV shows with ball gowns, and then he's gone down the hall before I can process what happened.

Nothing, I tell myself. *Nothing happened.*

I repeat it constantly, the *nothing* bit, but my stomach doesn't hurt the rest of the day.

★ ★ ★

Sam

She's in the back of my English class. She's at lunch. She's in the hallway, but we're not alone like yesterday, so I watch her pass by.

She's inside my football helmet, the inside of the T-shirt I throw on as fast as I can after my post-practice shower. She's a perfect blend of the before-Nova and the now-Nova with rounded cheeks and smiling eyes.

Sometimes when my brain is too loud, I'll stop at the nature preserve, walk around, and literally touch grass and bark and plant life until I feel like I can breathe.

But today my brain is loud for another reason. A Nova reason.

And when I get home, practically breaking the stick shift as I throw it into park at my usual spot on the curb, I can't wait a second longer for her to be beside me, not when I know that she's *right there*. Just beyond the fence. Not when I need to figure out what it is that makes her easy to smile at, easy to talk to in a way no one else is.

* * *

Nova

I'm sitting at my makeshift desk and waiting for my laptop to finish what must be seventy million updates, when the first pebble hits.

It doesn't hit my window—it lands somewhere closer to the front of the house—but I hear it anyway. At first, I think it must be a particularly large bug flinging itself against the brick, but then it happens again, and again.

I can't decide if I'm pleased or irritated when I finally rise from my chair enough to look down and see Sam Jordan standing in my backyard. Out in the open. Like he doesn't care that either set of parents might see him and then what will we say?

There would be too many questions, too many chances for the before and after to smack together in the worst way if his parents or my mom see us talking at my window like we're trying to sneak around.

Adults always think they know what's going on. That they *understand*. But they rarely do.

The window creaks when I raise it open.

"You're not supposed to be here," I tell him.

I can see his smile from here.

"You said we're not little kids anymore," he calls up.

"Because we're not."

He shrugs. "I'm not so sure."

"Well, I am." I should close the window, but I don't. Instead, I fold my arms and say, "Did you need something?"

"Yeah, a playdate."

I swear I try my level best to *Not. Smile. At. Him.* Because I know it will only encourage him, and that can only lead to him throwing more pebbles on more afternoons, which is definitely *not* part of the plan.

My face muscles have other plans, though, because I can't help stretching my lips up.

"I'm too old for those," I say. "I'm mature. Worldly. I have a savings account and everything."

That seems to draw him up short. He cocks his head. "Do you really?"

"It's got like thirty dollars in it, probably?" I tell him. "My great-aunt started it when I was a baby."

He grins up at me. "Come on, Nova. Play with me. Please? I've already got everything set up."

"Set up?"

Sam's smile widens, but he says nothing.

"What did you do?" I ask.

He's already ambling away, his arms swinging casually, *tauntingly*, like he knows I won't be able to resist following.

"I'm not telling you until you get down here."

* * *

"My mother is not going to appreciate that you dug a hole in our yard," I say, trying to sound stern and failing miserably. "She'll worry we'll lose our rental deposit."

"Technically, half of it is in my yard," Sam points out. "So it'll be half my fault."

"You broke the fence," I say.

Sam doesn't respond, sitting in the dirt instead. I wonder if he's worried about his jeans.

"I modified it," he finally says.

"Like, six pickets are missing their lower halves. Our parents are going to see and then we're going to get busted and—"

He reaches up, and, even sitting, he's tall enough to curl his hand all the way around my elbow and gently tug me downward, but I don't sit yet.

"You worry too much," he says. "Adults hardly notice anything. Are you going to play or not? I don't have long before my parents come home for dinner."

When I came down the stairs and into the yard, I expected snails. Maybe some old beat-up race cars.

I did not expect . . .

"Are those spaghetti noodles?"

Sam doesn't sound the least bit put off by my incredulity.

"Yep."

"And cat toys?"

"They're *mice*," Sam says. "I don't think they necessarily have to be 'for cats.'"

I finally surrender and sit beside him, my knee knocking his as I settle onto the crappy crabgrass.

"They have catnip in them," I point out. "They're definitely for cats."

Sam ignores that and uses an uncooked noodle to draw little zigzags in the dirt.

"So you're a night owl, too?"

I blink, not following. "What?"

"Ninety-nine percent match," Sam says, like that explains everything. When I just keep blinking at him, he clarifies, "I'm guessing that means we answered all but one question almost exactly the same. So are you a night owl or an early bird?"

It's my turn to draw with the noodle. I quit my effort to balance a cat toy on the end of one pasta stick.

"I don't remember what I answered," I say quietly. "I thought we agreed we weren't going to talk about that."

"You don't have to remember what you said on the test," Sam says. "You just have to answer *now*. No bubbles, no checks in the box. Just . . . talk about it."

My pasta noodle breaks. I reach for another.

"I bet you think it's weird that I can't give you a straight answer."

I expect Sam to say, *Of course not*, or maybe *Take your*

time, but Sam does that annoying thing where he's absolutely silent, waiting for my answer because he knows it will come just like he knew I would follow him down to this new hole in the fence.

He's right, of course.

But it feels strangely nice to say, "I don't really know. I went through a phase where I woke up early to run, joined the long-distance running teams at a couple of schools, that kind of thing. I *think* I liked it. I'm not sure if it counts if your body is just running—no pun intended—on autopilot until nine a.m., but I did it every day for months."

"And the night?" Sam asks. "You're a fan of that, too?"

I nod. "I also went through a board game period where most of the players were adults who met after work and kids were in bed, and I enjoyed staying up late. There was something nice about the world being quiet and empty when we left the board game store or the coffee shop or Denny's or wherever. But I guess I was a bit on autopilot then, too, when it got really late."

Sam is still looking down at the felt mice. He's trying to line all three of them up on a single piece of pasta by using two other noodles as chopsticks.

"Maybe you're an afternoon bird," he says. "No strong preference either way."

"Or maybe I just lack the self-awareness to know what kind of bird I am and I'm going to die from a messed-up circadian rhythm."

When Liam—the ex-boyfriend in Seattle I don't like to

think about—chuckled, it always sounded a bit dark, a bit *mean*. I told myself at the time that it was sexy and mysterious, that his personality wasn't like that. Because I thought he couldn't be. He was a *church kid*, the kind that gave me a promise ring, told me he wanted to marry me someday, that we could make my crazy living situation work long-distance and he'd wait for me and, blah, blah, blah.

But I should have heeded my intuition about Liam's laugh.

Maybe then I could have avoided the humiliation of finding out that my promise ring was actually one of five, part of a set he bought at Target and distributed in ring boxes he got from Amazon to me and four other girls.

So when Sam chuckles, I'm hyperaware of how it sounds hesitant, surprised, like he can't believe he has a reason to laugh but he's grateful to have found it.

There's not an ounce of meanness in it. No mystery.

Maybe it's because I'm so focused on his laugh, but I can feel myself slip, feel my guard come down an inch, my resolve flickering off and on like when the electricity blinks. It occurs to me that while Liam gave me a hokey ring and called it a promise, it meant nothing. It didn't even last two months.

But Sam gave me his word, and somehow it has followed us through the years.

His chuckle sounds like more of a promise than anything Liam could ever offer because they are *inherently* different people on the inside.

Not to mention the outside, too.

I blush at my train of thought, watching the way his hands—so different from the little-boy hands I remember—flex around cat toys and dry pasta. He's bigger than the Sammy Jordan of my memory—duh—but he's also *big*. He must live in the gym.

It wasn't that I didn't find Liam cute. I did, in that tall, slim, bookish way. I'm more into the insides—*ha*—than the outsides, but if we're talking pure aesthetic appeal . . . there's a pool of something in my stomach that certainly wasn't there when Sam and I were kids.

I'm not going to step into it. I don't want to drown. Not *really*.

Sam, oblivious to my dawning awareness of *him*, pokes me with a noodle that's been broken in half. Can he see how hot my face is?

"You're *not* going to die," he tells me. "I, a bona fide night owl, will always make sure to find you at the end of the day and get you back to your nest."

I find the other half and poke him back. "The whole point of figuring out your personality is to be a self-sufficient bird. I shouldn't *need* other birds."

Sam's answer is to untangle his legs and stand, holding a hand down to help me up and put an end to our short play-date.

"Everybody needs somebody," he says. "Even circadian-confused birds."

The sun is setting, the sky golden- and honey-colored above

the rooftops, and it feels like such a jolt back to our childhood that it makes me grip his hand tighter than I mean to. How many times was the sky this exact shade of warm yellow when we went back to our separate homes? Is this the hundredth time? The twelfth? The very first?

I let go first. I have to, otherwise I might never let go at all.

Chapter Seven

Sam

I'm annoyed that Nova hasn't said anything to me since Monday. Which isn't entirely fair. I've been putting in extra time in the fieldhouse gym trying to get ready for this week's game against Seraville, our rivals, so I haven't had the chance to throw any more pebbles against her window.

I *could* have gone yesterday, but when I was about to head home, I found myself staring at a text from Abigail that said #7 on the field, #1 in my heart no matter what Crush says with a string of poop emojis after it (an inside joke I've long since forgotten the origin of). Instead of home, I ended up at the ag barn beside the field house, where all the welding and woodworking classes are held.

Mr. Sumpter, the lord of the barn and its occupants, is used to seeing me ghost in and out. He doesn't say much. As far as I can tell—from the one class I took my freshman year where I spent all my free time in the barn—he mostly speaks in grunts and swats, quick to smack a hand that is getting too close to anything dangerous but just as quick to caress a lamb's head.

What he definitely doesn't do is comment when, on days like yesterday, I appear in the corner of the shop and dig out the miniature toy kitchen that I've been tinkering with since midsummer. I haven't taken a class with him since ninth grade, and yet I probably do more than his students.

The play kitchen was his idea, something he communicated to me by placing a hand-sketched blueprint on a workbench when I came in after practices just to—and this makes me sound creepy—get a whiff of the wood and the hay and get out of my thought whirlpools.

The little toy replica is almost done. I sketched my own improvements to it, measuring out a place to put in a plastic basin for the sink, redesigning the lower shelves so there could be more room for fake food and pans. It makes me feel like I have my life in order when I'm in the shop, like I'm a problem solver instead of a problem maker. I like having a plan, one that *I've* made, that I can follow and get the exact results I want.

But that was yesterday.

Today I am hell-bent on figuring out a way to talk to Nova,

and I have no blueprint, no Mr. Sumpter to guide me in his gruff way.

Nova and I only have the one English class together and *of course* it's also a class I share with Abigail, and of course we sit right next to each other, and of course it puts Nova in a weird position to try to talk to me when Abigail is constantly finding a reason to touch my arm or borrow a pen. It *shouldn't* be weird, but it is. Probably because it should be me going to Nova, but I can't. Not in front of everyone at school. Not when I can still see the way Abigail's face scrunched after the Crush results.

It's easier to *not* explain how I know Nova. It's easier to just . . . not be near Nova at all when Abigail is around.

A paper folded into a football hits the side of my head.

Oh yeah, Fox is here, too.

"Dude," he says, leaning forward in his desk. "Your hair smells *amazing.*"

I swat at him, grateful for the excuse to let go of Abigail's hand.

"Would you quit? I'm out of shampoo. I had to borrow my mom's."

Fox inhales deeply. "You smell like brown sugar and coconut. Lika a beach. A *sexy* beach."

Abigail leans over to flick Fox's arm with nails that match her blue-and-white cheerleading uniform.

"Stop molesting my boyfriend. Aren't you two supposed to be meditating on football plays for tonight's game or something?"

At the front of the room, Mrs. Trainer clicks on the smart-board with a sigh. "You're *all* supposed to be meditating on the main sources of conflict in *The Crucible*, but after grading last week's essays, I'm questioning whether you even read it."

The whole class groans, and Mrs. Trainer holds up a finger in warning before continuing.

"Which is *why* today we're going to watch selected clips from the movie adaptation and then spend next Monday reviewing AP questions before moving on to our next text."

The groans are immediately replaced with cheers. Fox leaps up to open the cabinet behind Mrs. Trainer's desk that holds extra school supplies, three emergency baseball bats, and an illicit stash of individual snacks. He comes away with a bag of off-brand Halloween candy with a big 75 percent off sticker on the front.

"Do *not* leave wrappers on your desks or the floor," she warns as she cues up the movie. "And, Fox, would you *please* hand those out to your classmates instead of hoarding them? Perhaps you should revisit your own excellent paper topic of the dangers of mob mentality in stressed populations."

Nova sits in the very back of the class, three rows behind me. I wish I could say I feel her eyes on me, that she's as drawn to me as I am to her, but every time I manage to steal a glance toward the back of the room—pretending to scratch my neck, to stretch my back, to get something from my backpack—she's looking at her desk or the board.

Not so with Abigail, though, who begins to scoot her desk closer to me, narrowing the gap between the aisles.

"Thank *god*," she says, trying her best to lean over the rail connecting her desk and chair to cuddle me. "I could use a movie day."

"Miss Shepherd, there is plenty of candy in this room without dangling from arms."

Behind me, Fox snorts and—so quiet I wouldn't catch it if I wasn't paying attention to her—Nova laughs.

So she *is* at least tangentially aware that I—and Abigail—exist in the same classroom as her.

Abigail, however, seems to be blissfully unaware of both Nova and the joke.

"Huh?" she asks, still clutching my arm.

Mrs. Trainer points to where Abigail's desk should be. *"Move."*

She does, sticking her bottom lip out at Mrs. Trainer in a protest our teacher pretends not to see and continues to ignore over the next forty minutes of *The Crucible.*

I, however, can't ignore Nova as easily as Mrs. Trainer ignores student moping.

While people on-screen begin planting insidious rumors and Fox loudly chews knockoff taffy in my ear, I try to come up with a plan to sneak to the back of the room. Because if I don't talk to Nova now, when will I have the chance? I have no idea what her weekends look like—if she spends them alone, with her mom, not at home at all—but I want to find out. I can't wait until Monday to see her again, and I doubt that she's coming to tonight's game.

Nobody questions why I need to go to the back of the

classroom to sharpen my pencil when I haven't taken a single note, not even Nova, whose desk is conveniently located right in front of the old-school mechanical sharpener. She continues to pretend I don't exist.

I whisper as quietly as I can over the slow, creaky grinding of the pencil I had to dig out of the crummy bottom of my backpack.

"What are you doing tomorrow?"

At first I wonder if she even heard me, but then she's slowly leaning back in her chair as if she's stretching.

Her answer comes out disguised as a yawn. "No."

It's not a firm *no*. There's no harshness to it.

My pencil is sharper than sharp, but I'm still cranking.

"Can I ask why?" I whisper back.

Her answer is just as quiet.

"Because," she says.

I wait for her to finish, but I guess that was a full sentence, and Mrs. Trainor has spotted me at the back of the class, so I go back to my chair, where Abigail has managed to scoot a few inches closer.

I don't see Nova again until the pep rally that afternoon.

Pep rallies are a big deal here. The whole town shows up to the high school gym to watch the cheerleaders perform a cheer specifically targeted at our opponents, a member of the community who is a big deal gives an inspiring speech to us players, and the marching band plays the fight song loud enough to bust eardrums. Fox always makes a big show of making sure he sits directly in front of Leanne and her clarinet section.

Friday pep rallies are part of my routine but not one I enjoy. And today—fuck, I forgot it was *today*—is when I'm formally being presented with my latest award, a Ford Player of the Week trophy. In front of everyone.

In front of *Nova*.

But I barely have time to register where she's sitting in the upper bleachers, her back to the gym wall, before cameras flash and my parents—proud as I've ever seen them—come to stand next to me and the hulking, wooden *Player of the Week* trophy shaped like Texas that somehow materialized in my hands. I wonder how they made it attach to the wooden base at such a small point. I'm examining it when the microphone feedback draws me back to the gym, to this Friday, to another football event in a long string of football events that stretch as far behind and as far in front of me as I can see.

An honor, Coach is saying into a microphone as the gym erupts in applause. *We expect big things from Mr. Jordan, here.*

On either side of me, decked out in the special #7 JORDAN jerseys Mom had made at the local spirit shop, she and Dad are smiling their widest smiles for the camera. They're doing that thing where their hands keep meeting on my back as they take turns patting my shoulders in pride.

When the photographer asks for a photo of me in front of the cheerleaders, Abigail's smile is even wider, her lipstick bright and her hair high as she ruffles her shiny pom-poms in my direction.

Proud of you, she mouths.

I can't help it: In between snaps and urges to *Look here, Sam*, my eyes find Nova. She's watching me, but so is everyone in the gym. There's not much else to look at because I'm *supposed to be* at the center of attention.

She's not so far away that I don't get chills when our gazes meet, not so far away in time or space that I can't close my eyes—just for a second—and put myself back in the hallway or at the nature preserve or in the front seat of my truck with her lips pressed to my palm.

I count to seven.

When I open my eyes, I am the Sam Jordan who is making his parents proud, who is making his *town* proud. It's enough. *More* than enough. This is what some people dream of, what I should be dreaming of.

When I open my eyes, I look away from Nova.

* * *

Nova

Fun fact: You can hear everything happening at the football game from my cracked bedroom window.

When I change into my pajamas for the evening, I hear the roar of the crowd at kickoff. At halftime, when I'm staring at the notebook I've dedicated to brainstorming ideas for my future, I hear a marching band performance, a cheerleader routine, and the announcer declaring the student of the week is a first grader named Skye.

In the final quarter, when my open notebook bears hardly any new marks, I hear the announcer declare that number seven is down and the medical team is entering the field. Idly, I hope that whoever the player is, they're okay. Football seems unnecessarily brutal with all that clashing and ramming. I've never understood it.

I'm back to my notebook, staring at the list of international universities I've been compiling for the last few months, when I hear the announcer again.

Looks like it's Tyler's running back, number seven, Sam Jordan.

I abandon my notebook and rush over to open the window wider so I can hear the already-muffled announcer a bit better. My entire evening has been filled with the racket from the game and now—*now* of all times—there's only silence.

Which has to be bad, right? If it's this quiet, it must really be bad. Running back? Isn't that what they said his position is? Is that the same as a quarterback? Frantically, I rack my brain for any football knowledge and come up empty. I've only been to a handful of games, and I was always there to socialize, not for the sport.

I'm halfway through googling "Can running backs die in football" when the announcer's voice echoes from the stadium finally.

A senior and our star Ford Player of the Week recipient, it looks like . . . Yes!

Then, moments later, a cheer that confirms he is okay to continue.

Number seven for Tyler, Sam Jordan, is reentering the field, ladies and gentlemen. It appears he just had the breath knocked out of him. Look at that double thumbs-up. A real team player. Let's give a hand to the medics and play ball!

The breath knocked from Sam must have been catapulted from the stadium, through my open window, and into my chest. I feel myself inhale sharply enough that I question if I've breathed at all since the announcer first said his name.

I wait for the rest of the game, leaning against the sill until the cracked paint chips dig into my arms and leave little red marks, but I don't hear Sam's number or name called again.

I tell myself it's enough to have heard that he wasn't taken off the field in a stretcher, and later, when I hear a car door slam that sounds suspiciously like it might come from Sam's overly large truck, I wait fifteen minutes, tiptoe out of my room, and escape into our backyard.

There are three upstairs windows in Sam's house that I can see above the part of the fence where he broke the pickets to re-create our childhood playground. Only one of the windows is lit from within, any actual shapes hidden by the blinds and curtains.

I should go home. What if they have those security cameras that alert you to motion? What if I get arrested for trespassing and Sam isn't there to defend me because he's sleeping off his injury?

I turn around to go back inside, but a memory stops me in my tracks. Another memory of before, with little Sammy and little Nova.

He was a grade older than me, so we almost never saw each other. It wasn't like high school where grades mingled based on schedules and advanced placements. Even recess was mostly separate, first graders sticking with first graders and so on.

But field day was different. All of us, from kindergarten through third grade, were thrown together with eggs on spoons and sack races and parents mingling with plastic cups of watered-down lemonade.

I was competing in the water balloon toss when a Frisbee came from out of nowhere and hit me straight in the temple.

I was fine but started crying immediately—the only appropriate response to unexpected cranial trauma at any age—so I was taken to the first aid tent and told to sit in the folding chair and hold an ice pack to my head and not to leave until I drank an entire bottle of water. The nurse didn't have time to listen to me explain that I had never drank a whole bottle of water in one sitting in my life. She quickly rushed away to address more important issues, like a kid whose hands were practically bleeding from rope burn.

There was no doubt in my little-kid mind that I was going to spend the rest of field day in the tent. The idea of disobeying and getting up while the nurse was busy did not even occur to me. And Mom wasn't going to come to the rescue— she had volunteered to help set up that morning because she had meetings in the afternoon—so there was nothing to do but feel my forehead go slowly numb and watch as my friends played without me.

But then there was Sam.

I remember he was wearing long sleeves that day when the rest of us were in short sleeves and tank tops.

I remember he had dark circles under his eyes, the kind Mom got when she stayed up too late working.

I remember the way he stood in the mouth of the tent and looked at me with wide eyes, like he was afraid of what he would see. But when I grinned at him, he smiled, too.

"I got hit with a Frisbee," I told him sadly. "But I'm okay."

I remember how he turned over my palm and kissed it. "It goes where it needs to go," he said.

It made me feel better, that he was there and I wasn't alone in the tent. I knew the tent was for sick and hurt kids only, but I didn't want him to leave.

"You should go play," I said. And then repeated, "I'm okay."

But Sam didn't leave. He sat next to me for the rest of the day, both of us quiet in the tent with the nurse hovering nearby and the other kids streaming in and out in a parade of bandages and ice packs and sunscreen. But we were together all the same.

The memory of his dark sleeve rubbing against my tanned arm propels me forward in the present. I'm scrambling up the fence when I hear someone clear their throat from the other side.

It's not Sam's face that I see when I disembark and lean down to look through the hole. Instead, it's a man who looks like he could be cast as a young version of Santa: pre beard, pre cookie belly, but with crinkles around his eyes and slightly reddened cheeks hinting at his jolly future. He's doubled over to look at me, his head slightly tilted.

"Hello there," he says, voice oddly cheery for it being so late at night. "Come to see my kid?"

He's holding a hose, one with a sprinkler attachment, and it's showering the ground between us, soaking the hole in the ground Sam made. I'm too busy staring at the water being drained into the dry, dry dirt to formulate an answer.

"I saw you out here the other day," he says. "With Sam. Unless you have a sister. Do you have a sister?"

I shake my head.

"Didn't think so. You *do* look exactly like your mother, though."

"You know my mom?"

He straightens with a groan, out of view from the hole, but I can still hear him clearly. "I've seen her walking the neighborhood."

Which checks out. Mom sometimes takes conference calls on walks to get out of the house on days she works from home.

"Gotta water these gardenias the same day each week or they wilt and my wife gets grumpy." Mr. Jordan says and pauses. "Like to keep her happy. Like to keep my *family* happy. Which is why, young miss, I think you oughta use the doorbell from now on. Lord knows his mother and I won't object."

He's one of those adults that doesn't seem to need to hear me speak to know what my response will be. Usually I find that irritating or uncanny, like they can't be bothered to actually listen to me or are some higher life-form with a better understanding of humans than I will ever have, but with Sam's dad it's . . . fitting. Maybe because of the Santa thing.

"I'm sorry," I say, because that is almost always a good response when adults go fishing for answers. "About the fence."

"Nothing to be sorry for," he says over the gentle sound of water hitting the flower vines. "Our Sam often forgets we have security cameras that can pick up a fly landing on these flowers. So you can imagine they have no problem watching a teenage boy dig a hole in the ground, break some fence posts, and invite a pretty girl to play with . . . What was it? Cat toys?"

He sounds like he's laughing so I say, "And spaghetti noodles."

"Ahh," he says. A pause. "You're the little girl from Providence Street."

When I don't answer, he amends, "You're the girl next door, the one who played with Sam when . . ."

He trails off, and I can practically hear him trying to find the right word. He finally settles on the same one I use, the one I think Sam uses, too. "The girl from before."

"I am," I say.

Sam's dad nods. "I thought so. I remember you. He insisted on saying goodbye, wanted to wait for you to come home from school and"—he gestures to the hole in the fence between us, an echo of the before—"return to your meeting spot."

I don't know what to say to that, so I say nothing.

"You look the same," he says.

Another pause, long enough that the silence expands to include the sound of water hissing through the hose, the crickets chirping around us, and the spin of the AC unit behind me.

There's a lump in my throat, but I push past it. "We moved," I say, because what else is there? This conversation feels like a twilight conversation, a discussion that makes sense but barely. "We moved after he left."

Some of the jolliness is missing when he sighs, long and low.

"He's a good kid, my Sam. Been through a lot, but I suspect you know that. I don't want to see him get hurt anymore. He's had enough of that to last a lifetime." Another pause. "Or more."

"Me either," I say.

"Things from before . . . Those tend to hurt him," he says. "But you're different. I can tell. Always have been."

I want to ask him *how*, because the way he says it makes me wonder if he knows something about me that I don't know myself. Like maybe he can see something I can't and it'll help solve the puzzle of *who* I am. Who I'm supposed to be.

But that's selfish to think about when we're standing in our respective backyards talking about his adopted son. I can tell his dad loves Sam with every cell in his body, but he would rather have had Sam start in a happy home with no need for sleeves or feel-better palm kisses.

So instead I say what I'm thinking, "I just wanted to see if he was okay. I could hear the game . . ."

The water turns off, the sharp *click* of the sprayer cutting off augmented by the squeaking of the faucet. The fence post between us moves as Sam's dad begins to store the hose, looping it round and round its holder.

"Front door next time," he reminds me when he's done. "But seeing as it's so late, I think it best you wait here."

Chapter Eight

Sam

When I shower, I make the water as hot as it will go. My pale skin is going to be pink for hours, but I'm hoping if I can make it scorching enough that it'll burn away the fear still ringing in my chest.

I was hit from the side in a faulty block, taking a fast-moving elbow directly to my helmet hard enough to see spots. The dark circles got worse when I stood to my feet, so I immediately sat down on the turf and closed my eyes to try to stop the progression from tough hit to tough knockout.

I've seen the spots before.

Before before.

And the memory of that alone was enough to keep me on the ground, waiting for the medics to come and give me the all clear. I needed a second to make the circles—and the memories—disappear.

At least this time I knew someone was coming to help.

At least this time I knew it wasn't *on purpose*.

I learned when I was younger how moments can stretch out and feel much longer than they actually are, and this was one of them. I had time to take multiple deep breaths, to push the anxiety and the quick rage to the back of my head and leave room for a different kind of fear, the football-future fear. But I welcomed it over the memories.

Usually, when I think about something jeopardizing my football career, I turn into two hundred pounds of nervous energy as Mom's and Dad's smiling faces flash through my brain, slowly changing from the way they looked when I was six and they pitied me and worried about me to what they look like now: proud, confident, *happy*. Usually, I go work it off, lifting weights and running on the treadmill until I out-exercise the fear of disappointing them. Because no matter how much I might dislike football, it's nowhere near as bad as what came before. Nothing could be.

But tonight, when I was lying on the field and the few seconds stretched into hours, I couldn't outrun my worries. And I was genuinely afraid this injury was *the big one*, the one that would make it impossible for me to play and get recruited into college next year.

And for a second—just a single second between the fear and more fear—I felt relief.

Because it wouldn't be my fault. Everyone would be disappointed, but not *at* me, because it wouldn't be my *choice*.

Dad's knock on my door is not unwelcome. There's no point in pursuing the relief. I'm never going to do anything about it.

"Hey, kid."

"Hey, Dad."

Dad does this a lot, coming to stand in the open door and look at me. It started right after the before, in the *new* after, when he was worried I wouldn't adjust well to living with him and Mom. But I adjusted just fine with him checking in on me, asking if I needed something, if I wanted to go for ice cream or maybe a drive. Dad has always been a fan of "going for drives" to clear his head, always happy to take me along, too.

I almost think he's going to offer to take me for a drive— even though I can go myself, now—but instead, after hovering for another half minute, he says, "Nice night."

Weird. He and Mom already checked me out and freaked out about my crash on the field, so I'm not sure why he's acting so strange. But Dad is always kind of strange. The fun strange. Kind of like Fox.

"Yeah," I say, confused. "If you don't count the near concussion."

Dad's face lights up. "You know what used to help me in my sporting days? Fresh air."

Weirder, still, but fine. I get up with a groan, cracking my window open just enough to let some of the nearly-cool-but-not-quite air into my room.

Dad nods encouragingly.

"Good, good," he says. "Yes, excellent idea. However, it would probably be much better, much more potent, straight from the source, yeah?"

Okay, we've reached peak weird. Even for Dad.

"You're being weird," I say. "Are you sure you're not the one who took a hit to the head?"

He holds up his hands. "I'm *just saying*: I think a walk in the backyard might do you some good."

I stare at him from where I stand by the window.

"By your mother's gardenias."

I shift my weight.

Dad's cheerful expression changes to one of exasperation. *"By the hole you forged in our lovely cedar fence, son."*

I'm trying to read his tone. I knew he and Mom would see it, but I hoped they wouldn't comment on it. It's one of the very few favors the before has afforded me. If it makes me happy and it's not hurting me or anyone else—no matter how weird or offbeat—Mom and Dad generally let me get away with it. And besides, I was extra careful to not harm the gardenias. I don't have a death wish.

"A science experiment," I explain. "Sorry, I can fix it—"

Dad mutters something under his breath I can't make out before stepping forward and putting his hands on my shoulders.

"*Son. I highly* recommend that you take a walk in the

backyard and go out the side door so that you don't squeak opening the back one and alert your mom. I also *highly* recommend that you hop to it because *the particular flower for whom you made the hole in the fence* will not stand there all night waiting to see you."

Nova.

I don't have time to wonder what Dad must be wondering about Abigail and Nova and the rest of it. I give him a quick hug.

"You could have said," I say, already squeezing past him to run down the stairs.

"I thought I did."

I don't stay to argue. And it turns out Dad was right: She almost didn't wait for me.

When I crouch beside the hole in the fence, Nova's turned toward her house, her feet still poised like she might stop and come back to me at any second.

Her arms are wrapped around herself, her back hunched like she's looking for something in the grass, which I guess she is, because a second later she bends to pick it up.

"What did you find?" I ask.

She makes a breathy little gasp, then jumps, nearly tripping over her slides. I feel so bad for startling her, I lunge forward like I can catch her, like I can fit through the hole in the fence by sheer will, which I can't.

Which is how, for the second time in one night, the unstoppable force of my head meets a relatively unmovable object.

I try not to cuss out loud very often, *definitely* not as much as I wish I could. For one, it upsets Mom, who grew up *super* southern Baptist, and even though she calls herself a "fan of Jesus but not Christians," she still has a lot of church habits that stuck.

Threatening to wash my mouth out with soap is one of them.

For two, it reminds me of the before, when *fuck* and *shit* and *asshole* and *bastard* and *son of a bitch* were so familiar I sometimes think I hear them coming from behind dark, closed doors even when I don't.

But *fuck* if this somehow doesn't hurt worse than what happened on the field.

And *fuck* if I'm not super embarrassed to have run into a *literal fence* like some kind of cartoon dog chasing a cat, especially in front of Nova Evans.

"Sorry!" she says, rushing toward me. "God, I'm *so* sorry. I—I heard what happened earlier. I could hear the game from my window and . . ."

She says more, I'm sure, but I kind of space out when her hands suddenly thrust through the hole in the fence and cradle my head. She runs light fingers over my scalp like she's looking for evidence of a bump.

Everything disappears when she touches me. It's not the same as when we were kids. I guess there's always been something there, but this . . . this kind of longing is different.

So much of my after has been working on physical affection, on not only tolerating it—which is all I could manage for a long time—but *enjoying* it, the connection to other people.

It's still difficult, though. I mean, it doesn't *bother* me when Abigail hooks her arm through mine or kisses me or pats my chest. But ever since our relationship started to feel like it was on a moving track that I have no chance of stopping, touches haven't been something I look forward to. It still makes me cringe a little on the inside, like I'm wasting my hard-won touch tolerance on something I shouldn't be.

It's not like that with Nova.

Not at all.

It almost *feels* like a cringe, what my insides are doing as she runs her hands over my face, the back of my head, my forehead. Like a tic, but a pleasant one, like my body is going into overdrive trying to comprehend the sensation of her fingers.

"I'm okay," I manage to say, proud that my voice doesn't shake. "It wasn't that big of a deal. The football stuff."

"They called the medics," she says, her voice the quietest I've heard it.

She's scared, I realize. Scared for *me*. Her concern shouldn't make me happy, but it does. Not as happy as the way her eyes shine green in the streetlights. Not as happy as the way that piece of hair curls just beneath her ear. Not as happy as it feels just being *near* her.

I'm starting to understand why moths will die throwing themselves against lightbulbs.

"They always call them," I tell her. "It's a liability thing. It happens all the time. I'm fine."

"*It happens all the time?*"

"I just mean—"

Nova sounds angry when she says, "If it happens all the time, should you be playing *at all*? Do you *have* to do this?"

Her hand is still warm on my cheek, growing hotter the longer she keeps it there.

"I didn't even know you wanted to play football," she continues. "You weren't really into sports when we were kids."

"I didn't know, either," I say. "Not until I came here. I didn't even know it was an option, and then I tried it and was *good* at it."

Nova lowers her hand from where it's resting on my cheek, and I impulsively reach up to stop her. Her eyes widen when she realizes what I've done, and I think mine do, too.

We stare at each other, two round-eyed deer caught in the spotlights of our own gazes.

"I should go back inside," Nova says, always the first one to cut us off. "I'm glad you're okay. Thank your dad for me. I . . . I hope he doesn't think we're . . ."

I can't help but smile. I'm still holding her hand against my cheek.

"Think we're what? Friends?"

Her fingers twitch beneath mine. She mumbles something I can't hear.

"What?" I ask.

"More than that," she repeats.

I swear her hand feels hotter beneath mine.

I'm trying to figure out what to say, trying to understand

what I'm *thinking*—traitorous thoughts, like I want to be more than friends, that I might be willing to nix the entire football-and-Abigail plan for her, that I've started to wonder if our promise, promise put some kind of cosmic plan into place and we were always destined to be here, now, beside another hole in another fence—when Nova spares me the trouble.

"But we can't," she says. "Because you have a girlfriend. You were happy before I got here, right? There's no need to ruin that when I'll be gone soon."

She's rambling. I let her.

"And I need to figure out who I am," she continues. "That was the whole reason I . . . I can't keep latching on to whoever's around me and making *that* my personality. I need to stop being a chameleon. Does that make sense? And I can't do that if I'm . . . If we . . ."

I should feel discouraged at her words, should take them as the final nail in the coffin of our promise, promise being anything more than ironic, stupid luck. And I would. I really, truly would, except . . .

She reaches back through the fence with her other hand so she's cradling my face. I quickly reach up to trap that one, too. Like maybe if I act fast enough, we can pause this moment, pause the world, and just be here. No plans. No responsibilities. Just us.

"We can't," she whispers again.

"We don't have to be more than we are," I say, my voice falling to match hers. "We could just be us. What's so wrong about that? You can figure out who you are, and I can stay who I am. But we could . . . see who we are together, you know?"

The crickets are chirping. The neighborhood dogs are barking. The sounds of a Texas suburbia night surround us, so it seems unlikely that the thumping I hear is Nova's heartbeat, but it exactly matches the pulse I feel in her wrists beneath my fingers.

The sound—and her pulse—quickens when she says, "I don't think we can. It's not possible."

"But what if it *is*?" I argue. "What if we keep everything else the same? And if that starts to change, at least we know we tried. We'll quit before anything really bad can happen. Deal? We can make it the new promise, promise."

She's biting her lip, considering.

Now all I can hear is *my* heart. Without thinking, I take one of her hands down from my face and kiss her palm. She inhales sharply but otherwise makes no sound.

"It goes where it needs to go," I say, unable to stop a huge, goofy grin that stretches my face like putty.

Nova looks conflicted for all of two seconds before taking my hand into hers and leaning forward to kiss it, too.

"We'll end it, though, right?" she asks. "If us being . . . 'us' near each other starts to break things, we'll end it, right?"

I curl my palm like I can hold on to her kiss.

"Yes," I say. "I promise, promise."

"And only outside of school," she says in a rush. "Because I don't want too much to change. I have school to worry about. And I don't want . . . I mean, I wouldn't want her . . ."

Abigail.

"I know." I say, sighing. "It's best that way. Ab—" I stop just short of saying her name and start again, trying my best to ignore the mental image of Abigail's face seeing my top match, the way she's called the Crush test *that stupid quiz* ever since we saw the results.

"We won't do anything at school," I promise Nova.

Nova nods, standing so I can see her only from the knees down.

"Good," she says. "Yeah."

"But not like a secret," I tell her legs. "Right?"

She thinks about that for a minute.

"Not a secret," she says. "Because we're not doing anything wrong. Just private."

Private. I like that. Because to me, Nova has always been private. From the start, she has been my private, safe place.

"Good night, Nova," I tell her, still crouched by the hole in the fence.

She leans over, her hair gleaming bronze in the moonlight.

"Good night, Sammy."

Chapter Nine

Nova

When I come downstairs Saturday morning, I expect any number of scenarios: Mom making pancakes in one of the two pans we lug from place to place; Mom in running clothes, either leaving or maybe just returning; or an empty kitchen because Mom has gone to the grocery store or is already holed up in her office for the morning.

Nowhere on my bingo card did I have Mom and Sam Jordan sitting at the little dinette table laughing over cups of terrible instant coffee. (Our Keurig is still yet to be found in the boxes.)

"Nova!" Mom smiles when she spots me. "I was about to come and get you. You don't want to be late for your first meeting."

I hope my wild glance toward Sam comes off to Mom as bewilderment from just having woken up and not from my obliviousness.

Sam's smile is easy as he raises his cup to me in an artificial *cheers* motion.

"Nature Club meeting," he says, like he's reminding me instead of telling me for the first time. "Starts at nine most Saturdays and goes until we've documented at least fifteen individual specimens." He drops my gaze and looks to Mom. "Does she need to be back by a particular time? Sometimes we go out for lunch afterward, but I am happy to bring her back whenever you think is best."

Mom smiles at Sam and then turns to me and waggles her eyebrows. She clearly thinks Sam can't see her, but *of course* he can.

"We don't have any plans today, so I see no problem with it. Did you remember to charge your phone?"

I always remember to charge my phone overnight, but I say, "Yes, Mom."

"Don't forget to text me every now and again so I know where you are," she says.

"Sure," I say. "Thanks, Mom. Sorry I forgot to tell you about this yesterday."

She waves me off, leaning over to pat Sam on the back.

"I've got to get in some extra hours today, anyways. Thanks

for taking her, Sam. It's one of the great things about Nova: She can find friends anywhere."

Her phone rings upstairs, and then it's only me and Sam. Sam and me. Sam sitting in a kitchen I hardly think of as mine, but it *is* and he's *here*.

We're smiling at each other, our grins growing the longer neither of us speaks.

"What?" I finally ask.

His smile impossibly widens. "What, what?"

"There's no Nature Club, is there?"

Somewhere in the universe, a star burns out with the energy that it takes to fuel the light in Sam's eyes. His gaze drops to take in my didn't-know-today-would-involve-nature outfit.

"I'd wear different shoes," he tells me.

I look down at my flip-flops. "Because we're going to Nature Club?" I ask, my voice teasing.

"Right," he says.

I roll my eyes. Our games are becoming more sophisticated, and I tell myself the rush that goes through me from sandals to ponytail is because he's an old friend, nothing more.

"*Fine*," I say, pretending to be put out. "I'll go change for *Nature Club.*"

"No air quotes needed," he tells my back as I go up the stairs. "That's where we're going."

"Sure."

* * *

We park in front of the spray-painted nature preserve sign again, but this time, the other spot is occupied with a golf cart that looks like it survived World War II.

I say as much to Sam, who smiles that star-burning grin at me again. It's like between last night's new promise, promise and today he found a whole constellation to burn and is hell-bent on doing it in one day.

"That would be the other half of Nature Club. They're probably already on the trail making out or something." He pauses, only for a second. "My girlfriend has never wanted to come to Nature Club. She's not a big fan of bugs. I think she got sick from a tick once? Anyway, I didn't want you to think she was, like, *not* here on purpose or—"

"No, I totally understand," I say, and something *does* ease in my chest. Hanging out in private is one thing, *excluding* his girlfriend from a normal activity would be another.

I don't have time to ask any follow-up questions, though, because from the overgrowth behind the makeshift sign springs a boy with leaves in his hair and a small but fresh scratch across his cheek.

"*Lizard*," he announces. "Come on. Before it leaves!"

Sam moves to follow and then, hesitating, holds his hand toward me. He looks apologetic.

"My best friend, Fox. His saint of a girlfriend, Leanne, is somewhere around here, too."

I take his outstretched hand.

"Nature Club is something *we* did as kids. I thought . . .

Well, I know you said we're private, not secret, but I thought . . .
I guess I thought . . ."

"No," I assure him. "No, this is . . . this will be great."

There's a new hesitancy between us that wasn't there before last night, before someone else—some *other* me who
is bold and unthinking—took control of my hands and ran
them through Sam's hair and around his face, like he was a
seashell I had found on the beach. Like he was mine to ex-
amine. Before we agreed *to just be us*—whatever that means.

I guess it means we're going to hold hands and play Nature
Club—which I am extremely suspicious of now that I know he
invited his *best friend* and his best friend's girlfriend, who surely
must have an opinion about Sam hanging out with a girl who
isn't Abigail—but I can't find enough resistance within me to
go back to the car and declare this a terrible idea.

Especially when my hand is in Sam's and he's tugging me
toward Fox's excited *whoops* and Leanne's tolerant voice saying, "You're going to scare it before they can *see* it."

"It" turns out to be a very spiky, very grumpy lizard that
looks more than a little irritated that his sunning was dis-
turbed. Leanne is working very hard to keep him on his rock.
She keeps moving her flattened palms to block his escape.

"Would you hurry up and just *draw* him already?"

I assume she's speaking to Fox, but Sam lets go of my
hand to reach into the pocket of his shorts and brings out
a small spiral pad with a red colored pencil. He crouches
down, eye-to-eye with the horned creature, and his hand
flies across the page. When he stands from his squat, I see

what looks to be an amazingly accurate sketch, from the tip of the tail to the grumpy, side-eye expression.

"Um, excuse me? Could you *always* draw like this?" I ask.

Sam's smile doesn't burn out a star this time. Maybe because it's the slightest bit smug.

"To be fair, this isn't my first time drawing one of these."

Fox has now picked up the lizard, which thrashes in his hand before settling down enough for Fox to bring a small tape measure to its side.

"Nearly four inches," he says, whistling low as Sam records the number beside his sketch. "That's gotta be one of the bigger ones we've found, right?"

Leanne plucks the pad from Sam and starts flipping through the pages—*many* pages, I realize—before handing it back.

"The last record was just over three. We've got a winner."

The lizard, freshly released, scuttles off. It does not appear to be a fan of Nature Club.

I wait for the awkward introductions, but they never come.

Instead, it's like I've always been here. Like *we've* always been here, the four of us, trampling through thin-trunked trees, tall grass, and dirt paths with animal footprints, looking for "friends"—as Fox calls them—or "specimens," according to Sam.

Leanne and I have settled on calling everything from animal to plant to geode "friendly specimens" because Leanne promises me it's best to remain neutral in this years-long argument.

"You and I will be long gone and these two will still be arguing over terminology for Nature Club," she tells me.

We're both perched on separate rocks, near enough to where Fox holds down a tree branch so that Sam can sketch some little round dots that Fox found and insists are "eggs from a friend."

Leanne declared this "too boring, even for naturalists," so she and I are picking at blades of grass and splitting them with our fingernails. We have an impressive pile of green shavings at our feet.

"How long have you and Fox been dating?" I ask her, surprised at how casually she mentioned leaving, that she doesn't seem to believe that love will last forever and ever.

"Oh, I guess it's been about two years," she says. She has the long, blond mermaid hair of my childhood dreams. She tucks it behind her ears without looking up from a grass blade. "We don't really keep track."

"That sounds . . . nice," I say. I mean it.

Lately I've wondered if my lack of permanence has damaged me somehow, like not belonging anywhere or to anyone but Mom broke something in my DNA. I suspect it's the reason I'm so obsessed with going to college and doing it right, fully committing to a major and clubs and a friend group.

"It is," she says. And like she could hear my true questions, adds, "We understand each other, Fox and me. You know? We both wanted a buddy while we're upperclassmen. Neither of us wanted to bother with asking someone new out to every single little dance and formal and football banquet and band banquet and shit. We're buddies that occasionally kiss and like it, so it really worked out. But next year we'll go our separate ways with good memories and no hard feelings."

I like Leanne. Maybe it's because she's going along with *this* game, the one where nobody questions me and Sam and what we are to each other, but I trust her. And I can tell she's one of those people who are like open books, which is why I feel comfortable enough to ask, "And you're okay with that? The goodbye?"

I've always assumed my ease at saying goodbye went with the territory of my broken DNA, or maybe I just got the worst farewell out of my system when Sam left to live with his aunt and uncle, but maybe it's not. Maybe lots of people are comfortable with the idea of temporary and I'm rebelling against something that is perfectly normal.

But when Leanne looks up toward Fox, and their eyes connect across the grass and rocks, and he picks up his hand in a little nerdy wave, it makes Leanne smile in that dreamy, lost kind of way you see in movies, and I feel both happy and a little sad for them.

"I'm going to have to be," she says, but her tone and smile are more of an answer than her words.

★ ★ ★

Sam

Fox is watching me out of the corner of his eye like I don't notice his stare.

"Dude, what? Stop looking at me like that. It's creeping me out."

"*You're* creeping me out," he retorts.

I wait for him to say more, but when he doesn't, I feel like I have to say something to fill the silence.

"Do you like her?"

Fox angles another leaf my way so I can sketch the spider veins branching out from its center. We've moved on from the "eggs"—which are *not* eggs. They're some kind of pest, I think, but not eggs. Now we both know we're buying time alone to discuss the frantic text I sent him at five o'clock this morning. The one where I begged for a grand reunion of the Nature Club after multiple months of not meeting and how I was bringing a girl and no, it's *not* Abigail and please be cool.

"Nova?"

I groan. He's not going to make this easy.

"No, I mean Leanne, your true love. *Yes*, Nova. What do you think of her?"

Maybe Fox isn't such a terrible nickname, because when he focuses completely on you, it feels a bit like a hunting animal staring down its prey.

"Do you really want to know?"

This time I groan *and* throw an acorn from my pocket at his head. I had meant to give it to Nova, but I'll find another one. This one needs to be a missile for Fox's stupidity.

"That's why I asked."

Fox throws the acorn back. I pocket it.

"She makes you different," Fox says. "You're Sam on steroids around her."

He wants to say something else, but he bites it back.

"What?" I ask. "Just say it."

Fox doesn't hesitate. "Nova is a stimulant, and Abigail is a depressant."

There it is.

Impulsively, I draw a long, thick red line across the leaf I just sketched, ruining it. Fox notices, of course, but says nothing.

"So many drug metaphors," I say. I try to keep my voice casual, but it comes out a little strangled.

"Are you going to break up with her?" Fox asks, his voice lowering further. "Abigail?"

I pocket the pencil and the pad before I can do something worse. "No," I say. "We're not like that. Nova and I are just friends. Sort of."

"I find that hard to believe," Fox says with a snort. "You act like you've known each other for years."

"*We've* known each other for years," I point between us, "and we're not dating."

"We're both woefully hetero," Fox says. "Besides, Leanne smells better than you. *Unless* you would consider switching to that delightful coconut-candy shampoo you used before class the other day . . ."

"Shut up." I laugh, shoving him. And I can tell we're shifting away from the initial topic, but I know I'm going to have to tell Fox everything at some point: about the before I've never outright mentioned though I'm sure he suspects, about Nova, and about how I can't deviate from the plan.

For now, I settle for the other important thing.

"I don't want Abigail to know."

I say it directly. It's the best way to make sure Fox really heard me and isn't going to accidentally spill when he's hyped on energy drinks after practice.

My words make him drop the leaf he's been shredding with his nails.

"What are you doing, man?"

I snort. "Man? What are we, Californians? I don't know, *dude*, I just want to . . ." I drop the playful act. "I don't know. We click, you know? Nova and me? Always have and still do, I think. I just want to see how she is."

Fox looks past me to where Leanne and Nova are sitting on rocks, having their own conversation.

"From where I'm standing, it looks like she's doing fine. No need to check up on her in any special way."

"You *know* what I mean."

He raises an eyebrow. "Actually, I don't. Because it *looks like* you're hanging out with a girl who isn't your girlfriend *and* keeping it from said girlfriend."

"It's private," I tell him. "Not secret."

Now Fox snorts at me. "Sir: You *know* there's no difference when it comes to this kind of thing. How hard was that hit you took to the head? Abigail is cool, but how cool do you think she'll be when she finds out you've been hanging out with a *childhood girlfriend* on the sly?"

"Nova and I weren't dating. We were *five*. And Abigail isn't going to find out, because we're keeping it from her to avoid complicating things. Not because we're embarrassed or doing anything wrong." I swallow. "Nova leaves soon, anyways. So it's not like . . . It'll be over before . . ."

I sigh. I can't find the words, and I've got that wrung-out feeling in my chest, so I don't want to try.

Nature Club isn't always full of heavy conversations with Fox and me, but almost every talk we've had of substance has been at Nature Club.

It started out because I missed being outside. When I first moved in with Mom and Dad, the outdoors was familiar in a way their house was not. I didn't want to hurt their feelings and didn't want to be in the way, so I went outside. Eventually I became old enough to bike to the nature preserve and would meet Fox there to climb rocks, jump into the nearly nonexistent streams, and draw the cool stuff we found.

As we got older, it turned into a mishmash of the new and the old: the play we never quite grew out of, and the big discussions and feelings that were easier to talk about beneath trees than in halogen-lit classrooms. Out here, it was easier to admit when the girls we liked didn't like us back, to talk about how sometimes we wondered what it would be like to live *not here* and if that meant we were terrible people for wanting more (or different) than our parents had.

Nature Club was where Fox first told me he was going to ask Leanne out—who, at first, would join us because she said she was bored. But I think she was half in love with Fox already.

And now Nature Club is where I will ask him to make *me* a promise, promise.

"I don't want her to know," I repeat. "It would just confuse her, and I don't want to hurt her."

Fox got his nickname when we were little. No matter the sport, he could find his way out of impossible holds, blocks, and situations. It's like he saw what others couldn't, even when we were seven.

Right now, though, his eyes are the most foxlike thing about him: narrowed, shrewd, and aimed directly at me.

"You could just tell her," he says. "She's a big girl, a *smart* girl. And if you can't tell her everything, why are you in a relationship at all?"

I dig the pencil back out of my pocket for something to do, somewhere to look that isn't Fox's face.

Fox gets me better than almost anyone, but he doesn't get my need to adhere to the plan and to not upset my parents or Abigail or *anybody*. Maybe he *thinks* he does, but if he really understood, he wouldn't be asking me to throw everything back in their faces after all they've done for me.

Even the thought makes my stomach churn.

"Can you just trust me on this?" I ask him, a cop-out, but it's what I need. "If I *did* tell Abigail, then Nova and I would be a *thing* to her, and I would feel paranoid every time I saw Nova, and I don't want that. Not when she's here such a short time . . ."

I trail off, words failing again.

When I make myself look up at Fox, he nods once.

"Okay," he says. "It's your call. None of my business, really."

I try to keep my sigh of relief quiet, but I know he hears it.

"Thanks. You're sure Leanne won't say anything? To anyone?"

Fox slaps a hand on my shoulder, angling us both toward where Leanne and Nova are still chatting.

"Leanne is too busy practicing for her first-chair audition to worry about anything else. Besides, you know she can hardly stand Abigail."

"She can't stand *anybody* but band kids," I say. "And you, on a good day."

Which is true, but I say it mostly to defend Abigail.

But that's all I have time to say because Leanne hops down from her rock and comes over.

She kisses Fox in greeting. "We gotta go," she tells him. "Remember? I'm supposed to help the incoming freshmen with marching techniques and I—"

"—need to practice for my chair exam," Fox finishes in unison, wrapping his arm around her shoulders. They're almost the same exact height, Leanne a tiny bit taller. "I know."

Leanne punches him playfully in the arm and turns to me. "Bye, Sam. I like Nova. Don't scare her away, please. Much less boring coming to Nature Club when I'm not outnumbered."

If Nova and I were something other than . . . whatever we are, I'd put my arm around her, too, where she stands beside me. Maybe she'd pat my back, say, "He can't get rid of me," and we'd all laugh and it would feel like a tiny piece of forever.

But we are what we are, so Nova stands awkwardly away from the group and says, "It was nice to meet you." Then

Leanne and Fox are gone, trekking back to Leanne's parents' golf cart that is broken more often than not. Even so, it goes so slowly they would have been better off walking the ten minutes to Leanne's house.

I wait until I hear the cart rumbling away before saying to Nova, "I can take you home, too, if you want."

She shrugs, and I can tell she's trying to look nonchalant.

"I've got nowhere better to be. Didn't you tell my mom something about lunch?"

I take out my phone to check the time. It's only eleven o'clock. I say as much.

Nova shrugs again, a smile tugging at her lips. "Well, we have to drive at least an hour out of town, right? Isn't that rule number one of private-not-secret?"

Fuck, she's right. I hadn't even thought of that. I had figured we would go to Sonic. Maybe Braum's if we wanted to sit somewhere *not* in my car. Those are the only two options in town that serve more than ice cream, and I am so, *so* bad at this.

Sometimes, even when the situation shouldn't be overwhelming, I *feel* overwhelmed. It's like one second the world is fine—there are waves, but it's mostly chill. And then, all of a sudden, those build into one massive tidal wave that comes crashing down on me.

Fox and his concern; Leanne and the way I saw her look at me and Nova out of the corner of her eye; Nova and how she scrambled up a tree to look at a squirrel's nest like Nature Club was actually a *good* idea and not a stupid game Fox and I have played since we met; Abigail and her perfect snare on my future that I helped her set; the football training I could be doing but instead I'm here, getting hit by tidal wave after tidal wave.

Nova notices. Of *course* she does. This isn't her first time functioning as a life preserver.

"Hey," she says, reaching for my hand. Her fingers feel natural between mine, grounding. "Come on. We'll find some place just out of town."

When we get to the car, I still haven't said anything, still trying to get my head above water. I open the passenger-side door to my truck for Nova, but she gently pushes me forward instead and holds out her hand for my keys.

"I'll drive," she says.

I don't argue.

She looks so small in the driver's seat. Even though it's a standard-size steering wheel, she looks like a sea captain behind an overly large helm, especially when she curls her shoulders down to type something into her phone.

After a second, she laughs.

"Some Place," she says. "Ever heard of it?"

I find there is enough breath in my lungs to say, "What?"

Nova smiles. "It's a barbecue joint called Some Place. Literally. It has really good reviews. It's a little over an hour's drive. Wanna go?"

I do want to go. I really, really do. But sometimes when I feel the crushing weight of everything, it's hard to talk.

My yes gets stuck in my throat, but I try to tell Nova with my eyes, *I want more than anything to go with you. I want to watch you drive behind the wheel of the truck I don't let anyone touch but me. I want to eat barbecue and sit across a table from you in a restaurant on our own. I want to know that everything has worked out and you don't have to leave after two months, and that we'll do this every weekend instead of only once.*

She must understand, because she puts her hand on my headrest to back us out of the parking spot and point us toward the road.

Nova waits until we're well out of town before darting her eyes toward me and to the road again.

"So," she says. "Wasn't there a question on that stupid quiz about toys from when we were kids?"

My voice feels raw in my throat, but it *sounds* normal enough when I say, "I thought you didn't want to talk about the quiz."

Nova shrugs. I'm obsessed with watching her lips curl up knowing I can stare at her profile without her seeing me. She is a *very* safe driver. Her eyes have left the road only once to look at me and once to change the radio to some horrid country station.

"I just want to talk," she admits. "And if that means talking about the quiz, that means talking about the quiz."

I wish she hadn't remembered *this* specific question.

If it was anyone else asking, I would lie, make something up about a teddy bear or an action figure.

But it's Nova, and she already *knows*, which is both a relief and a burden.

"I called it Blanket," I tell her. "One time after my parents fell asleep, I watched some old cartoon movie about a toaster who goes on adventures and one of his friends is this mustard-yellow electric blanket named Blanky. My pillowcase used to be white, but it had yellowed over the years. I pulled it off the pillow and called it Blanket."

Nova's eyes shoot to mine for the second time and immediately back to the road.

"Why not call it Blanky, then? Like the movie?"

"My father didn't like baby talk," I tell her, which is true. I remember him flying into a rage after I said "froggy Christmas" instead of "foggy Christmas" when singing "Rudolph the Red-Nosed Reindeer."

I shut the door on the memory as hard as I can and brace myself for Nova's pity. But it doesn't come.

"Blanket," she says. "Very distinguished. Way better than my rabbit named Rat because I couldn't say my *b*'s properly."

Her answer surprises a laugh out of me, and she quickly joins in.

"A rabbit named Rat." I chuckle. "It sounds like a weird kids' book. Where is Rat these days? In a box? On your bed every night?"

"No, he didn't make the cut in like fifth grade or something."

"The cut?"

"Yeah, Mom and I both periodically purge our stuff so we have less to shuttle around when we move from place to place."

Because I'm watching her so closely, I expect to catch a

speck of sadness in her expression, a subtle twitch that might indicate that she's not happy about her nomadic lifestyle. I wonder what else she's had to cut that she regrets. I wonder what else she has had to sacrifice.

But there's nothing. Not even a twitch of the lip for Rat the rabbit.

"You like it, I guess?" I ask. "The moving around?"

Her fingers tighten on the steering wheel.

"Yes." She thinks better of it. "Well, maybe. I'm not sure anymore. I used to love it, but . . ." She trails off, picks back up again. "Lately I wonder if it broke me or something. Like, maybe I would know who I am by now if I hadn't been trying out so many different personalities and aesthetics and hobbies at every new place. Because I've never stuck with anything for more than a few months, it's like that phrase—what is it? Master of none."

"Jack-of-all-trades, master of none."

"Yeah, that."

I adjust my seat belt so I can angle toward her better. In her lap, her phone screen declares we'll be at Some Place in ten minutes.

Ten minutes doesn't seem long enough to loosen her fingers from the wheel, but the king of Snailopolis should try to help his coruler, right?

So I do. Even though I'm pretty sure I'm going to suck at it. Fox would know the exact thing to say to give Nova a blast of confidence, to help her feel like she *does* know herself, that she's the master of herself.

But I don't.

"Jack-of-all-trades," I repeat. "I like the name Jack."

Super helpful, Sam. Well done. Very insightful. God, it's a good thing Nova and I are not more than whatever we are now. Nova deserves someone who can carry on an actual important conversation with her.

Because I'm still watching her closely, I see the smile crinkle her eyes, the way her cheeks rise up like a sunrise as she laughs a sharp, loud laugh that echoes in the cab of the truck.

"Maybe that's the answer," she says. "I legally change my name to Jack and she'll know what to do. A girl named Jack and a rabbit named Rat: two weirdos take on the world."

"You'll have to find a new Rat, though."

Nova waits a beat. "Maybe we can do that next weekend? After Nature Club."

She's not looking at me like I'm looking at her, but she must be able to feel the way my entire body smiles.

Next weekend.

There is going to be a next weekend with Nova Evans.

I don't feel overwhelmed for the rest of the day.

Chapter Ten

Sam

School has never been my favorite—sometimes it seems the walls of the building were created just to make me feel claustrophobic—but it's even less bearable after a weekend of Nature Club and Nova and Some Place barbecue. Which ended up being delicious.

I try to keep myself occupied during lunch while Abigail talks about homecoming and the dress I already know she found this weekend because she texted me *about* it, but not pictures *of* it because she "wants it to be a surprise."

"You're going to love it," she says, poking me with the handle of her fork.

"I'm sure I will," I say. "But I'd love it just as much if you showed me now."

Abigail laughs. "That would ruin the surprise!"

I'm not a fan of surprises that I know are coming. They don't feel like surprises anymore, then. They feel like dread. Even if I know it's going to be something as simple as a dress, it gives me anxiety trying to figure out how I'm going to react, what I'm going to say. Because surprises are as much for the person giving the surprise as the person receiving them, and I'm always worried I'm going to miss the mark, not play the part well enough.

To keep myself from thinking too much about it, I search the internet for the perfect rabbit stuffed animal. I want to find one and buy it a little tag that says "Rat" on it for Nova.

As a joke.

Like friends do.

A joke.

Ha.

I can see Nova nearby, sitting at a different table than us. It's like she's one half of a magnet and I'm the other. I can't help but look at her no matter how we try to distance each other in classes or hallways or cafeterias.

I think she notices me looking at her. Actually, I *know* she notices, because at one point she narrows her eyes and shakes her head and moves from the table in my direct line of sight to one behind me.

It's a bad move, but I switch to the other side of the table under the guise of copying Fox's math worksheet so that Nova is directly in front of me again.

Only this time, I have to look right past Abigail to do it.

Fox tries to warn me with a jab to the ribs the third or fourth or twelfth time I look Nova's way, but it's too late. Abigail follows my gaze and twirls in her seat to look behind her.

"*What* are you looking at?"

I know Nova heard her because her eyes widen and she instinctively drops to the floor like we're in a bad spy movie. She seems to realize how ridiculous a move this is if the goal is to avoid notice, because she starts patting at the perfectly empty linoleum around her and saying, "Glasses? Glasses?"

Fox hides his laugh as a cough as I stand to come help her, explaining to Abigail, "I saw them teetering off the edge of her table. I should have warned her."

It's a stupid explanation—why would someone take off glasses during lunch—but Abigail buys it.

"Poor thing," she says to Catherine, her best friend, and then they're talking about homecoming again and how it's *just two weeks away* and how they want to coordinate their hair appointments for the same exact time so they can make a TikTok of before and after.

It doesn't matter to me, though, as I stand and move away from the table. Abigail and Catherine can talk all they want about whatever they want.

I'm crouching on the ground next to Nova *during* school.

"You don't wear glasses," I whisper, though I don't know

why I bother. We're too far away for my lunch table to hear and the only other person anywhere near Nova is a girl reading a book, who, from what I can tell, has not looked up *once*.

"You're right. I wear contacts. And don't worry, Holly can't hear you," Nova tells me, nodding to the girl who migrated tables along with her. "I sit next to her in Spanish. Every day before last period she finishes a book and then she must start a new one every night because there's *always* another book in her hand. She's too far in to hear anything we're saying."

"That's not true," Holly says, still not looking up as she flips a page. "I just don't hear anything worth *responding to*."

Nova smiles at her like my grandma used to smile at her old, crotchety cat that hated everyone but my grandpa.

"Holly's the best," she says.

But then the fond smile drops from her face, and I can tell I'm not going to like what she says next.

"We agreed," she said. "Not at school."

We don't have much time, I know. There's only so long we can pretend to look for nonexistent glasses before even homecoming-distracted Abigail starts to ask questions.

"I know," I say. "I'm sorry."

Which I'm not.

Nova's lip curls up, and her eyes glow in the cafeteria lights. "No, you're not."

I smile back. "I'm not."

I stand and reach down to help her from the floor and then, feeling like little knives are stabbing me in the heart, I let go of her hand and head back to the table that two weeks ago would have been my best-case scenario and now magically—or maybe cursedly—feels like a consolation prize.

I hide it well, though. Or, I think I do, but Abigail gives me a once-over when I sit back down beside her that makes me second-guess my acting abilities.

"Everything okay?" she asks, an echo of her question the other day in my room when I realized that it was Nova, my Nova of Snailopolis, who I had matched with on the Crush test.

It's not a crossroads, this one second in the school cafeteria, but it *could be.*

I could tell Abigail, just *tell* her, that I'm not sure we're meant to be together. And I know it sounds stupid to use the *It's me, not you* line, but maybe I could find a way to make it genuine, because it is actually the truth.

But then I remember how she was when her ex broke up with her last spring, how strong, confident Abigail did her best to not look broken when she came to return her extra ticket and get her money back.

I had been sitting next to Fox at the little card table he lorded over the two weeks before prom. As junior class treasurer, he was in charge of the money box, printing the tickets, and—as is his way—making a *huge* deal and ringing a cowbell every time a ticket was sold.

"Come on, come on, come on!" he yelled before the bell rang to move us to fifth period. "It's *prom.* The more the merrier! There's going to be an *actual* DJ this year instead of Mr. Callahan and his iPhone. No offense, Mr. Callahan! You're the MVP!"

Amid this particular bout of showmanship, Abigail stepped quietly beside me, trying very obviously—and fruitlessly—to avoid Fox and his cowbell. I knew her, of course. It was impossible not to. She was popular. She was nice to *everybody*. Always smiling even if you weren't really friends.

"Hey, Sam," she whispered. "Look, I need to return—"

"Abigail Shepherd, what a surprise," Fox interrupted, his voice still stuck in sportscast-announcer mode. "You bringing *more* than one date to prom?"

He lifted the cowbell to ring it, but I stopped it with a hand to the clapper.

"Dude," I said, dropping my voice when I noticed Abigail tearing up. "Quit it."

Fox, finally catching on, lowered the bell with an equally quiet, "Oh."

Abigail's eyes might have been watering, but she was fighting like hell to make sure not a single one fell. She was doing a tactic I recognized, the one I called breathing through the eyes, where you widen your eyes as far as they can go and try to will the tears back into them.

Maybe it was that.

Or maybe it was the way she straightened her shoulders and looked Fox in the eye and held out her printed ticket and said, "I need to return a ticket. I no longer have a date for prom. Can I get a refund for it?"

Whatever it was, the next thing I knew, I was digging fifty bucks out of my own wallet—the last of my Christmas money—and giving it to Abigail.

"I'll buy your ticket," I told her. "And . . . we can go to-gether? If you want."

I thought it would be enough forever, the way her shoul-ders drooped in relief, the smile she gave me that wasn't her *everybody* smile but the one that was already only for me. I'd had a few girlfriends here and there before. None of them lasted more than a few weeks, always amicably broken off be-cause *it just wasn't working out.*

I guess part of me figured . . . She was alone, Abigail. She was alone, and I was alone. If it was never going to click with anybody, if it was always going to feel a little bit forced, a little bit off, shouldn't it be with someone I at least liked?

And I *did* like her. I still do if I make myself sit down and look at her objectively. She really is kind to everyone. She lis-tens to *everything*. If it's music, she'll give it a shot. It doesn't matter the genre, the artist. Once, when we were in my truck, she turned on the latest album from a pop artist I knew she hated. When I asked her why, she said, "Every creator de-serves multiple chances. Maybe this album could be my new favorite album!" It wasn't, but I admired her for thinking it could be.

In the span of the one second it takes for Abigail to ask me if I'm okay and for me to answer, I imagine all of this: our beginning, our hypothetical end. And I tell myself not for the first time these last few days that Abigail and I *are* enough. We have plans, mutual goals. If that's not love, what is?

"Everything is fine," I tell her.

And when she smiles the same smile she gave me last spring before prom, I almost believe it.

* * *

Nova

Mom is in one of her moods today.

It's easy to tell when she gets like this because I can smell lasagna and homemade garlic knots and her Nova salad—which is what she calls Caesar salad with the extra cheese I like—when I walk through the door from school.

Every once in a while Mom has a full-on panic that I'm not having a normal enough childhood and she's not having a normal enough motherhood and aren't mothers and daughters supposed to sit down at the table and discuss their respective days over a straight-from-the-mother's-heart-to-the-daughter's-stomach meal?

I stopped trying to assure her a while ago that she didn't need to make up for anything or that I haven't been irrevocably damaged because of the job she loves. Maybe because I worry about that last part being true. Or maybe because she makes really, *really* good garlic knots when she remembers to follow Grandma's recipe.

"Hi, honey," she calls when she hears the front door shut behind me. "In the kitchen."

I put my backpack on a box in the entryway. It's still taped up.

"I figured," I say. "I could smell it from the corner."

"*Lasagna*," Mom announces with what I assume is *supposed* to be an enthusiastic Italian accent. "Wrapped up this assignment early today and thought you could use a home-cooked meal."

Everything inside me freezes.

Mom very rarely finishes up at a client early, but it's mayhem when she does. It usually means we're leaving in less than a week. It usually means she's already got her next assignment lined up and we're going to box everything back up and check for the cheapest moving options so she can submit the receipt through her company, and then, and then . . .

And then we leave the latest place behind like it never happened.

It's always hectic, always something I'd rather *not* happen. Moving is hard enough when it's as frequent as it is for us, but this time, it feels like a cosmic punishment.

I haven't even spoken to Sam since he almost outed us— whatever *us* is—to Abigail on Monday in the cafeteria when he was *staring* at me so hard it drew attention. He's been busy with practice, I know, because every day when I leave school I see him and the rest of the team on the field on my way to the bus line.

We've texted, though. Last night he sent me a picture of a

southern flannel moth with the message, Professor Fox says we should be able to find these this time of year. Have to go at night because they are nocturnal. Can you get permission from your mom to go this weekend?

Mom barely even looked at the flyer "Professor Fox" made to make it look like an official club campout that may or may not be sponsored by Tyler High before agreeing. Now I know she was distracted from finishing up the last bit of work for the client.

I've been trying to *not* look forward to it, even though I totally am. It's all I've thought about.

And now, maybe, I won't get to go. Because Mom's stupid job is—for once—going to be done *early*.

"You're *done* with the company?" I ask. My voice sounds garbled. "Already?"

Mom pauses, the salad tongs suspended over a serving bowl I'm pretty sure we've had since I was born.

She's confused, trying to make sense of my tone. I know, because I am, too. Neither of us know what to do with the level of panic in my voice.

"No, honey. I just finished one of the presentations for the client today a bit ahead of schedule. We're still here for another few weeks. We've got the house rented through the end of October, for sure, so even if I finish up early, we'll camp here until the next bit. I don't start for the Walsh Webb Group until the first of November, and they won't even need me in office until December, so . . ."

I guess my exhale of relief is a little louder than I intend it to be, because it makes Mom pause and raise an eyebrow. She sets down the tongs completely, wiping her hands on a dish towel.

"Everything okay?"

I try to make my voice casual, unreadable. I try to remember what it's like to anticipate the next move rather than dread it.

When we were nearing the end of our time in Seattle, I couldn't wait to leave. Putting as much distance between me and he-who-must-not-be-discussed-or-thought-of was appealing obviously, but also I look forward to going somewhere new. Usually, that is.

It's so much easier to go with the flow than it is to waste time wishing things could be different. I stopped worrying about leaving friends and hobbies and clubs behind sometime around fifth grade and started looking at moving as an adventure, a chance to re-create myself or perfect my latest persona in a new environment.

But since coming here, it feels . . .

"Everything's fine," I tell Mom, and before she has a chance to question my answer, I move to the oven and grab the mitt to open the door and peek inside. To mix a bit of truth into my reaction, I add, "I was just looking forward to Nature Club this weekend and didn't want to miss it."

She's still looking at me funny, so I add, "The cheese is bubbling. Want me to take it out?"

"It should be ready in ten," Mom says. "Also that reminds

me, will you take the other lasagna out of the fridge? I made one for Sam and his parents as a thank-you for driving you. Tell him to tell his mother to bake it at 375 for forty minutes or so."

I don't want to see Sam just now, not with the confusing adrenaline still seeping out of my veins. But I can't think of a good enough excuse to get out of it that wouldn't make Mom more suspicious, so I take the dish and make my way to the Jordan house.

His dad answers the door when I arrive, and I wonder if this is going to be a new pattern, Mr. Jordan and I meeting again and again in doorways and fence-hole-ways. I wonder if he's always going to have that knowing gleam in his eyes that all adults have when they think they have "us kids" all figured out.

But maybe he *does* actually have us figured out, because the first thing he says after "Hello, fence girl," is "I can see that you've learned how to use the front door, for which I applaud you. Did you also wish to see my son, or would you like to leave the dish your mom had you bring and disappear into the twilight?"

I wonder if the indecision is written that plainly on my face. I'm trying to think of my answer when Sam comes down the stairs, our eyes instantly snapping together.

"Hi," we say in unison, which makes us both laugh.

I hold up the aluminum pan in explanation.

"Mom sent this to you guys. It's lasagna. Oh, I'm supposed to tell your parents how long to heat it, but I forgot what she said."

I turn to Mr. Jordan. "I forgot," I say again, this time directly to him. "Sorry."

Sam comes to stand beside me, a hair's breadth between us. If I twitch my fingers, our hands will touch. But I don't.

"I should go back with her," he tells his dad. "To get the temperature and stuff, right?"

Mr. Jordan nods and reaches forward to take the lasagna from me.

"Yes, but then straight back. *Your* mom will be here soon, and we're going out to celebrate her promotion at work. We'll write it down and eat it tomorrow, Nova. Thank your mom for us."

"Sure," Sam says. "Right back."

His dad's smile looks *so* much like Sam's. If I didn't know, if I didn't remember the before, I wouldn't think twice about them being biological father and son.

It's a short walk between our houses. Too short. Sam seems cognizant of this, too, because his usually long stride looks ridiculously slow and shortened.

"You look like a clumsy ballerina," I tell him.

"I *am* a clumsy ballerina," he retorts. "Coach has us run ballet drills on the regular to improve footwork. I'm always the worst at it. Well, maybe not *the* worst, but pretty close."

We're already much too close to my house, and with time nipping at my heels, I blurt, "This is nice."

Because it *is*. Walking beside him, not feeling pressured one way or the other. It's the closest I've felt to before, when we were young and promise, promises didn't have to exist yet because we knew we'd see each other nearly every day.

"You're just saying that because I didn't make you go back home through the hole in the fence." Sam laughs.

There's a beat of silence after that, but it's not uncomfortable. It's the kind of quiet we used to be as kids in the lulls between making loud proclamations for Snailopolis and crashing matchbox cars together with noisy *bangs*.

I'm enjoying it, actually, the silence. I'm thinking about ruining it by bringing up a Crush question when the quiet is ripped to shreds by a high, Disney-princess melodious voice calling, "Sam! *Sammy!* Wait up!"

It's not as if I haven't seen Abigail Shepherd. There was my first day at Tyler High when she stood at the front of the room and issued the personality quiz, and there's been all the moments since when I've seen her beside Sam and haven't been able to help *watching*.

She's pretty, which is an understatement. She's got long blond hair that reminds me of Leanne's, except Leanne's was more mermaid-in-a-lagoon and Abigail's has the glossy shine of undiscovered supermodel.

Right now she's in a tube-top romper and flip-flops that if *I* tried to wear would look like a little girl dressing up to play Barbie but on Abigail looks casual and natural.

People follow patterns, too. I've seen a dozen Abigails in a dozen cities: popular, genetic lottery winners who coast through life in a way that few others do. They almost always pair up with someone just like them.

She pulls Sam—who is very tense beside me—down to give him a kiss on the cheek.

"Hey, babe." She smiles. The smile sticks when she turns to me, not a hint of suspicion or bitterness so much as flickers. "Oh, hi! You're the new girl, right?"

I think my face does some version of a smile in return, but I can't be sure.

"Hi, yeah. I'm Nova." Then, because I suppose this moment is already too awkward and I might as well make it worse, I gesture between Sam and me. "We're neighbors."

"Yeah," Sam echoes, his voice strange. "I'm walking her home to ask her mom about the lasagna she sent."

I wait for it, the look of betrayal, the flare of insecurity turning into a raging wildfire of anger and hurt when Abigail realizes that her boyfriend is hanging out with another girl *alone*, the literal girl next door.

It doesn't come. Instead, Abigail looks like I just told her the sky is blue, water is wet. She's completely indifferent.

"Cool," she says. "Is it okay if I tag along?"

She falls into step beside us, seemingly unable to hear the notes of deranged panic in Sam's strangled yet overly enthusiastic "Sure!"

I expect an awkward sixty seconds of silence and maybe Abigail talking to Sam while pointedly ignoring me, but instead she walks on the outside of *me* so that I'm between her and Sam.

The metaphorical resonance is exquisite and awful, even though I remind myself that she really, truly has no reason to be concerned. Sam and I have discussed ad nauseum how we want nothing to change, most especially my singledom and his and Abigail's not singledom.

"You're in English with us, right?" she asks me. "You sit in the back? I didn't know you were neighbors with Sammy! You should come sit with us during class. Oh!" She gasps like an idea has just occurred to her. "Lunch, too! I can't believe Sam hasn't invited you before now." Here, she pauses and glares up at him. *"Rude boy."*

"There's no room," Sam says.

His tone is carefully neutral, but his comment still stings a little. Even though it's perfectly reasonable, even though we're walking the tightrope between secret and private and wobbling the whole way, part of me feels a certain kind of way that he didn't leap at the chance to have me closer in the one class we share. Even though we both know it's a terrible idea. An agreed-upon, shouldn't-act-on-it terrible idea.

But still.

Abigail's laugh is like bells and birds and all things twinkling and lovely.

"We'll move Fox," she teases.

"I'm okay in the back," I say. "I don't want to take someone's seat when I'll be out of here in less than a month anyway."

I'm not sure what I said, but Abigail reaches toward me and clasps my upper arm like we've been friends for years, stopping me before I can walk through the white picket gate that leads to the front door.

"Oh. *My god,*" she says. "You're going to be here for homecoming!"

I obviously can't see my own face, but I'm guessing my expression is as cartoonish as Sam's, who is blinking at Abigail like she took all her marbles and chucked them into the nearby storm drain.

"She doesn't want to go to homecoming," Sam tells Abigail.

Which is true, but again, why does he have to say it like *that*? Like it's the last thing I would ever want. Like it is a universal impossibility that I, Nova Evans, would want to attend a dance. Like it's beneath me.

That's what he makes it sound like, and for some reason—maybe because I'm thrown off by Abigail's presence—it makes me mad.

Because if *I* don't even know who I am, there is no way he does. What if Nova Evans *likes* going to dances and getting dressed up and putting on flashy makeup? Does it make me any less a kind, benevolent ruler of Snailopolis or a good friend if I, god forbid, want to know what it's like to participate in a normal, pattern-adhering school function?

I don't think so.

"Sure she wants to go," Abigail retorts. "There's going to be a s'mores bar this year."

I wish the cracked pavement leading to the front door that is mine for now felt familiar instead of foreign, that Sam and Abigail and Fox and Leanne were all friends I would actually consider finding a fancy dress for instead of just placeholders in a long line of placeholders.

But it *is* foreign, and they *aren't*.

Which is for the best, I know. Trying to put down roots means broken promises and inevitable lengthy silences between texts until they stop showing up as "read" anymore.

I'm teetering on my own tightrope, caring about Sam and our stupid quiz results and my curiosity about the boy who was and the boy who stands awkwardly in front of me now.

I fear I'm going to topple over at any second.

"I really can't go," I tell Abigail. "I haven't got a dress and—"

"We can *get you* a dress," she says, like it's easy. "Say you'll come with us! We still have room in the limo!"

Sam's look of alarm is almost enough to make up for the rest of it, which—among other reasons that I swear to myself are mature and worldly and not petty and childish—is why I shrug and say, "Maybe I will, then."

Chapter Eleven

Sam

Abigail doesn't stay for dinner, but she does walk back with me from Nova's house, slowly, her arms dangling at her side and then coming up to fiddle with her necklace before dropping back down again.

She's agitated.

She wasn't when we said goodbye to Nova. Abigail insisted on hugging her, Nova and I sharing a glance while Abigail squeezed her like they were long-lost friends. Like *they* were the ones being reunited after years and years. But no, that's just Abigail. She's friendly. She tries to put you at ease.

It's my turn to return the favor.

I reach over to grab her hand where it's fidgeting with the necklace clasp. It's fallen to the front near the little yellow rose charm. When she lets go, I straighten the necklace for her.

"My mom used to say that means someone is thinking of you," Abigail says.

"*I'm* thinking of you," I say.

And it's true. For as much as I've thought about Nova, Abigail is always there, hovering on the edges.

I'm still holding on to the yellow rose, looking down at it when Abigail reaches up to kiss me.

"We're okay," she says.

It's not a question, but I answer it anyway.

"We are," I say.

* * *

Dinner is a mix of celebrating Mom's promotion and my Ford recognition, and despite my best efforts to turn the conversation back to Mom's thing, we always end up at *my* thing.

"We'll have to have a family meeting soon," Mom says, her voice chipper. "It might be best to put the house on the market in the spring, and we can always stay with my parents for a couple months if we—"

"Wait, wait," I break in. "Since when are we selling the house?"

Mom and Dad both stop, mid bite, to look at me like *I'm* the crazy one.

"Depending on which school you pick, we want to be able to see all of your games," Mom says, her tone suggesting I should already know this. "We can't afford two homes *and* a college tuition." She laughs.

"We'll move close enough to drive to games but far enough that you don't feel like good ol' Mom and Dad are breathing down your neck." Dad laughs. "Don't worry. We're not going to randomly pop up on campus. We just want to see our boy play. Might be our last chance if you decide against going for pro, and we want to enjoy every minute of it."

I decide against going pro. Like it's up to *me* whether that happens. Like they're considering it as a possibility.

"Signing day is the first day of February this year," Mom reminds us, as if it's not tattooed on our brains.

My stomach is gurgling. I don't think it's from the garlic knots. "Yeah, but I have until April to decide if I go with a Division I program, right?"

"Oh, you'll know before then," Dad says. "We've got it narrowed to your top three, so all that's left to do is decide and—"

He keeps talking. I stop hearing what they are saying and smile my practiced smile and nod my practiced nod. I vaguely hear them say something about *Seattle* and *Alabama*. Mom laughs at a comment from Dad like it's the funniest thing in the world. Maybe it is, so I laugh, too, just in case.

I used to fantasize about standing up during a dinner like this, putting my hands flat on the table, and saying, "Mom, Dad: I don't want to play football anymore."

But I'll never do it. They're willing to move from the town

and house they love to make it happen. Mom's willing to leave her gardenias and her new promotion. Dad is willing to leave the friends he's had since before I lived with them.

I can't tell them no, now. Not after the money and time and effort.

So instead I let my mind wander to the hole in the fence and the girl on the other side.

If I was a reasonable person, I would wait until this weekend when I'm supposed to see Nova for the late-night Nature Club to try and talk to her.

If I was a *good* person, I would just . . . not at all.

But the minute we're home and Mom and Dad go to their room, I find myself crawling through the fence to stand beneath her window, whisper-shouting her name.

She doesn't answer.

Not even after four perfectly placed pebbles that I borrowed from Mom's gardenia landscaping.

But I *have* to see her. It's like dinner with my parents knocked me out of my regular orbit and I'm careening through a universe with no roots, no companion, no memory of ever having spun around another person.

Which is my entire argument for doing the stupid thing and—instead of knocking on the door and possibly having to ask her mom for permission to talk so late at night or just *texting Nova*—climbing the spindly tree nearest her window.

At the beginning of each season when we're all sweating to death working on two-a-days on the field before school starts, the coaches always give us lots of lectures—especially the seniors—about "mitigating risks" and "your body is your instrument" and blah, blah, blah. Usually they mean drugs and alcohol and not getting people pregnant, but this year Coach Pemberton gave us this whole spiel about driving recklessly and—weirdly—climbing trees and playing on trampolines.

"You boys don't want to risk a chance at playing college ball by doing something stupid, and sometimes something stupid is climbing a tree and breaking an arm and benching yourself for half the season."

His words were already echoing in my head, but they turn into a roar when—halfway up the tree—the branch beneath my right leg buckles and in a split second flat, I find myself on the ground looking upward.

Nova's bedroom window opens with a flash of dim light from a lamp. From where I lay on the crunchy brown grass, I can see her silhouette outlined in a ring of light that makes her look like one of those saint candles in the grocery store.

"*Sammy*," she hisses. "What the *actual* fuck is wrong with you?"

It's the second time I've heard her curse, and the memory of the first time makes me laugh instead of answer her, which I guess makes Nova worry that I've knocked my brain loose because she does this cute little growl in the back of her throat and says, "Stay there. Don't move. I'll be right down."

The first time she cursed, we were in the hole beneath the fence in the before times. We were trying to name a beetle that Nova had found at school and "kept in her empty lunch box all day," she was sure to tell me proudly, so that it could come live with us in Snailopolis.

"It needs a name," I told her.

"*He* needs a name," Nova said, "and I think his name should be Son of a Bitch."

I'd choked on my saliva, surprised to hear such an ugly word come from Nova's mouth instead of my parents'.

"Do you know what that word means?" I asked, certain she did not.

"It means someone you love," Nova said. "I heard it on a movie my mom was watching. A lady slapped a man and said, 'I love you, Son of a Bitch,' and then they kissed a lot so he must have liked it."

"It doesn't mean that," I told her, hoping to avoid her next question by hurrying past it. "What about Alvin? Like from the Chipmunks?"

It didn't work.

"What does it mean, then?"

I didn't want the ugly words here with me and Nova, but I heard them anyway, from my mom, my dad. I hated that phrase more than *fuck* or *shit* because it was the only time they really called me "son" and I didn't want to give it to this poor beetle.

"It means something bad," I finally told her. "It's not nice."

Nova blinked, and I thought she would ask something more, but she shrugged.

"Okay," she said. "So what do we call him?"

Now grown-up Nova is beside me, her breath coming out

a little fast, her cheeks a little redder than they should be, but that might be a trick of the dim light from the distant streetlamp.

"Sam," she says, and her hands are on my face, just like last Friday. I could *really* get used to this. "Sam, are you hurt? Did you break something? Should I—"

"Do you remember the beetle?" I ask.

Nova cocks her head. "Oh my god," she says, her voice low. "You're concussed. Really truly concussed. I'm calling nine-one-one. I'm getting your dad. I'm—"

She stops talking when I pull her hand from my cheek to my mouth to try to muffle my laugh. It doesn't work.

She yanks her hand away and stands quickly to her feet.

"I'm going to get your parents," she says.

"No," I groan, pulling myself into a slouched sitting position. All my bones hurt at once, but in an achy-too-many-reps kind of way, not in a broken kind of way. "I'm okay. Just sore."

Nova is still pointed away from me, angled toward the hole in the fence as if she can run through it like a rabbit and alert my parents.

"*Nova*," I say. "Really. Come on. Just . . . sit with me for a second. I'm okay."

She does, slowly, cautiously, like if I make one wrong move she's going to bring an ambulance herself.

"We have to stop meeting like this," she jokes, but her voice is shaky.

I've scared her.

I turn—ignoring the burning in my core as I do—and pull her against my side.

It's the most we've touched in terms of body-to-body percentage, and I can't tell if it hurts because I fell down a tree or because I know it can't last, but either way I ignore it and keep holding her.

"I'm sorry," I tell her. "It was stupid of me to climb the tree."

"I should have come to the window," she says into my shoulder. "But I was being petty and sulky. And I was working on my college list and my major list and my hobbies list so . . . I ignored you."

Her hair smells like a cinnamon candle. Her head is buried somewhere near my armpit and it tickles when she exhales, but I wouldn't move for the world.

"Why were you being petty?" I ask.

I think I'll have to wait for her answer, but I don't. Evidently she's been dying to say it.

"Because you did what we promised to do and treated me like a normal person in front of Abigail instead of . . ."

My heart is in my throat. "Instead of what?"

Now she makes me wait and, worse, she straightens so my arm falls from her shoulders and we're separated again.

"Instead of the queen of Snailopolis."

"But you'll always be the queen of Snailopolis," I say. "I thought we didn't want to share that and—"

"We don't," Nova interrupts. "Well, didn't. *Don't.* I just . . ."

She stands up, but because she doesn't look like she's going to dart to my house and drag my parents through the hole in the fence to lecture me on the dangers of climbing trees outside windows, I stay where I am, already missing the way she was pressed up against me.

"I don't know what I want," she admits. "That's the problem. If we keep trying to keep our friendship private, we're going to get hurt and you might *literally* keep getting hurt. *Abigail* could get hurt. And I know we've done this . . ." She pauses and laughs, but it's the bitter kind of laugh. "I *know* we keep going back and forth, but maybe it's because this is all wrong. Maybe me coming here was a mistake. Like, maybe if Mom had taken another assignment, maybe if we hadn't moved onto this street, we could still exist in each other's memories. We wouldn't have to do . . ."

"This," I finish for her.

"This," she echoes.

I'm starting to think whoever designed human bodies was right to keep the heart in the chest because the beating-in-the-throat thing is really not working for me.

It feels like another end, what she says next, though I guess it's not so different from everything that came before.

But this time there's no promise, promise to bring us back together.

Just Nova's—reluctant, I think—compromise of "We'll still see each other and talk and stuff. But we probably shouldn't do . . ."

"Holes in fences?" I ask. "Weekend Nature Club? Window versus tree meetings?"

She shrugs a little, looking down. "Yeah."

It was a mistake to come to her window. If I hadn't, maybe she would feel differently in the morning. Maybe she would have realized that the Abigail encounter meant *nothing*, it was fine.

Instead, it spooked us both, and now we're facing the consequences.

"Can you get home on your own?" she asks. "Do you need me to help you?"

"I'm all right," I tell her.

Which is a lie, and she must know because she flinches toward me like she's going to take my hand but stops herself.

"Okay," she says. "Um, text me when you get back inside. Just so I know you didn't, like, faint going up the stairs or something."

"Okay," I say. "Will do."

"Okay."

Neither of us is moving, standing in front of each other with our arms crossed. A car drives down the street with its bass thumping.

I realize I'm waiting for her to walk away. I'm waiting for her to cut the thread between us, to call it done. And—in a moment of self-reflection—I realize that it's not *just* because I want to go on standing here with her for as long as she'll have me, but it's also because I want her to do the hard thing, the inevitable thing. I want Nova to be the one to shoulder the goodbye.

I wonder if that makes her tired. I wonder if that makes this so much worse for her.

What a sucky king of Snailopolis I am, always making her bear the load.

"Good night," I tell her, even though it kills me. "I'll text when I get home."

"Don't crawl through the fence, please," she says, her voice relieved. "I don't want you to hit your head."

"Okay," I say. And it's the last thing I say besides my one-word text of Home.

Chapter Twelve

Nova

We said what we said. And I know we both meant it, but it's been days without any rocks at my window, no prolonged pencil sharpening near my desk as an excuse to whisper to me (he's been using a pen), not even chance run-ins in the hallway even though I've left class to go to the bathroom more than usual.

Which is what I wanted, but now I am *drastically* reconsidering my life choices when Abigail, closely trailed by a pained-looking Sam, comes to corner me at my locker before first period.

It's the first time we've been this close to each other since Romeo fell from the turret and Juliet told him to go back to Rosaline to save them both from a painful death.

"No. *Va*," Abigail stretches the two syllables out to two words. "Sammy says you don't want to go! Tell me it's not true."

I try my best not to make direct eye contact with Sam, but it's hard when he's *right there* and his girlfriend is acting like we're friends, like we've *been* friends.

Which is, surprisingly, a pattern. I hear adults talk about "how mean" teenagers can be, and I'm not saying people can't be cruel, but overall people try to include me. Maybe it's because of the new-girl thing—they're curious where I fit in, and the only way to find out is to pretend I'm a puzzle piece that belongs in their box—but I really don't think so. I think there are finders in the world who for whatever reason or motive want to include the ones they find.

Abigail is a finder.

"She doesn't have to go, Abigail," Sam says. He is working *so hard* to not look at me. "It's not like we have to fill up the spots in the limo. We already split the cost and paid for it in the group."

I went through a brief cheerleader-adjacent period a few years ago. It was the dance team, but still, same vibes, same patterns of having life rotate around football and all its many splendors and celebrations. They're like holy holidays in towns like this, things like homecoming and senior showcase night and playoffs. Tyler High is no different. The signs have started popping up *everywhere* reminding people to buy their tickets before the dance because you save five bucks if you do. Even the teachers are reminding us before class begins, some of them sure to tell us they'll be in attendance as chaperones but not to worry because they'll "be cool."

It's not just at Tyler High that I would be sticking out like a sore thumb for not attending.

Abigail looks up at Sam like he's lost his mind for fighting her on this.

"All the more reason for Nova to come! It's a *free seat* for her and her date," she says.

"I don't have a date," I rush to say.

"Well, now you're *definitely* coming in the limo," she says, like my not having a date settles it. Which I guess it does because then she says, "You can be Hayden's date. He's on the football team and going solo, too, so y'all can dance the slow dances so you're not by yourselves."

I can't help it. I look at Sam. I look at him, and I wish not for the first time since arriving that I hadn't come *at all*.

Because in a beautiful, perfect world, he would be single and I would have my shit together and we really could go back to the way it was before.

But he's made it clear that he's on his path, I've made it even clearer that I'm trying to find mine, and I believe this is what the people call an impasse, and this is not a beautiful, perfect world.

Sam is not Liam. I know that. Sam is naturally good and kind in a way that Liam was not, but I'm starting to wonder . . .

if Liam felt half as confused as I do about Sam, maybe he wasn't being purposefully cruel when he made promises to so many.

Sometimes you can't know the promise you're making when you make it, but then, *that's the point* of promises: to keep them no matter what.

I don't want Sam to break any promises on my account. Certainly not to Abigail, who, despite my reluctance and Sam's grimaces, I'm really warming up to.

But not enough to want to go with them *as a group* to homecoming, and certainly not enough to go with this random boy who I don't even know.

"I don't know . . . ," I say, still looking at Sam.

Sam, for his part, looks like he's going to have a jaw ache before the bell rings if he doesn't loosen up.

"Dress shopping," Abigail declares, taking my indecision as confirmation that I *want* to go to homecoming. "Today, after cheer practice. Deal? You absolutely should go to your senior—"

"She's a junior," Sam interjects.

"—junior homecoming dance. Come on, it'll be fun!"

I blink. "Um, maybe . . ."

I shoot Sam a look that I hope says *Help me get out of this* but I guess actually says *Help, I guess we have to do this,* because he says, "Maybe you could invite Leanne, too? Fox mentioned she doesn't want to shop for a new dress, but maybe if you invite her along she'll come, Nova."

I wait for Abigail to find a polite but firm way to reject inviting Leanne, because that can be a pattern sometimes, too, the cheerleaders feeling superior to everyone, especially band kids. No need to find those who have been found by a different group.

But Abigail keeps surprising me.

She practically *prances* away from me and Sam down the hall, not pausing to see if we're following, which we do at a distance. We've gone back to not looking at each other, even though I swear my arm burns where his hovers beside it.

"*Leanne Abrams,*" Abigail yells. "Please report to the front of the hallway."

Leanne's voice comes from behind me.

"Is somebody going to tell her that *front* is relative?"

"She wants you to go dress shopping for homecoming with us," I tell her. And then, suddenly feeling desperate to not be alone with the complete and total stranger that is Sam's girlfriend—because I guess this is happening—I add, "*Please* come with us."

Fox comes out of nowhere to stand with us. It's like we're in some high school sitcom where friend gangs just assemble on-screen as if everyone doesn't have different, conflicting schedules.

"Go where?" he asks.

Leanne rolls her eyes at him. "Did you put them up to this? I told you I'm not going dress shopping. I'm only going to be at the dance for, like, twenty minutes.

Sam turns to Fox. I can feel his relief at having a reason to turn away, or maybe I'm projecting my own feelings.

"You scared your girlfriend off from the dance already?"

Fox throws up his hands, the picture of righteous defense. "The marching band has some sort of practice competition in Enfield Sunday morning. *She's* the one who wants to be responsible and, like, get sleep or whatever."

Abigail has finally figured out that we're all at the other relative front of the hallway and has looped back.

"Twenty minutes is long enough to make an *impression*," she tells Leanne. "Besides, if you get something without too many sequins, you can wear it again to senior tea or something later this year."

This practicality must appeal to Leanne because she looks half convinced from that alone.

"*Fine*," she says, turning to Fox. "But it'll cost all of you a stop at the mall pretzel stand. And I am *not* buying my own pretzel if I'm going to have to buy another stupid dress."

"As if I would pass up cinnamon nuggets." Abigail scoffs as Fox says, "Why do we have to go?"

"Because you are loyal and true boyfriends," Abigail says.

"And because you can have mall pretzels, too," Leanne adds.

Fox perks up at that. Sam looks no more convinced that any of this is a good idea, but I can tell he's trying to play along.

Above us, the bell rings, and we all disperse to our first-period classes. I don't have time for more than a wave in Sam's general direction before Leanne and I head toward the science lab in the back of the school.

"So how did you get roped into dress shopping with Abigail?" she asks.

I'm pretty sure I can trust Leanne, and this seems as good a time as any to tell her a sterilized, cleaned-up version of our past.

I'm not bringing up what he hid beneath sleeves, the palm kisses that go where they need to, or even Snailopolis. It's easier to just write us off—write off what we were and might still be—as old childhood friends. No need, either, to bring up the may-or-may-not-be cosmic interference in making sure our promise, promise came true.

"She ran into Sam and me walking outside my house." I pause, thinking. "Sam and I knew each other when we were kids. Abigail doesn't know, and Sam wants to keep it that way."

I expect Leanne to be surprised that this didn't get brought up during the entirety of Nature Club, but she isn't. She also doesn't seem particularly prone to prying, because she doesn't skip a beat.

"That makes sense," she says with a careless shrug. "I mean, I thought it was weird when Sam randomly decided that we should do Nature Club out of the blue. They've been doing it since they were, like, seven, but I've only been invited along like—"

"Wait, it's been going on that long?" I ask. "Really?"

"Oh, longer than that," she says. "He and Fox started it back when Sam first moved to Texas. I guess he wanted to go snail hunting or something and then Fox got *really* into it and *then* they found out that Sam could draw and . . ."

Her voice fades away, and if we weren't already pushing

the boundaries of tardy, I would probably excuse myself to go to the bathroom.

He kept playing with snails after the before.

Oh, Sammy.

"I wouldn't have *gone* to Nature Club if I knew it was going to lead to me being roped into dress shopping with Abigail Shepherd, though," Leanne says, interrupting my thoughts. "No offense to you or anything. Like, I'm glad we met, but this is going to seriously cut into my evening practice time."

It's not Leanne's practice time I think about for the remainder of the school day, though. It's the montage I'm building in my head, the one of Sam—little and long-sleeved like the day he said goodbye—growing up here with Fox and Leanne, romping through the sort-of-kind-of nature preserve in search of snails.

Did he think of me, I wonder, when he found them? Did he remember what it was like beneath the tree, beside the fence, beside *me* when he sketched them into his book?

Later, when Abigail and Leanne find me in the library with the boys in tow after their respective practices, it feels full circle for the montage in my head to see Sam with hair wet from the shower, a short-sleeved shirt, and shoulders wider than the length of his little-boy legs. Abigail has her arm wrapped around his middle, and his face has the not-in-the-eyes smile plastered onto it. It almost makes me wince.

"Look who I found," Abigail singsongs. "Let's *gooooo*, Nova. We want to get to the mall before all the good stores close."

"Don't Sam and Fox need to rest after practice?" A last-ditch effort to save Sam if I can't save myself.

Leanne looks at me and laughs. "If we have to suffer, the menfolk should, too."

Abigail pats Sam's chest. "Nobody is going to *suffer*. We're going to find amazing dresses for you two, the boys are going to go ogle expensive sport's equipment at Dick's Sporting Goods, and then we'll all celebrate with mall pretzels."

"Whose car are we taking?" Fox asks.

"There's no way we're all fitting in one car," Leanne answers. "We'll have to take two."

Which is how I end up in Abigail's back seat while she drives and Sam rides shotgun. There was an awkward shuffle about this, with Sam insisting I should ride up front since it's technically a girls' outing, and then I called him sexist, and then he said I was being stubborn, and then *I* said, "It's your girlfriend's car, you should sit up front," which ended that conversation rather abruptly.

Abigail is breaking every recognizable pattern template I have. When she presses the button to start the car, instead of the pop music I expect to pour from the speakers, out flows a literal symphony. As the music fades, a nice old man voice tells me it's the local classical station, and if we want to "keep good music free," we should consider donating to their fundraising drive by going to their website and signing up for a monthly gift.

I've never been a huge fan of classical music. I get that it's important and smart, but it's not my style. At least I know *that* much about myself.

I think I could grow to like it, though, if I was real-life friends with Abigail, instead of a reluctant tagalong.

When the next piece starts at the red light, she excitedly leans over and slaps Sam's arm before twisting in her seat to look at me.

"*This*," she declares with what I'm learning is her natural propensity to add vocal gravity to everything, "*is a bop.*"

The "bop" ends up being some violin something or other by Tchaikovsky, which Abigail hums along to like it's Lizzo and she's Tchaikovsky's number one backup singer.

Sam turns, nearly missing her swaying shoulders, and is about to tell me something when Abigail says, "No! Wait, wait, wait! Here comes the good part. You don't want to miss it."

She's not wrong. The music plays the same theme it's been repeating for the last couple of minutes, but at three times the volume and with the entire orchestra. It's hard not to feel swept away, even though it's a bunch of strings with no Taylor Swift in sight.

"You're right," I tell her. "A bop."

"Oh god," Sam says from the front seat. "Don't encourage her."

It *almost* sounds funny, his tone, but I can hear the hard edge beneath the surface of his words.

Abigail slaps his shoulder again, seemingly oblivious to Sam's sharpness.

"*See?*" she says. "Nova agrees with me because Nova is *smart.*"

"Nova is agreeing just to be nice," Sam says.

Abigail doesn't seem to catch his slight tone of combativeness, but I do. Come to think of it, he's acted half-grumpy since we got in the car. Maybe even three-quarters-grumpy.

I wonder if he is regretting blending the before with the now. I wonder if he wishes we had stayed . . . whatever we were and gone on pretending like neither of us planned on doing anything about it except for pining and making sad faces at each other in the hallways.

Sam and my thoughts must make me grumpy, too, and I find myself matching his tone when I say, "I'm *not* just being nice. It's a good song."

"Movement," Abigail corrects.

"Movement, right," I say.

We make our way into the mall parking lot, in front of a looks-abandoned-but-isn't JCPenney. I should let it go, the way Sam is taking out his feelings on Abigail, but I can't.

Especially when he adds, "I'd rather listen to literally *anything* else."

There it is again, the jackassery. I can practically feel it crawling into my bones. He sounds so disdainful, so . . . Not Sammy.

It scares me a little, like it's somebody else in the front seat who doesn't know about Snailopolis or field days or anything.

Like it was all pretend and now that it's out in the daylight and not hidden away beneath fence posts and Nature Club outings—acknowledged by its lack of acknowledgment—it's not going to last.

My fright makes me snap, "Then you can ride with Fox and Leanne on the way home."

Abigail seems to think we're play-fighting, lion cubs batting at each other with claws drawn in.

"You two." She laughs, like Sam and I have been a "two" for as long as she can remember. "No fighting in my car. I just got it detailed."

And maybe we are fake-sparring. Maybe this is what it is. But it doesn't *feel* like playing.

Playing is digging holes in the dirt for our snails. Playing is looking at each other and laughing over nothing at all.

It doesn't feel like glaring at each other over median consoles while Sam's girlfriend enthuses about the joys of classical music.

If anyone notices that Sam and I don't speak to each other as we walk into the mall as a group, they don't say anything.

* * *

We've been trying clothes on for what feels like hours but has only been thirty minutes according to my phone, when Leanne leaves to find shoes "to get the full effect" of the dress she's trying on, leaving me and Abigail in the fitting room.

I can hear Sam and Fox and their low voices out in the waiting area, but they're far enough away that it feels like Abigail and I are truly alone.

She's in a dress a size too big that she's folded into itself somehow to magically fit her torso. I watch as she sits up straight and continues to tuck in the mirror, intent on making the outfit she has no intention of buying look perfect. It occurs to me, her sitting on the tiny excuse of a chair in the corner of the largest fitting room while I lean against the wall in an equally fancy pink dress, that we could be in an episode of *Bridgerton*.

"I'm sorry about Sammy," Abigail says.

It startles me so much, the apology that shouldn't be coming from *her*, that I don't have a chance to say anything before she continues.

"Sometimes he gets that way, kinda frustrated. He's not usually like that, I swear. It's just sometimes . . ." She trails off.

I know the answer to the question—or at least Sam's answer—but I want to hear Abigail's.

"How did you two get together?"

Abigail smiles. "It sounds cliché, but I swear that kid saved me. He asked me to a dance right after I got cheated on, but it was more than that, too."

She gets a funny faraway look in her eyes.

"Not to get too deep on main"—she laughs—"but, like, are you freaked out? By being an upperclassman? I know you're not a senior but . . ." She pauses, breathes. "Anyway, sometimes I feel really, really, *really* overwhelmed by the future and not knowing where I'm going or what I'm doing, but Sam helps bring balance to that. Because no matter what I choose, I know he'll be there for me like I'll be for him, you know?"

Leanne will be back any minute. I'm sure there's a more eloquent way to say the words in my head, but I can't find it so I just let them out.

"I was dumped, too," I say, scrunching the pale chiffon

skirt in my hands. "I get that part. But mostly I get the part about being freaked out about what comes next."

And I do get it. It's like Abigail and I are parallel versions of the other when she lays her fears out on the table between us. Both for different reasons, both frightened of the future that we can't fathom that lies outside of high school.

"Hopefully you find your own Sam to help you through it." Abigail smiles up at me. "Not all guys are like those losers who cheated on us. It's their loss. We are *awesome*."

A bold statement for someone who doesn't know me at all, but I smile at her anyway, something in my stomach sinking with the increasingly undeniable truth that Abigail is amazing and she doesn't deserve to have her boyfriend and her boyfriend's old friend doing . . . whatever we're doing behind her back. Not that she would deserve it if she *wasn't* such a nice person, but she is, and that makes it feel worse.

Leanne knocks on the fitting room door to be let in, and as I turn to open it, I get a clear view of my frozen smile in the mirror.

* * *

Sam

The tidal wave is back, and my way of handling its resurgence seems to be devolving into my father.

Not my uncle-dad. My biological father. The one who

shouted and threw things and was generally a terrifying, horrible person to be around.

I've had enough therapy to know that turning into my father is a choice, but I've also had enough therapy to know terms like *generational trauma* and *reactive* PTSD and worry that despite my best efforts to stick to this plan, this timeline, I'm going to lapse into something that resembles my father.

I've never physically hurt anyone, not intentionally. (Football is a rough sport, and we all get beat-up from time to time.) But I know better than anyone that it can hurt just as badly for someone to hit you with words as with fists. Which sounds like something from a fortune cookie or a kids' show, but it's true.

Nova hasn't said a word to me since we left Abigail's car, which is more than fair. I wouldn't say a word to me either after I acted like a complete jerk over a *stupid* radio station.

It's not an excuse—but sitting in Abigail's passenger seat like I have dozens of times before, this time with Nova in the back seat, felt like an alternate universe, like one where everything I wanted and everything I felt trapped by were thrown into a blender and spit out to make *this* happen.

We knew this was inevitable, Nova and me. We knew we couldn't keep on pretending to ignore each other in school, knew that someday Abigail's presence or Fox's questions or our parents' confusion would catch up to us and we'd have to figure out a new course of action, a new game plan.

Dad hasn't acted quite right since the night Nova waited to see if I was okay after my game injury. He keeps looking at me a second too long, and I know it's because he's worried

I'm going to throw it all away, that I'm going to miss a pass or a block or something because I'm too distracted by Nova. He hasn't *said* as much, but I know. It's the most logical conclusion with the information he has . . . And he's not wrong.

Reality got here too quick, and now Nova and I are being forced to interact with each other in the setting we tried most to avoid, but while she's adapting, I'm still stuck running defense for a play we have long since abandoned.

I'm too unreliable, too volatile.

This is why I should stick to the plan: Because it makes my parents happy and it limits surprises. And surprises are what make me lash out, turn me into someone I don't recognize.

Once, when I came to Mr. Sumpter's shop after school, he gruffly suggested I would have more time to woodwork if I "didn't practice football so much."

I'm sure he meant it as an observation, an offhand comment, but I was shocked at how swiftly the anger boiled up in me: at him, at my parents, but mostly at me. Because I was too cowardly to change the plan, too afraid of hurting Mom and Dad even if the thought of not running drills anymore was so appealing it made my heart hurt.

I didn't say or do anything to Mr. Sumpter, of course, but I used more force than necessary for the hammer. It's the force of the anger that scares me.

I shift on the couch cushion to recenter myself in the here and now.

Nova, Abigail, and Leanne are in a department store changing room. I can hear the sounds of Abigail's squeals, of zippers and the cursing of zippers when they get stuck on fabric, of Leanne questioning whether it's ethical to buy a dress she'll wear only twice, of Nova insisting everything she tries on looks the same while Abigail insists it doesn't, really it doesn't.

Fox and I are in the waiting area on couches that look comfy but aren't. Fox alternates between typing on his phone—notes for his English essay, the nerd—and shouting words of encouragement down the hallway as if the girls are in a sporting match and not a marathon of changing outfits.

"You've got this, Leanne!"

"You have *trained* for this!"

"First chair in the clarinet section, first chair in our hearts!"

This last one earns him both a *look* from a passing employee in a blazer and a chorus of laughter from the dressing room. Not for the first time, I envy the way Fox operates in the world.

This whole evening feels like an out-of-body experience because one second I'm trying to figure out if I need to tell Mom and Dad I want to see a therapist again, the next I'm laughing and sharing mall pretzels with Fox, who swears he can't eat a full cup by himself but keeps eyeballing every nugget I take from his large stash.

In another cluster of dressing rooms—this one in a small specialty store that seems to *only* sell fancy event dresses—it sounds like we're finally nearing the end of the shopping expedition, which is a relief.

I want to go home. And I wish I could say it's so that I can sort out my feelings, but really I'm just bone-tired from practice, from the car ride here, and of pretending that everything is fine, that the plan is fine, that *I'm fine*. I want to stuff my face into my pillow and inhale the weird musky damp-hair smell until I fall asleep.

There's some commotion from behind the curtains of the two dressing rooms. Nova is in one, Leanne and Abigail in the other. Apparently there is a decision being made and that decision is that Leanne and Abigail should run back to the department store to get a dress that Leanne passed on but is actually apparently *the dress* but it was also the last one and they *must* go fetch it tonight before the store closes in— there is a scramble to check watches and cell phones—oh my god, *five minutes*.

"What color is it? I can run and grab it!" Fox says, all too happy to buy into their—well, Abigail's—urgency. Leanne has said twice already that she'll come back later this week, which Abigail assures her is "not a risk worth taking."

"Blue, blue, blue!" Abigail calls to Fox like an army sergeant. "With a halter top! *With a halter top!*"

Fox takes off like a shot. I watch him leave the store, run in the wrong direction, and then double back.

"He is *not* going to know what a halter top is," Leanne says, emerging from the fitting room in her regular clothes.

Abigail comes out behind her, batting the curtain out of the way.

"Shit, you're right," she says. "Come on, if we run we can make it on our own. Sam and Nova can catch up."

Leanne looks like there are hundreds of things she'd rather do than run from one end of the mall to the other, but Abigail isn't leaving her much choice.

"I would have worn different shoes had I known this was going to be a cardio activity," Leanne tells me with an eye roll. But she jogs after Abigail all the same.

Which leaves only me and Nova, separated by a curtain and my anger from the car ride.

She doesn't say anything, though I know she heard every word. I know *she* knows we're alone, now.

I finally open my mouth to say something, anything, and my "I'm sorry" comes out at the same time as her irritated admission of "It's stuck."

"What?" I ask.

Nova sounds annoyed . . . and maybe a little sad.

"It's stuck," she repeats. "The zipper on this dress. I can't get it on my own. Is that sales lady still out there?"

These dressing rooms are in the main part of the store, so I look around from where I stand by the couches Fox and I were occupying for a sales associate and come up empty.

"I don't see her. She must be in the back room," I say.

A pause.

"You'll have to do it, then," Nova says.

Christ.

The thought of being in a tiny, enclosed, relatively private space with Nova *while helping her remove a nice dress* is making my brain go haywire, the tidal waves growing in the distance and threatening to come crashing down.

"Stick to the plan," I mumble to myself, but I guess I say it too loudly because Nova says, "What?" from the other side of the curtain so I have to say, "Nothing." And there's nowhere to knock, and, god, whose idea was it to make dressing rooms with curtains? Couldn't just anyone come in if they wanted to?

"You can come in," Nova says. "I'm not indecent or anything."

When I push back the curtain, there is Nova, trapped in a sea of stars.

It doesn't look like the dresses I've seen at homecoming in years past. It doesn't look like a dress I've seen *at all*. It's like someone took the view from a telescope aimed at the night sky, put it on some fabric, and turned it into a flowy dress that somehow both envelops and hangs off her. It's black—or blue, or purple—with glittering yellow stars and sparkling crystals sewn into the gauzy overlay.

And it's stunning.

She's stunning.

I haven't moved, the curtain still clutched in my hand. My knuckles feel tight. Nova's expression is impossible to read.

"It's not bad," she tells me.

I say nothing, so she rushes to fill the silence.

"A little on the nose with the stars, considering my name. *Nova*. That alone is reason enough to pick something else."

She's rambling because she's nervous.

I don't want to stop her.

Nova turns toward the slim mirror propped against the wall and extends her arms. The sleeves drape down like a mage's from a video game.

"Still . . . I like that it's different. I tried some of the more traditional-looking ones, and the cocktail-length ones didn't look right." She pauses, fluffing the skirt. "See, the problem is, I really like stars. I always have. I wish I knew why. It's not like I wanted to go to space or anything, but . . . Yeah."

I still can't say anything, my everything frozen as we stand in this tiny space, together. And I didn't know she had a smell until now, but Nova *does*. It's not perfume or shampoo or anything, but her. It's not floral or sweet or citrus. It's just Nova.

How weird that of all the places in the United States, all the places in the entire world, we end up here, together again, in these five square feet of changing room.

"Speaking of stars, did you know that the earth always sees the same side of the moon?" In my silence, Nova's words continue to tumble out like she can't stop them. "It's locked in the same orbit, so something about the time it takes to spin around us and the time it takes us to spin around the sun means we're always seeing the same face, no matter what. Isn't that weird?" Her words taper off as she squints at my face. "Sammy, are you okay?"

Maybe it's because she looks so concerned. Maybe it's because of the way her nose scrunches a little. Maybe it's the way she says the name I hate others using but love when she does. Maybe it's because I know that fixing us—Nova and me—and making it so that we can be more than friends would mean destroying everything else, of admitting to myself and everyone around me that I don't *like* the plan.

Maybe it's the tidal wave.

Whatever the reason, I tell the truth. Well, a version of it.

"You were right," I say. "At the beginning, you were right."

She must know what I mean, but her face doesn't move, not so much as an eyebrow shift.

I keep going.

"This is . . . it's not right. I'm sorry."

Nova is suspended in a galaxy and instead of pulling her toward Earth, toward *me*, I'm pushing her farther away.

"We shouldn't . . . We can't . . ."

When Nova moves toward me, the stars in her dress shimmer. She puts both her hands on my face, and the heat from her palms makes it harder to say what I'm thinking.

"I'm sorry," I say. "You were right. The promise, promise will have to be enough, enough that we found each other. It's . . ."

"It's okay," Nova says. She's not crying, but her voice sounds a little like she is. "Really. I leave in a few weeks anyway. Seeing you, knowing you're okay . . . It's enough."

"I'm sorry about the car," I say all in a rush. "I was a dick. It's just—"

"Abigail is *great*," Nova interrupts. "You know that, right?

It doesn't matter what you think about me or . . . whatever. But if you don't love her like she loves you, that's not fair, either."

Something in her face, her voice shifts. I swear her shoulders straighten when she says, "She deserves to know the truth, no matter what that is for you. No matter how hard it is for you to say it, either way."

She looks like an empress of stars, a ruler of space.

If only she was a ruler of time, too, and we could go back and unravel the past few weeks, the many years we were apart, and get to the root of the promise, promise, of the 99 percent I'm beginning to wonder might have been a fluke.

Because if we were really 99 percent compatible, if we were cosmically destined to be together because of a promise I made when we were kids, wouldn't it all have fallen into place? Wouldn't Abigail have decided suddenly that she's not interested in me and Nova's mom have bought the house behind ours? Wouldn't it all have worked out without any of this angst?

"Sam," Nova says, her voice hesitant. "Sam, I'm sorry, but I still need help getting out of my dress."

I sigh, closing my eyes, regrouping.

Okay, then.

The zipper in the sea of stars is not on her back, but on her side. I try to pretend I'm a doctor who sees a ton of bodies in a clinical setting every day. I try to think dispassionately, *academically* about Nova's well-proportioned arms, the way her elbow hooks just above her rib cage. When part of her bra peeks out—plain and nearly the same color as her skin—I tell myself that it's *good* I'm seeing it because it means the zipper is working and I'll soon be out of this dressing room, out of Nova's life. We can go back to only being in each other's before, where we belong.

"Thanks," Nova says, holding the dress up at her shoulders. "I'll only be a minute. You can go catch up with the others, if you want."

I don't.

I want to stay here and wait for her to come out with a galaxy of stars slung over her arm and follow her to the register, where she declares to the salespeople that it's perfect, it's exactly what she wants, and then she'll turn to me and ask if I will wear a tie to match it.

I want to drive her home and "accidentally" loop one, two, three times around the block to prolong our goodbye while Nova laughs and says, "Okay, but the *last* time for real. I need to sleep. You'll see me tomorrow, you know."

I want to know what it's like to know the girl who is my 99 percent match—the one who felt like home from the moment I saw her again—*and* the girl who is the queen of Snailopolis without constantly feeling like I'm stuck between the two of them. I want . . .

It doesn't matter what I want. Because I'm being greedy. There are only so many extraordinarily lucky things that can happen to one person, and I've maxed out with Mom and Dad, with football scholarships on the horizon, and a girlfriend who everyone says is perfect.

So even though I don't want to leave Nova, I do.

Because we've agreed, finally, and it's better to do the right thing and be miserable than to do what you want and ruin everything else in the bargain.

Chapter Thirteen

Nova

It's been three days since the mall. Sam and I have gone this long without talking since I moved to Texas, obviously, but those times felt anticipatory because I figured we *would* talk again. Now I'm not sure we will. We've nodded at each other in the hallway, but there hasn't been much beyond that. Abigail has been tied up in student council responsibilities—I've seen her darting around with stacks of papers and the council badge that lets her use the printer in the teachers' conference area—and so she's not available to accidentally-on-purpose throw Sam and me together, either. And I seriously doubt the late-night Nature Club meeting is still on.

Coasting is going abominably, obviously, but I decide that I can still try to figure out what it is I'm supposed to *do* with my life. Maybe it will serve the dual purpose of keeping my thoughts from running back to the mall to relive the part where Sam stood too close, said too many things.

Because it's a good thing. *This is a good thing.* I had been looking forward to this chill period, this designated Nova-figures-her-shit-out time before Sam and promise, promises and holes in fences.

I'm determined to look forward to it again.

Hence the piles of lists on my desk—not to mention the dozen or so in my notes app—that all say different versions of the same thing: Nova Evans has no career-able hobbies, no direction, and no prospect of suddenly obtaining either in time to declare a college major.

But I want roots. I want hard, fast plans and spreadsheets and rubrics and road maps that will take me from point A to point B in an orderly fashion. My entire life has been like a dandelion seed trapped in a gust of wind, blowing from one town to another school to a new hobby, and it seems silly that I don't have an answer for who I actually am at the age of seventeen.

Silly and terribly inconvenient.

Because what if I pick the wrong school? What if I put all my eggs in the wrong basket by going to a school with a great theater program or a university that specializes in psychology and get there only to find out that the thing I am *actually* interested in isn't offered?

College will be the first time that *I'm* in charge, and I don't want to screw it up because I was too busy obsessing over Sam Jordan to figure out the correct path forward.

I'm going to spend my evening systematically working my way through lists of majors, and if they sound the *least* bit interesting, I'm going to mark them and research the crap out of them.

Which all seems very practical, very grown-up, until the universe or whatever god is in charge of promise, promises decides that three days is much too long without Sam and me seeing each other.

Sometimes I wonder if I'm psychic. Not enough to see huge life events or solve wars before they begin . . .

But just enough to *not* be surprised when the first pebble hits my window.

I'm the opposite of surprised—I'm resigned. Maybe recognizing patterns is its own form of being clairvoyant. For every *This is it, this is the final goodbye* I've shared with Sam, the final closing of the book, he comes moments, hours, days later to reopen it, insistent that we are being too hasty. *Even though we both agreed this is for the best.*

Which is exactly what I say when I open the window.

"We can't keep doing this."

I expect Sam to look chastised, rueful, but he's grinning his blinding smile and it catches me off guard.

"Why are you smiling like that?"

His grin widens.

"You came," he says. "I wasn't sure if you would."

I gesture behind him to the broken fence.

"You've damaged enough property without adding a broken window to the list."

★ ★ ★

Sam

It's been dreary since the mall. Not just because Nova and I aren't talking, or because the weather has been dull and rainy, or even because Mr. Sumpter has been sick so the ag barn isn't open after school for me to hide away and work on the little-kid kitchen set.

I think it's *me*.

I wake up each morning and tell myself that nothing has changed, and really? It hasn't. Nova was always going to be temporary. Us speeding that up is jumping to the inevitable. But the past three days have felt like drinking flat soda: almost right, but not quite.

I'm trying to remember what brought me fizz before Nova came to town.

I'm trying to remember if I had it at all, or if Nova *is* the fizz and now I'm just miserably aware she's missing.

It's another night of willing the clock to tick faster so that I can go to sleep and hope that the next day is a better one, but I'm not tired. Eventually I give up on keeping my eyes shut while begging for rest and turn to my phone, idly clicking through social media. Maybe the repetitiveness of it will help me drift off.

The internet has just about managed to bore me to sleep when I see one of those posts that *looks* like a regular feed post but is actually an ad for an account I don't follow called Did You Know?

It's an infographic, and in huge bold letters it says, "Did you know the earth always sees the same face of the moon? They're locked in the same orbit. The more you know!"

After staring at it for a bit, I click away.

Coincidence. Just another coincidence.

But I can't ignore what comes next, a notification for an email with the subject line: More stats about your Crush results!

I can't help clicking on it, thinking it's going to tell me I can buy more matches or something, but instead, it says, *Of all the schools that participated in this year's Crush, your #1 top match is in the upper 2 percent of all Crush results. Congrats and happy Crushin'!*

Then it does offer to let me buy more slots, but I don't.

I'm already out the door, under her window, and not *really* aware I've done it until she says, "You've damaged enough property without adding a broken window to the list."

She's not smiling—not exactly—but she *came.*

It makes me grin.

"This has a 99 percent chance of failure," I remind her. "Us not seeing each other."

She runs her fingers along the windowsill, her eyes focused down but not at me.

"I told you that test was stupid," she says.

"And I told you it's *a sign*."

When she flicks her eyes to mine, my stomach sinks at the sadness there.

"I'm going to need a much, much bigger sign if we're . . . if there's . . ."

Nova pauses and blows air through her lips. I don't rush her, which is killing me because it looks like she's about to confess something, and I am *dying* to know what it is, but I know if I try to force it out of her before she's ready, she'll retreat.

While I wait, my mind wonders if she went back to get the dress of stars, the galaxy she left behind in the fitting room of that little store in the mall. I wonder if she's still planning to come to homecoming. I wonder if she's going to agree to be Hayden's date. I wonder if, no matter how this conversation ends, she'll dance at least once with me. I wonder if that will be enough to satisfy me, even while knowing it absolutely won't. If that's how this ends—with one dance—it will be like giving a starving man a mint and telling him to be happy about it because *at least it's something*.

"Everything points to this being a bad idea," Nova says.

I wait for her to elaborate. She does.

"It's not fair to anyone for us to keep trying to make

something from when we were little fit into our high school lives. It's not fair to me *or* you."

She pauses and then echoes her words from earlier.

"It's not fair to *Abigail*."

Now it's my turn to be quiet, which isn't difficult because Nova's eyes feel like two weights pressing down on my chest, and I have no spotter to help me push them back up.

"Are you going to break up with her?"

"No."

There is no hesitation, not a bit, and I think it takes us both aback. I can see Nova's throat move as she swallows.

"Do you love her?"

She's asked me this before, the first day, but it was round-about and not specific to Abigail. This is direct, piercing. Half accusation, half question.

I'm surprised by how quickly this *no* leaves my mouth, too.

I'm not sure what I thought Nova's reaction would be, but it's not what I see on her face: disappointment, maybe even a little heartbreak.

I'm wondering if she thought I said I don't love *her*—which is another question entirely, one I don't have an answer for, but I know it's not *no*—when she sighs again and says, "Then why do you stay with her?"

And now I'm scrambling to find the right mix of words, ones from the same universe that linked the earth and the moon together and the same universe that brought me the *two signs*, back-to-back, that told me to leave my room and come over here.

What is the answer to make Nova do what she has done every other time we've promised to stay away from each other? How do I make her stay?

* * *

Nova

I know the answer to my own question.

He stays with her because it's easy.

He stays with her because he thinks it's what he's *supposed* to do.

He's said as much, acted as much. It was never more abundantly clear than when we were at the mall and it looked like he was trapped in his own skin anytime Abigail was near.

Maybe if not for Liam, I would consider pursuing this pseudo-dating relationship, this half-nostalgia, half-curiosity mishmash we've been dancing around since I got here.

If not for college and the future roaring down the tracks toward me at one hundred miles per hour, maybe I'd say *Why not?* and give Sam and me a go at figuring out what we could be other than defunct rulers of Snailopolis.

And maybe if I hadn't spent time with Abigail, who is bound to the same patterns we all are but breaks some of them, too, I would feel neutral instead of angry.

Maybe if she wasn't so kind.

Maybe if she wasn't so quick to include me.

I wonder if Sam sees any of that on my face, because his answer sounds extra careful.

"Abigail is . . . she's nice," he says. "And we look good together on paper, but that's it."

I can feel my heart breaking as I say, "Maybe we're only good on paper, too."

Sam steps back, like I've punched him, and the implications of that make me want to cry, but I don't.

As if the weather is upset with me, too, the rain that has been threatening us all day begins to fall.

"We were good friends, Sammy," I say, and I swear that even though I'm up here and he's down there, it feels like we're standing directly beside each other. I swear I can feel his breath coming in quick spurts on my cheek. "Great friends, but that's . . . it was a long time ago. The quiz meant nothing, and we can't keep pretending it does. It was just one of those random things. It's not a sign or . . . or anything else."

We've said all this before, but it's always been with half smiles, maybe with our hands held together; we haven't actually *meant* it.

I mean it.

I say it aloud to Sam as much to myself.

"I mean it."

Even from up here, I can see his chest rising and falling with his fast breaths.

"What if I did leave her?" he asks. "Would that change anything?"

My heart flutters, but I ignore it.

"No," I say honestly. "No, I don't think so. Because you don't *want* to or you would have said so. And I would still be leaving soon and we would still be . . ." I trail off, looking for better words than the ones that come. "We'd still be grasping at straws, trying to make something from the past fit *now*." The tears start, now, but I'm proud I don't let them make my voice wet, too. "No matter how much we want to. Don't we have enough reasons to *not*, Sammy?"

Sam's hands have gone to his ears. His covering them uncovers a lost memory, from before, when he would drop whatever he was holding if a car backfired or if someone dropped a bag of heavy trash into the dumpster. Once, he did it while we were riding bikes and fell, letting go of the handlebars without thinking and skinning both of his knees in the process.

It pings around the hollowness in my chest, the knowledge that I am a loud, sudden noise to him in this moment.

But like the backfiring cars or the taking out of trash, I mean him no harm.

And unlike the backfiring cars or the taking out of trash, I know what I've done.

When Sam turns back toward the hole in the fence, his hands are still covering his ears as a roll of thunder skitters across the sky.

It's loud enough that I almost don't hear him say, "I wish you had never come here."

The Middle

All stories have middles. All middles are murky, unruly things that take the dirt of conflict and the water from the story's current and fashion them together to make a beast of mud that prowls the pages until the very end.

This particular middle beast had been coming for the little girl and the little boy beneath the giant oak tree for a very, very long time. Even when they were small and his little-boy curls tangled with her stick-straight pigtails, even as they moved snails through dirt roads and placed kisses on palms, their middle beast was coming.

Energy can be neither created nor destroyed. So this particular beast—a specifically placed lightning bolt on a specifically placed chimney—could very well have held bits of the little girl's laughter, the little boy's tugging of his sleeves. It could have been made up of stars burning to Earth or vile shouted words or the distant flap of a butterfly's wing.

It doesn't matter what atoms and molecules were hewn into the lightning bolt that came down from the sky and into the chimney of the little white house beside the hole in the fence.

It matters that it did.

It matters how the little boy and the little girl, all grown up and full of their own ideas of patterns and stories, reacted.

Chapter Fourteen

Sam

I haven't run like this in a long time. It's been a while since I felt the need to push myself to the point of exhaustion for the sake of outmaneuvering my emotions, and I could have dressed better for it. Or at least changed out of my jeans.

But there wasn't time for that.

Not with Nova slamming the door closed on everything. *Everything.*

I didn't mean what I said, *I wish you had never come here.* Not really. But I still said it and even though I turned away before I could see if Nova heard me, I know she did.

I should have known this grand break was coming, should have seen it coming *miles* away that this would never work the way I wanted it to. You can't have your cake and eat it, too. You can't make everyone happy and do the right thing by your coaches and your parents and your *life* and also be lucky enough to have everything you want, even if you aren't quite sure *what* you want.

It's too much. It's not fair to ask that much out of life.

Whatever promise, promises we made, it was too good to be true.

But I can't think about that. It might break me if I think about it too much, so here I am, running through the increasingly heavy rain in a drenched tee and denim that sticks to my legs like glue. I'll keep running around the neighborhood—avoiding the street with my house, the street too close to *her*—until the water floods the roads and takes me away or I pass out in someone's soggy yard from overexertion. Whichever comes first.

It turns out to be neither of those things.

The storm has turned angry and loud, loud enough that I keep having to peel my hands away from my ears, and I decide that passing out in a neighbor's yard—while never a *good* idea—is probably an especially stupid one when there is lightning spidering through the sky almost as soon as the thunder finishes rolling from the last bolt. Nova or no, I need to head home.

I'm about four blocks away, on a street with a hill that makes my legs burn as I run up, when I feel it.

Not relief from my tidal wave thoughts or some kind of supernatural peace that everything is going to be all right.

No, I feel the wet hairs lift on my arms, the back of my neck. The air is thick with energy that, if I didn't know what it can mean, would make me feel like a superhero.

I do know what it means, though. I felt it once before, when Fox and I were playing at the neighborhood playground and lightning struck a tree half a football field away from where we stood.

I feel it now, and in an instant of pure panic, my eyes immediately go down the hill toward my house, toward the hole in the fence, toward Nova.

It's probably the adrenaline, but I swear I can see her at her window watching the rain when a flash of light comes from the sky and—like a well-placed neon sign—points directly to the chimney of her house.

Once, when I didn't clean up the bottles of beer my father left beside his recliner fast enough, he hit me so hard my ears started ringing. After, I couldn't hear for nearly two days.

I think of it now, my ringing ears from the deafening *crack*. I'm screaming Nova's name over and over in my head as I run down the hill, trying my best to get to her as fast as I can and promising whatever god is listening that I'll never ask for anything again if they can do me this one favor, if they can keep her from getting hurt, if they will give me a chance to apologize and take back the words I didn't mean.

* * *

Nova

The crack is deafening, but I don't have time to process it because Mom is yelling, I can smell burning, the electricity went off in a flash, and there is ominous creaking just above my head.

Fire.

"Nova!" Mom is yelling from downstairs. "*Fire! We have to get out now! Do you hear me?*"

It's like she's far away, and I can't figure out why until I make my way to the door, pull the handle, and find myself faced with a wall of smoke.

If there are flames, I can't see them yet, but they must be there. This smoke is thick, pitch-black, and *moving*. It looks like something out of an apocalypse movie, the kind where not everyone survives.

Mom is still shouting, but I'm not listening. There's no point. She must have been downstairs when whatever happened happened—lightning, maybe?—so I'm up here on my own.

I close the door to my bedroom, earning myself a slight reprieve from the smoke. Stupidly—is this shock?—I put my laptop, my notepads, and the rest of my school stuff into my backpack, slinging it on my back.

That's done.

My brain thaws from its stupor enough for me to go to the window, to pull on it like I did earlier when the pebbles hit. How long ago was that? An hour? Five?

The window does not budge.

I wipe my sweating palms on my shirt and try again, panic settling into my bones, into my muscles that clench at the bottom of the window like my life depends on it. Because maybe it does.

Nothing.

I go back to the bedroom door, this time determined to brave the smoke and—hopefully—small flames, but they are more than visible now, angry and orange and surprisingly cartoonish this close, this dangerous.

My brain is going back to its numbed state. My two exits are blocked. What am I supposed to *do*? Stop, drop, and roll only works once you are *on* fire, and I'd very much like to avoid that.

I can hear the sound of sirens drawing closer. I hope they get here in time. The room is slowly starting to fill with smoke and—in a moment of clarity—I stuff my bed sheets at the crack beneath the door to slow it.

I'm starting to cough when the window shatters behind me, glass and bits of what looks like wood skittering across the floor toward me.

"*Nova.* Come here."

His voice is calm. Instead of a specific memory, I float in time on a gentle breeze, watching as Sam—Sammy's—face watches me back beneath the oak tree, at field day, from the front of English class, from my broken window.

"*Nova!*"

His voice is less calm, now. He's using a branch to clear

the rest of the glass from the frame from where he stands precariously on the tree he's already fallen from once before.

There are angry, red scratches on his arm as he reaches out toward me.

"We have to go," he says. "Please."

The sirens are closer. I hear slamming doors, my mom, other voices, but all I see is Sam, arm outstretched, bleeding, soaking wet.

I don't even think. I take his hand and let him guide me out the window, my backpack snagging and nearly toppling us both.

Firefighters are racing toward us, helping us dismount from the tree. Sam's parents and my mom are clutching one another like they're in a soap opera. Both our moms are crying, and they let out identical sobs of relief when our feet touch the ground.

Sam tries to let go of me, to let me go to my mom and the paramedics, who I'm sure are ready to haul us to the ambulance for thorough inspections, but I can't let go of him, can't make my arms loosen from around his waist.

"Your arms," I whisper. It's still raining, still loud, and the roar of the firehose behind us isn't helping, but he hears me.

I've wondered these last weeks which one of us attracted the other. Like, if this really is some sort of cosmic fulfillment, did one of us have a homing signal?

Maybe it's both of us, like calling to like, because something in him snaps and suddenly his arms are everywhere and nowhere at once: on my face, my back, my arms in nervous sweeping motions, my neck. The urgency is unnerving, almost as confusing as being frozen in my room with the smoke and stuck window.

"The lightning," he says.

I reach up and hold his hands where they are resting on my face, stopping their roaming.

"It's okay," I say, my voice shaking. "We're okay."

"I didn't mean it," he says.

"It's okay," I repeat. "I know."

"I didn't mean what I said about not seeing you again."

"I know," I say.

Our moms are here, pulling us into their arms, away from each other, away from the house.

"I'm sorry," Sam says to me, before we're split up.

"Me too," I say.

Chapter Fifteen

Nova

Mr. and Mrs. Jordan must be taking the whole Southern hospitality thing to another level, because they are literally treating us like family.

We can't stay in our house obviously. From what I gathered in between the paramedics clearing me for release, putting antibiotic ointment on Sam's cuts while I held his hand, and our parents darting in and out of view of the back of the ambulance, the fire was out less than fifteen minutes after Sam broke the window.

"Lightning," the fire chief tells Mom. "Super rare, actually.

Must have had faulty wiring to begin with, or else shitty—beg your pardon, ma'am—materials. Wrong place, wrong time."

Apparently the only parts of the house that actually caught fire was a bit of the attic and the part *literally* outside my bedroom door.

Mom tried to book us a motel in the next town over, but their electricity must be out, too, or else they just weren't answering.

After much back and forth, with Mom insisting we could stay at the motel once it was able to book us in and the Jordans repeating *absolutely not* in increasingly determined tones, Mom finally folded and thanked them, promising we'd move to the motel tomorrow.

Sam and I are standing in the corner of the Jordans' kitchen, watching our parents sort everything out.

They're too busy to see Sam and me holding hands or the way he keeps running his thumb over and over mine.

"You can't stay in that motel, Mara," Mrs. Jordan says, not for the first time. "*Ever*. It's been tented twice for bedbugs."

I guess I wasn't paying attention during the name exchange, but it must have happened because Mom sighs and says, "You worry too much, Dawn."

Mr. Jordan has become Keith and there is an air of familiarity around us that I hadn't expected.

But Mr. Jordan—*Keith*—was kind the night Sam got hurt and we spoke through the hole in the fence. More than kind. It makes sense that his wife and his household aura would reflect that.

Mrs. Jordan—*Dawn, honey, call me Dawn*—puts her arm around my shoulder.

"You okay, hon? That had to be scary."

"I'm okay," I say. "Thanks for letting us stay here."

She waves me off, giving me a squeeze before releasing me in Sam's direction.

"It is *no problem*. You two stop apologizing. We're more than happy to have you. Now, our guest bed is in my craft room but it's just a twin. Why don't we treat that as your homebase so to speak, where you can store your bags and have some privacy. Mara, you can sleep in there. Nova, you can sleep in Sam's room at night and he'll take the couch."

More good-natured arguing ensues. Mom says we couldn't possibly inconvenience them like this. Keith says Mom is being a nuisance by not accepting.

All the while, Sam and I stand off to the side, our parents remarkably fine once we were both given the all clear from the medics.

"I'm sorry it freaked you out," I say, low enough that our parents can't hear. "The lightning."

I try to make it sound like a question, that last part, because it is. Because even if we have homing beacons buried beneath our skin, *how did he know about the lightning right when it happened?*

But Sam doesn't say anything,

"How did you know?" I ask.

He takes a second to reply, and when he does, he sounds resigned.

"I was out running the neighborhood," he says.

I look up at him, trying to read his unreadable expression. His eyes are clear, he's still dripping wet like he was when he ran to our house, and his lips are set in a straight line that could mean he's stressed or angry or bored or nothing at all.

"How would you have had time to go for a run after we . . . talked?" I ask.

Another pause, this one much longer than the first. I guess he was deciding how honest to be because I can tell it costs him something to say, "I went running *because* of our talk."

"*In the storm?*" My tone is incredulous, a little angry. "And I thought the tree climbing was stupid."

"Where else could I go?" His whisper borders on anger, too. "I couldn't go home. I couldn't go to the fence. I couldn't—"

He cuts off abruptly, takes a deep breath, and appears to be counting down, his lips moving silently, methodically.

"Sorry," he says. "Sorry, it's not your fault. I acted on impulse, and it *was* stupid. But I was at the top of the hill and I saw the bolt and got there as fast as I could."

I want to say something, to tell him that *I'm* sorry for how our conversation went—the same one we've been having in circles, but still—or that I should have invited him inside and none of this would have happened.

But I don't. Thunder crashes and the lights in *this* house flicker ominously once, twice, before settling back into their regularly scheduled programming.

Our parents' voices have paused, too, all of us staring up

at the ceiling-fan bulbs like fortune tellers looking into crystal balls, trying to predict our chances of hot water and television in the immediate future.

I've gotten used to seeing Mom among sets of parents where she's the third wheel. She's always okay with it, or so she has said every time I've asked her if she misses Dad in those situations.

"I don't know what he would be like as a parent," she says. "I've only ever known motherhood with just you and me. I miss *him*, of course. Every day. But when it comes to parenting, it's always been me. I'm never uncomfortable being your mom."

She says that, but I wonder if it's true. Sometimes I catch her stuck in a conversation she wants to escape and there's no adult to save her, or I'll notice most of the other parents have someone to sit beside them at school events while it's only her and she looks a little lonely for it.

But here, in the dim light of the Jordan's no-longer-flickering living room lamps, she looks the opposite of lonely. She still has that weird look on her face—the one I suspect is from probably a stressful workday and then *the* most stressful evening ever—but her posture is relaxed and the smiles I've seen since we got here don't look like her fake ones.

Despite our electrical husk of a rental home and my near-death experience, despite the storm and the inconvenience of shuffling enough belongings for the next couple days along soggy concrete, and even though Mom's hair is limp and dangly and touching her chin because of it—which she hates—she looks . . . almost happy here. At home.

Which makes no sense, but when I remember Mr. Jordan's—*Keith*, I sternly remind myself in his voice once more—smile beneath the fence, his laugh, how much his eyes look like Sam's when Sam is properly happy, I get it. Dawn, too, seems to be one of those Southern hospitality machines that exudes warmth and comfort like a chocolate chip cookie personified.

It's already late, too late for cooking as Dawn declares, so while Sam helps Mom and me to the guest room, all of us carrying bags the firefighters were kind enough to help us get, Keith takes our pizza orders. While we wait for the delivery to arrive, Sam gets mismatched clean towels from a linen closet at the end of the hallway and points Mom and me to the upstairs bathroom so we can take turns rinsing off the exhausting day.

We all sit in the living room around the TV blaring a show about an American football coach in Britain. We eat our pizza and cheese bread from plastic plates with Christmas scenes on them. Mine has a little boy and girl building a snowman. The boy looks nothing like Sam, but the little girl could almost be me, pigtails and all.

Dawn nods at me when she notices me staring at the illustration.

"That has been Sam's favorite plate since he was a kid. He'll *still* go through the stack of plates to find it if he knows it's clean."

"*Mom*," Sam groans. "Can you *not*?"

"I'm only making conversation, Sam," she says.

His cheeks are bright red, and he avoids my gaze. It makes me laugh aloud. When I make eye contact with Dawn, her facial expression goes from teasing to fond, like she's happy that I'm here and isn't just being a good neighbor.

I like days that stretch out in front of you, the kind that unfurl like your favorite blanket and you can see how every hour will go, what you'll do, and you're excited for all of it.

I like days like this less, usually, the kind that stretch out behind you and it feels like you're winding yarn from what was once your favorite blanket but now is an endlessly long unspooled blob of thread. Everything has been exhausting from the argument with Sam to the fire to this.

But sitting on the couch in a stranger's house with a stranger's dishes and eating pizza from a place I've never heard of feels strangely comfortable, even though the day was *so long*.

So when we help clear the plates and switch off the TV, and Keith instructs Sam to show me to his room and help me change the sheets, I'm too grateful at the prospect of sleep to be interested in Sam's room. The adrenaline rise and crash has finally found me at the end of the spool.

At least that's what I tell myself.

I've been in straight-boy rooms before. They almost always have a solid color comforter with no decorations or embellishment. *Maybe* a stripe along the bottom, but usually just a uniform boring blue or green or gray.

The pattern dictates trophies on the wall of indeterminate age: They could be as old as T-ball or as current as last week's sporty something or other championship, but they're always lined on wooden shelves either directly above or beside the bed.

Sometimes the bedside tables are remnants of a nursery or a toddler's room, an off-white ranch-style, two-drawer affair that everyone has owned at one point but that everyone bought from different places. Maybe there's a computer—decked out with backlit keyboards and mouses that have extra buttons for gaming—and maybe there's a couple of old, assigned-reading books shoved in the cubby of the nightstand.

I don't know what I'm expecting when Sammy Jordan opens the door to his bedroom and gently pushes me in with a hand to my back, but it's not this.

It smells like a candle; a fancy one I can see burning on the desk in the far corner that looks nothing like a remnant from junior high or something found on Facebook market-place. It looks custom-made, actually, with its metal-rimmed drawers and legs.

Because it's the first thing I see, I go to it, walking toward it under the guise of setting my little zipper pack of toiletries on its surface, but really I want to get a closer look at it.

"I made that," Sam says.

He hasn't left the open doorway.

I gasp, which I find immediately embarrassing—What am I? A cartoon character?—but when I turn to Sam, he's smiling, a little smug.

"And the bed frame," he says. "The trunk, too."

When I spot all the pieces, it makes sense. They have the same flow to them, which I'm sure isn't the right word, but it's what comes to mind. It looks like they were drawn by the same hand, all created in the welding shop of the same brain.

"They're beautiful," I say. "I had no idea you liked making stuff like this. I had no idea you *could*."

Which sounds silly as soon as I say it. I actually have very little idea what Sam is up to these days. That's the problem of losing touch for nearly fifteen years.

But it makes sense, the making things, when I stop and consider it. Sam was always the one to construct the architecture and infrastructure of Snailopolis. Dirt piles meant to be castles went here, little roads drawn with sticks there. Once he made a tent out of broken fence post slivers and a tissue I dug out of my backpack that I was *pretty sure* was clean. It had a working flap and everything, and I remember he lit up when I told him it was better than the one I had for my Barbies.

Sam shrugs, more evasive at my praise than he was when we were rulers of Snailopolis.

"I took woodworking and metalworking classes as fine arts credits freshman year. It was supposed to be so I could get them out of the way and have more time for football as an upperclassman."

I stop from where I'm running my hand along the trunk. "What stopped you? If you're this good, why quit?"

He steps into the room, holding my shoulders and gently turning me so that my back is to his front as he wraps an arm around me to point at the . . . Ah, yes. There they are. The pattern holders. The typical shelves holding the typical line of trophies and medals and ribbons above his bed. There are *a lot* of them. I hope the shelves hold and don't decide to fall and end this weird day by crushing me to death beneath plastic and metal.

"Because of football?" I ask him, just to confirm, my eyes still trained on the trophies.

Sam nods behind me, dropping his arm.

It is a testament to the loveliness of his furniture that I didn't see the trophies at first. They really do look more numerous than they should be. I wonder if he never bothers to take old ones off or if they all really matter to him.

"Because you love it, right?" I ask him. "Football?"

I know humans aren't just patterns. I know that there is nuance and a whole host of things that could be causing the prolonged silence from Sam after what should have been the easiest of questions.

But I also know that his silence is all the answer I need, that his, "Of course I do," is much too late, much too quiet, much too rehearsed.

It shouldn't change anything about what we decided— what *I* decided—earlier, but standing in his room, his private space, and fully realizing what I've suspected since we fulfilled the promise, promise is making me reconsider everything, all of it.

Especially the part where it's better for us to go our separate ways.

Somewhere downstairs, a clock chimes. It's late. Late-late,

and this isn't the time to have a huge conversation about futures and expectations and whatever else.

"The furniture is beautiful," I say. "You've got a lot of talent."

To that, Sam says nothing, goes to stand on the opposite side of the bed, and strips the sheets.

Chapter Sixteen

Sam

It feels like I'm seeing her for the first time, or at least for the first time since elementary school. Nova looks different in my bedroom, and not in a creepy, what-if-we-both-got-in-the-bed-at-the-same-time kind of way (which I'm not thinking at all about, of course).

Here, she could be anybody, a houseguest friend of Mom and Dad's, maybe a cousin crashing for a couple nights.

She leans forward to stretch the fitted sheet along the

mattress, and I watch as her hair falls over her shoulder and strands land just below her collarbone.

Definitely not a cousin.

Everything has been surreal since she got here. Like, *here* in town, at school, but even in the last couple of hours of being *here* in my house.

I don't entirely like it. Even if she does look both more and less like the Nova of Snailopolis and palm kisses when she's standing in my bedroom, looking at the furniture I made.

I don't like seeing my room through her eyes. It makes me feel both proud and angry, and I shouldn't have to feel that way about my bedroom. This is supposed to be where I come home and sleep, not some pit of existential crisis.

But that's exactly what she's turning it into, because it's written on her face in the way her lips twitch down when she looks up at the rows of trophies and the way her eyebrows raise and her mouth softens when she looks at the stuff I've made.

I wonder what Nova would say if she knew I was sneaking into the ag barn as frequently as I do just to feel the material in my hands, to see if Mr. Sumpter has something else for me to fiddle with.

She says I have a lot of talent, but she says it in a way that feels like a prompt, like she's asking one of the damned personality questions.

It's been a minute since we brought it up, the 99 percent

quiz. I guess because Nova has been ignoring it at every turn, insisting it means nothing.

"Do you remember any of the other questions?" I ask her. "From the personality quiz?"

Nova pauses mid shake, my favorite pillow halfway in its fresh pillowcase.

"I think one of them was 'Do you consider yourself to have a good memory?'" She laughs. "Which I guess means we can both safely answer no, right?"

She means it as a joke, that surely we must not if we can't remember more questions from a quiz we took only two weeks ago.

But I remember that question, too. I remember the panic that laced through me, the panic I always feel when I see the word *remember*. It feels like an edict, a command, like I'm powerless not to drag up every terrible thing that's happened to me because of one little word.

I remember hurriedly answering yes, hoping if I answered and moved on I might avoid the boogeymen busting their way from the closet in my head and the monsters slipping out from beneath my bed.

Nova is looking at me, now, and maybe it's because when our eyes connect I realize that these are the very same eyes that looked at me through the hole in the fence, but whatever the reason, I *do* remember.

It's a good memory.

I remember the way my heart would feel too big in my

chest when I got off the bus and ran from the stop all the way home on days where I was a little bit late. I remember knowing that Nova would be there waiting for *me*, maybe already setting up Snailopolis beneath the fence, maybe picking the touch-but-don't-eat berries from the bush beside the road so we could pretend they were marbles.

But she would be there, a safe spot.

For the first time maybe ever, I remember I used to sing her a song I heard the couple of times my father decided we would attend church, the one about the little light that shines.

"'This little light of mine,'" I would sing-tell her, and Nova would always laugh.

"I remember a lot of things," I tell her.

I expect her to argue with me, that this is going to be another night-bird, early-worm situation where I'm not sure if she really *doesn't* know the answer or if she just wants to be a contrarian and prove we have less in common than the quiz claims, but she doesn't.

"I do, too," she says, and it's almost a whisper.

She would say more, probably—I *hope* she would, anyway—but we don't get to find out because Mom knocks on my open door to deliver fresh towels and ask if Nova needs to borrow toothpaste, and then I'm being pulled from the room and given my own armful of blankets to take down to the couch.

* * *

Nova

"Sam?"

He doesn't stir on the couch, but I see the dim glow of a phone screen, so I creep a little farther down the stairs.

"Sam," I whisper a bit louder. "Are you awake?"

Messy hair and eyes peek over the couch.

"Night owl," he says. I think he's smiling, but it's hard to tell through his yawn. "Remember?"

I snort at him managing to fit two question references in one sentence.

"Yeah," I say. "I remember. I wanted to say good night. It felt weird not to."

It feels like we're always like this, separated by so many feet and inches. This time the distance between the couch and the stairs feels like miles, like we're looking at each other through binoculars and are glad for the chance, but we can't really comprehend what it would be like to stand side by side.

And maybe that's enough, I tell myself. Maybe this—the lightning, the fried wires—is a way to tell us we are meant to be adjacent to each other now that the promise, promise has been fulfilled.

Maybe we're twin planets and our options are either to distantly orbit the same star or else collide and take everything down with us.

I'm tired. That's the reason I'm being too fanciful and too metaphorical and too—

My thoughts fade as Sam stands from the couch and comes to stand in front of me, where I can feel his gravitational pull. It's strong. *Too* strong. But I manage to resist his tug until he leans forward and physically pulls me into a hug.

"Good night, Nova," he says.

His head is bent down to my shoulder. His hair is tickling my ears, my cheek. It's finally completely dry, the long wavy strands. It doesn't smell like coconut, unlike what Fox said in class the other day, but it smells *good*, and I could fall asleep with the scent alone.

"Good night, Sammy," I whisper.

"Do you need me to walk you back to your room?"

I laugh. "Your room, you mean?"

It's too dark to see much beyond his eyes when he straightens from our hug and looks down at me, but I swear he looks like he wants to say something but doesn't.

I put him out of his misery, answering his question with what I hope is a nonchalant, "I can find my way back."

"You know where I am, now," he says. "I mean, if you need anything. Like water or . . . towels."

Even though we're the only two in the living room, our voices keep dropping. And we keep getting closer together. I tell myself it's so we can hear each other's whispers, that the pull isn't *really* a pull but a convenience thing.

Except he's bent his head so low he's nearly even with me and I feel myself rocking forward to the edge of the balls of my feet like I'm trying to propel myself upward and . . .

With utmost slowness—and staring into my eyes the entire

time he does it—Sam leans forward and picks up my slack arm from my side, gently bending my elbow until my knuckles are at his lips.

I think he's just going to hold them there, but then he bows his head completely, and I feel his lips move over my hand in slow, near-reverent kisses. One after the other, one on each finger, a slight turn for my thumb, and then two in the palm of my trembling hand.

"It goes where it needs to go," he whispers.

"Does it?"

I sound breathless, airy in a way that I didn't know I even could. I sound like a damsel, like a princess after the knight saves her from the dragon. And I know I'm empowered and can fight my own dragons, but is it so wrong to *want* him here kissing my hand in the dark?

And then I think of Abigail and the way she envelops those around her, and I feel the ground shift beneath my feet.

Sam already has a princess, and I'm not going to be the one who stands between them and their happily ever after.

Even if he wants me to.

Even if *I* want to.

"I should go back to bed," I say.

When I take a small step backward, he doesn't let go of my hand, and now it feels like we might dance.

Instead, I pull my fingers from his, but he, too, must be stuck in some other story, some other painting of nobility and knights, because his hand stays outstretched, lingering like I might bring mine back.

But I don't.

"Good night, Nova," he says. He bends at the neck a little, the slightest of bows for the slightest of side steps into another dimension, another life where maybe we were also unable to do anything about the *it* neither of us is willing to name.

* * *

Observable pattern: Fairy tales are too good to be true in this timeline or in any other.

Our post-hand-kiss-good-night version of a storybook only lasts—according to the old-fashioned alarm clock with actual bells on Sam's bedside table—about three hours.

The dream wakes me up, the same dream I've been having on and off since Seattle, since it felt like everything, but maybe especially my judgment, had been called into question.

It's boring as most dreams are by day—a pieced-together series of semi-stressful events that culminate in me falling into a deep, dark hole, which is always what startles me into waking. But by night, when childhood monsters still lurk in unlit corners and new, eerie nearly-adult ones stand ready to spring, it's terrifying.

I'm still thinking of the sensation of falling into the hole, how each time I actually lose my stomach like the downward slope of a roller coaster, when I drag myself down unfamiliar stairs to an unfamiliar kitchen with the now-empty water glass Dawn insisted I keep with me.

I don't even remember drinking it.

Distantly I know that Sam is asleep on the couch. I know that I should be quiet, tiptoe, and certainly shouldn't get ice for my water because the grinding of the machine and the clinking of the glass could wake him.

I don't even bother with the fridge dispenser, going straight to the farm-sink tap. The handle squeaks—*barely*—but all the same, I hear a rustle of quilts against leather as Sam stirs on the couch. I stop the tap—it squeaks again—hoping it won't wake him up completely, but my hope is dashed when the same mussed head of hair from earlier peeks over the couch in the same exact spot.

"You should use the fridge-filtered water," he says, his voice husky. "The tap water tastes awful."

I do, and then—because he's still watching me over the couch and doesn't look particularly displeased to have been woken—I come to sit beside him on the couch with my glass.

"People always say that," I say, "but I can't taste the difference in water."

Sam leans over and takes my glass. I can see prints on his hands from where he's been sleeping on rumpled blankets. He takes a swig and makes a face.

"Half-tap, half-filtered. Not a good combination."

I roll my eyes. "Like you would have known that if you hadn't watched me pour it."

"Could too."

Sam's middle-of-the-night laugh is intoxicating. My traitorous brain wishes he would kiss my knuckles again, but I quickly throw that thought into the deep, dark hole from my dream and tell it to stay.

It's after three in the morning. We have to wake up for school in less than four hours, and yet I slit my gaze at Sam as I lean over and take the cup back.

"Don't look," I threaten. "Or you'll ruin the experiment. And cover your ears so you can't hear where I'm getting the water from."

Sam's smile is crooked. "Yes, ma'am."

When I reappear in front of Sam with my glass—another exactly-the-same half-filtered, half-tap combo—he is still sitting with his eyes shut and his hands crammed over his ears. He doesn't seem to realize I'm here.

I watch him for a second too long before tapping his knee and offering him the glass.

"Totally different glass," I tell him. "Is it filtered or not?"

Sam takes a drink, pretends to think, and then takes another.

"Both," he says. "Same as before: half and half."

"There is *no way* you know that," I say, playfully hitting his shoulder. "You cheated. You're a cheater."

I'm joking when I say it, of course. It echoes down the timeline of childhood taunts on playgrounds, of fake accusations with laughter and smiles.

But Sam isn't smiling. His face falls, his entire face going still, and he looks frozen somewhere between horror and anger.

It's a little frightening. And I think it would still be that way even if it were day instead of night.

Not because he would hurt me. Never that. But it looks like he just fell into his own pit, the deep, dark, wake-you-from-sleep kind. Sam isn't sleeping, though. He's falling in real time, wide awake and totally aware of his plummet.

"Sam?"

He doesn't react, not at first, but he eventually says, "Sorry, Nova. I'm just really tired. Good night."

His voice is cold and distant and . . . not Sam.

"I feel like I should stay with you," I say. "I didn't mean to—"

Sam interrupts by mechanically returning the glass to my hand, a dismissal. I would do more harm than good staying here. He's going to have to dig himself out of whatever hole I made beneath him.

I knew better, I tell myself as I head back upstairs, than to bring our two planets this close again.

But I did it anyway, and now the pattern of fairy tales with kings and queens of Snailopolis crumbling falls totally on me.

Chapter Seventeen

Sam

My father was a lot of things, but one of those things was a cheater.

It's a trigger word for me, *cheater*. Probably because I've blocked certain things out—or my brain has blocked things out for me—but something that lingers is the sound of my mother crying, screaming the word over and over at my uncaring father.

Try as I might, my brain can't make the hole in my memory from last night make sense. There was Nova and the tap and the water-test game and her calling me a cheater and then . . .

This is why I don't like things from before. This is why I stick to the plan.

This is why Nova was right and I am wrong and I just need to *stop*.

We talked about it this morning, sort of. The kitchen is always chaotic before school, even though it's roughly the same routine each day. Mom starts to make green smoothies for the three of us until she eventually wonders if she turned off her straightener and runs upstairs to check. Then Dad comes in and sees the smoothie ingredients and starts to take over as Mom comes back downstairs and yells, "I've got it! I've got it!"

My job during all of this is to stay out of the way at the kitchen table, listening to the same banter every morning as Dad begs to grab Starbucks on the way to work, for the love of god, and Mom says it's too expensive and besides, didn't his doctor say he needs to ease up on his caffeine intake?

Eventually I'm presented with a smoothie that somehow never tastes the same way twice, my regular three hard-boiled eggs and piece of whole-grain toast, and a couple strips of microwave bacon Dad thinks he's being sneaky by making after Mom heads upstairs to finish getting dressed, even though the kitchen constantly smells of bacon because he does this every morning. Mom refuses to make bacon because she says she can feel the grease in the air, but I guess she just lets Dad do his pseudo-secretive bacon making anyway.

The rhythm is all off today, though. Mom is trying to make five smoothies even as Nova and her mom insist they can pick up breakfast on their way out. Mom latches on to that last part, insisting that I can take Nova to school, and she doesn't know why I didn't start doing that earlier anyway.

At one point, Nova and I are awkwardly at the table together with our matching smoothies, and she says something that sounds like *Sorry about last night* and I say something that sounds like *It's okay,* and then we ride in silence to school and go our separate ways immediately upon stepping foot in the parking lot.

I'm afraid if I say more, I'll have to explain everything, and the thought is too exhausting.

When Abigail rushes up to me first thing, I tell myself I feel relieved. I tell myself that my girlfriend is here now, and the world's strangest weekend is over, so I can get back to normal.

I tell myself this is the normal I want, the one I will choose and keep choosing.

"Sam-*my.* You didn't return any of my calls! If you're not careful, I'm going to think you're avoiding me." She laughs.

Abigail's hair is down today. I like when she wears it down, I remind myself. We kiss, a quick peck that I tell myself is nice, and then I smile at her, the one I've practiced in the mirror.

"Sorry," I say. "Weird weekend. Nova and her mom had to come stay with us because their house was—get this—struck by *lightning.*"

Abigail looks appropriately shocked.

"The poor *thing.* Does she need clothes? Do they have enough food? Well, of course they have enough food. Your mom will make sure of that. Oh my god, we should take her shopping again. She probably has *nothing*."

I manage to talk over and around her stream of consciousness enough to convey that all their belongings are fine, their house is just internally fried, but Abigail doesn't stop.

"What class is she in right now? Is she freaked out? She's probably freaked out."

Abigail's concern for Nova is opening up the pit in my stomach again, so I do my best to shut her down.

"It's all taken care of," I tell her. And then, because I know it'll work as a distraction technique, I say, "Ready for homecoming this weekend?"

It works. Abigail verbally runs down a list of things she and Catherine want to do this week for what she calls "the final prep."

I tell myself this is what I wanted, and I repeat it to myself through the school day with Abigail at my side, and later through football practice, where scouts sit in folding chairs directly beside the field.

But somewhere between the bear crawls, the crossing drills, the punishment push-ups when some of the freshmen won't quit goofing off, and the scratching of the scouts' pens on their clipboards, both the hole in the fence *and* the ag barn appear in my mind, and I find myself wanting—again and again and again—what I shouldn't.

★ ★ ★

Nova

Mom texted to let me know she's going to work until dinner at a coffee shop and tells me to tell Dawn and Keith she's bringing home dinner for us all from the local Mexican place and to ask if everyone is okay with enchiladas and tacos.

But when the bus stops at the corner and I walk the short distance to the Jordans' house, I find the door is locked tight, the shades are closed, and I realize I wasn't given a key because Sam's parents probably expected me to come home with Sam.

But he has football practice. He has a girlfriend he probably wants to spend time with after school. He has a whole life that was in motion and will stay in motion when I leave next week.

Next week.

I haven't reckoned with anything I was supposed to, least of all that I'm leaving for the second move of my junior year. I don't even remember *where* we're going this time. Somewhere north, maybe, which will be especially jarring since here in Texas the temperature still hovers around ninety degrees *in October.*

I'm not sure why I gravitate toward the hole in the fence. I guess it's as good a place to wait as any, and the gate to the backyard is the only thing unlocked. I put down my backpack, careful not to encroach on Dawn's gardenias, and sit beside it.

I should use this quiet time out in nature to work on my lists, but something about the heavy smell of flowers, the gentle hum of bees buzzing from bloom to bloom, and the way the air is a tinge too hot combined with the sun warming my skin makes me contemplative in a different way.

For some reason, I find myself imitating Nature Club. I take out a half-used spiral from my bag, one of my crappy pens, and begin to sketch.

I actually did some drawing when I played certain tabletop games that required you to create your own character. I dabbled a little bit, too, when I tried my hand at sketching clothes designs that I then attempted to make on an old sewing machine at the local library. We were only in that town for two months, though, which was *definitely* a good thing because whatever my future holds, it's not going to include a sewing machine. I broke like five needles and tangled more thread spools than I can count.

Based on my drawing of the gardenias, my future probably shouldn't include drawing in any capacity, either. At least not drawing where it needs to resemble something.

My flowers are too small, their pistons disproportionately large, especially when next to a bee that looks more like an angry black ball than an insect.

Sam comes up behind me a few minutes after I've turned the page and begun doodling my true artistic specialty: little 3D boxes. His shadow falls across my notebook. Even though he doesn't say anything, I know he's waiting for me to give him permission to sit beside me and the hole in the fence he created.

I've tried my best not to think too much of him today, which is another way of saying I thought of little else. In English, when Abigail begged me to leave my seat at the back of the room and switch with Fox instead, I playfully pretended I couldn't hear her, silently begging her to leave me alone. At lunch, I avoided the Sam situation entirely by going to the library to eat an old granola bar at the bottom of my book bag while browsing the shelves and wondering over and over what I said last night that made angry Sam come back.

And now he's here, normal Sam, hesitant Sam, simultaneously cooling me with his shadow and warming my cheeks with his presence, and I can't avoid him any longer.

"Hi," I say, not looking up.

"Hello."

He doesn't move to sit beside me.

"I should have given you my key," he finally says.

My boxes are turning into their own blob. I'm making them too fast, too sloppy. They resemble my bees from the last page more than anything, now.

"It's okay," I say. "I don't mind waiting."

Sam's legs brush mine as he squats beside me.

Why is this the most awkward thing that has ever happened to anyone? Is this what happens when you force planets together into the same orbit and then send them spinning away again? Are you just forever scraping to find your equilibrium?

"How was practice?" I am desperate to fill the humid air with something other than the endless droning of the bees.

Sam shrugs. I don't see it so much as feel it.

"The usual," he says.

I wait to see if I have to prompt him again or endure the sounds of the bees, but instead he adds, "There were talent scouts there today. It's that time of year."

"Oh," I say. "That's . . . exciting?"

Another shrug from Sam.

"It's just another practice with extra sets of eyes on you."

Silence falls again, and it's my turn to say something, so I say the first thing that pops into my head, which is regrettably, "You don't need to worry about me messing anything else up. We leave next week for Mom's new assignment. Two weeks at the latest if she has to sort out this rental house."

Sam doesn't reply. Instead, he reaches over and takes my pen from where I've set it on the open spiral, using its closed point to draw hatches in the dirt in front of us.

"And we're leaving for the motel after dinner tonight. Mom booked it this afternoon, so you won't have to see me around your house, either. Or at night."

In my head, I play out the pattern I know is coming: Sam will say he doesn't want me to go, that he's sorry for how weird things have been, but maybe now is the *best* time to be friends since I have to leave anyway. Everything will go back to the way it was before when I go, so why not stay here and stay with him and pretend for a while longer that we are in the before instead of the now?

Sam doesn't say any of that, though.

"There was a question on the quiz about how you handle

making tough decisions," he says. "Do you remember what you answered?"

It's such a shift from what I was expecting him to say, it takes me a minute to recall the quiz's existence at all.

"I don't even remember the question," I admit. "What were the options?"

"Check with your friends, check with your parents, go with your gut, ignore it and hope it goes away. Something like that."

"There should be a check-with-yourself option. I don't like any of those."

He sets aside my pen and begins to trace circles in the dirt with his finger, destroying his careful rows of hashes and tallies.

"Isn't that just going with your gut?"

"Not really," I say. "I mean, you can research yourself and come to your own well-thought-out, educated decisions, right?"

I mean it as a hypothetical question, but Sam takes it literally, shrugging again.

"I don't know," he says. "You can't really make decisions in a vacuum. You have to take into consideration everyone around you."

"Do you, though?" I ask. "I'm really not trying to play devil's advocate here, but aren't you supposed to make most decisions based on what's right for *you* and not other people?"

Somewhere, we've lost the thread. Somewhere, instead of explanations and apologies for last night, we circled back to the 99 percent.

"I'm not saying you're wrong in theory," Sam says. "What I am saying is that it's impossible to make decisions in a bubble. Unless you're, like, a sociopath or something."

"What did *you* answer?" I ask, not meaning to sound accusatory even though I do.

Sam is quiet so long, I think he's not going to tell me.

"The last one," he says. "The coward's choice."

Somewhere behind us, there is the faint sound of a garage door opening, the slight acceleration of an engine pulling over the garage lip, and then the sound of a car idling as its occupant gathers everything from their day.

"Mom's home," Sam says. "We should go inside."

Chapter Eighteen

Nova

Tonight we sit around a table-clothed dining room table instead of the TV. Styrofoam cartons of rice and beans and salsa are scattered around, and the fresh guacamole is already beginning to brown.

"You really didn't have to bring food," Keith tells Mom, not for the first time.

Dawn makes a moan of appreciation for her beef fajitas. "But we're glad you *did*."

"Nova and I will be heading on after dinner, but we wanted to say thank you so much for your hospitality."

Keith puts his fork down. "You are *not* going to that motel, Mara."

"*Bedbugs*," Dawn reminds us. "*Multiple* bedbug incidents."

"We'll be fine," Mom says, laughing. "We're only here for one more week, and then it's off to Massachusetts to cure some tech company of excess cereal bars and other unnecessary budget strainers."

Right. Massachusetts. I remember, now.

Directly across the table, Sam is picking at a bit of corn tortilla. We keep accidentally making eye contact with mouthfuls of food, which is embarrassing, at least to me. Sam's still wearing that carefully neutral look, the one that makes me frustrated. Like being unable to decipher him means we really *aren't* 99 percent anything anymore.

"We can't have Nova getting ready for homecoming in a motel," Dawn adds. "All the kids are coming here to take pictures on the staircase. She might as well start out here. *Much* less hassle."

"Not to mention all of your stuff is still at the rental house, correct?" Keith asks, not waiting for an answer. And then, widening his eyes at Mom a little, he says, "Mara. Please stay. Really."

Sam and I are both looking at each other, now, no chewing in sight.

They're being weird, right? my face asks.

Definitely, his face says.

* * *

Sam

Nova comes down the stairs earlier this time, but not so early that any of our parents are awake to eavesdrop.

She must have known that I'd still be awake, because she doesn't tiptoe and creep like she did last night. Instead, she comes directly to the couch and, when I don't sit up fast enough, perches in front of my feet on the edge of the cushion.

"Our parents are weird," I say, which seems a fairly safe opener.

"Yeah," she says. "They use each other's names a lot. They say them so much, it's like they're worried they're going to forget if they don't."

Which is funny because to me, it seems like Dad in particular is trying to break some sort of spell the way he says *Mara* as two syllables instead of one. Like if he can speak her name clearly enough, the curse will be broken. But it's probably just him doing his usual thing of trying to make everyone around him comfortable. It's something he and I have in common, our obsessive need to try to make everyone around us happy because if everyone is happy, they won't have any need to be angry with *us*. Which one of my therapists said was a codependency thing, but whatever it's called, it works.

"So parents are weird and you're staying," I say. "Here, I mean."

Nova nods. "Only for a week," she reminds me. "We leave next Wednesday."

"Yeah," I say. "Yeah."

She's still not looking at me, staring straight ahead at the turned-off TV.

I like looking at her, at the way her nose slopes downward, at the way her hair comes out of its messy bun like she's been tossing and turning for the short time she would have been in my bed, at the way her chest—which I swear I'm not looking at to be pervy; it's just nicely silhouetted in the light—rises and falls as she breathes.

It's weird to think of your heart moving your entire body, but I guess it does. Or, at least, Nova's does.

"It's not a long time," I say.

"Not at all. Long enough to say goodbye, I guess," she says.

Maybe it's the nighttime sounds, the kind of muted soundtrack that only has the random mechanical noises from the refrigerator, the dishwasher running in the kitchen as its instruments, but something about the way Nova says *not at all*—regretful, I think—makes me answer without much thought. Or any thought at all.

"Or long enough to say hello," I say.

Nova turns her head sharply toward me.

"What do you mean?"

"I mean we should start over," I say. "Just for a week. Just until you have to leave."

"Start over how?"

"Like . . . We . . ." I groan. The idea is so perfect in my head, and I can't think of how to explain what I mean, so I show her.

I stick out my hand. When Nova tentatively reaches back, I grasp hers and shake it.

"Hi," I say. "I'm Sam Jordan. I'm seventeen. I play football. I used to make things in woodshop, but I don't anymore. I like to draw, but I don't do that very much anymore, either. Sometimes I'm a jerk, but I'm working on it."

Nova is smiling, slow and shy, so I keep going.

"I took a quiz in school that matched me with this girl named Nova. Do you know her?"

Nova shakes my hand back, her grin white in the darkness.

"I'm starting to," she says. "There are lots of things I *think* she likes, but I'm not sure."

"What kinds of things is she sure about?"

"Holes in fences."

I'm grinning, now, too. "What about lightning storms?"

She scrunches her nose. "Used to be a fan, but now I'm reconsidering. They can be . . . interesting, though."

"Interesting good or interesting bad?" I ask.

Nova lets go of my hand. "Ask me at the end of the week," she says. "I'll tell you then."

Chapter Nineteen

Nova

Tuesday dawns bright and clear, a perfect blue sky shining with the early-morning light that reflects off Sam's truck as we pile into it, smoothies in one hand and doughnuts Mom bought in the other.

"Careful," Sam says as we walk down the path from his front door. "Mom missed a couple blueberry stems."

"What makes you say that?" I ask, before taking a swig from my straw after I buckle my seat belt and—with perfect comedic timing—something small and wooden gets lodged in my throat and I nearly choke to death on my last days in Texas and my last days with Sam.

"Oh my god," Sam says, throwing his car back in park and leaning over to slap my back. "You *cannot* die in the front seat of my car."

He slaps *hard*, football-weight-lifting hard, which makes me cough for a different reason, the reason being my spleen has been shoved into my lung.

When I finally recover my breath, eyes watering, I take a swig from a half-empty water bottle I find in his console and manage to say through my now-raspy throat, "Is it okay for me to die in the *back* seat?"

"I feel like it would break the integrity of whatever agreement we've made if you end our hello day prematurely by dying from one of my mom's smoothies."

I snort as he puts the car in drive.

"At least if I died then I wouldn't have to figure out where I want to go to college or what I want to do with my life. Or spend the *rest* of my life worrying that I made the wrong choice."

I expect him to say something goofy, because that seems to be the mood he's been in since yesterday's late-night agreement.

"I know you're kidding," he says, his tone wry, "but you *do* know it's better to be confused and alive than certain and dead, right?"

"Of course," I say.

From there, our day truly begins with what I see as an obscene amount of questions from Sam, all mundane, all non-related to seemingly anything.

"Favorite color?"

"Green."

"Favorite song?"

"Um, I don't know. It changes based on my mood, I guess."

He blinks at me. "You *have* to have a favorite."

"Mom has a playlist she's always used for long car rides. Does that count?"

Sam sighs. "I don't think you should be able to claim an entire playlist I've never heard as your favorite song, but I'll let it slide."

"What's *your* favorite song, then?" I ask.

I wait for the pause, the same fumbling around as me, but it doesn't come. Sam is ready.

"'Have Yourself a Merry Little Christmas.' The Frank Sinatra version."

"That's . . . oddly specific."

"It's supposed to be," Sam says. "It's *a song*, not a playlist."

I laugh. "Fine, fine, I suck at questions. We knew this, though. But why is that your favorite song?"

Sam looks over at me. We're at a stoplight—he hasn't told me where we're going, and I haven't asked—and his long arm is stretched out casually on the wheel and covered in the ever-present letterman jacket.

It occurs to me that these types of jackets have been around for decades, since my grandparents were alive. I wonder if my great-great-grandma ever looked over from the shotgun seat and saw a boy in this same pose with the same leather sleeves and felt her heart flutter.

"Do you really not remember?"

His question jerks me from 1950.

"Remember what?"

There's the not-cruel laugh again, the one that is finding joy in the moment, in you and not *at* you.

"You really do have a terrible memory," he jokes.

Even as he says it, though, a glimmer comes back, racing forward from the before to sit between us in this truck cab.

It was nearly Christmas. The weather was sweater-cool, the tree above us—usually full and green—barren. I had smuggled extra cookies and candy from my classroom's winter party to bring to the Snailopolis Christmas Ball we had been planning for weeks. Well, in my memory it was weeks, but looking back, it was probably a couple of days.

I remember running home from the bus stop, careening into our backyard and skittering to a stop beside the hole in the fence, eagerly setting out the cookies on brown-gray leaves so they "wouldn't get dirty" and placing a piece of candy next to each of our snail residents.

From the front pouch of my backpack—the *special* pouch with extra padding where I hid my most delicate of treasures during the school day—I pulled two perfect construction paper crowns, one big and blue, one small and yellow with sequin-gems glued meticulously into diamond shapes I drew with my ruler.

And then I sat on the ground and waited.

And waited.

And then Mom called me in for dinner, and the ants had found the cookies, and there was no sign of Sammy.

I managed to hide my sadness throughout our meal of takeout and premade Christmas sugar cookies, but the minute she told me good night and turned off my light, I cried.

I didn't think I would stop crying, in fact, until I heard music outside my window.

It was a one-story house, so Sam didn't have to do unnecessary tree climbing. Just a tap on the window, the quietest of taps, and then his foggy, cold breath against the glass as he held a small radio aloft and gestured for me to open the window.

"Come on," he said. "It's coming. The song. Hurry!"

He helped me move the screen, helped me crawl out in my pajamas and run across the yard to the hole in the fence where he had brought a key chain flashlight, the radio, and a glass of milk with an opened bag of mini Chips Ahoy!.

Now, in the safety of the cab of grown-up Sammy's truck, I want to cry just thinking of it.

"You brought more cookies," I whisper.

He's actively driving again, his eyes on the road.

"Yeah," he says.

"We . . . we danced? Is that right?"

"You insisted," he says, and his voice is doing something weird and deep, like he might cry, too. "You had watched *The*

Nutcracker at school and said dancing was Christmassy and that I owed you for missing the Snailopolis Christmas party."

It's like looking at a picture through a cloudy snow globe, the memory of Sam awkwardly holding me not quite at arm's length, but not close, as we danced with the paper crowns on our heads. (Sam's was *much* too big and kept slipping over his hair into his eyes.)

Beside us the little radio was on a local station solely playing holiday music. It was playing . . .

★ ★ ★

Sam

"Sinatra," I finish for her. "Cheesy, really."

I didn't mean for the question to turn into another walk into our past, which I've done so well at avoiding until she got here.

But for this memory, I don't mind.

I don't mind at all when it comes to Nova, I think.

"It's not cheesy," she says. "It's a classic."

"Do you remember what came on next?" I ask her, because I do.

Nova does, too, singing instead of answering.

"'*Grandma got run over by a rein-deeeer.*'"

"I think you can safely cross world-famous singer off the list of potential future careers," I say.

"Ballroom dancer, too." She laughs. "If I'm remembering correctly, it's a miracle you have toes left to play football with. How did I not break every single one?"

"I have very strong feet."

"You should have put an end to it," she says.

I don't mean to, but I say it anyway, another hallmark of Nova careening back into my life, I guess.

"Never."

* * *

I want the day to go slowly, for it to stretch out in both directions to make up for all the time we lost before and all the time we will lose after.

It doesn't.

Instead, it goes by second by freakin' second, my endless questions and our endless memories of our time in elementary school on loop until suddenly we're eating barbecue at Some Place, and Nova is ordering extra macaroni and cheese and making me try it with barbecue sauce drizzled on top, and just as quickly we're standing up as our chairs scrape against the sticky floor, and I'm walking our discarded paper boats to the trash can on the dull red tray, and . . .

"Hey, you okay?"

Nova's hand is on my arm, and I realize I'm frozen in front of the bin, tray suspended above it.

I dump the trash.

"Sorry," I say, hoping that saying something out loud will stop the loop in my head. "Sorry."

"You zoned out there for a second." Nova laughs. "It happens."

When we return to the truck, Nova moves to hop in the passenger side, but I stop her and hand her my keys.

"You want me to drive?" she asks.

I nod.

We're on the road before she glances over at me and says, "We're going to have to stop coming here if it gives you existential crises."

"We're going to have stop coming here anyways," I say. "You're leaving."

Nova closes her eyes in a blink slow enough that I know she would keep them closed if she didn't have to pay attention to the road.

"I know," she whispers. She reaches over and brushes my arm. "But we have today."

"Yeah," I say, reaching over and making myself *not think too much* about taking her hand in mine. Friends do this. We're friends. "We have today."

"And tonight!" Nova says, her voice perking up, and I can't tell if it's for my benefit or hers that she's trying to be cheery. "I mean, we're going to be in the same house and all. Maybe we can . . . I don't know. Watch a movie or something after the parents are asleep?"

The thought of sitting next to her on the couch beneath

a blanket while the rest of the house is oblivious is enough to make me reconsider the plans I already begged—*and begged and begged*—my parents' and her Mom to agree to before she woke up this morning. But not quite.

"I had something else in mind," I say.

* * *

Fox is doing a bit where he yells words and phrases that sound like he fell out of an old black-and-white TV show.

"WHAT IN TARNATION IS WRONG WITH THIS HERE TENT?"

This is yelled at full volume in Leanne's ear, who does not take kindly to the bit as she struggles to anchor her parents' fancy camping tent to the ground.

"That's *it*," she says, throwing down a pole and whirling toward Fox. "I know we agreed we wouldn't discuss our impending separation until the spring, but it's over starting fifteen minutes ago. Sorry not sorry."

"Aw shucks, Leanne. You can't go telling a fella something like that in the dead of night. He might take it personally and get his feelings hurt, wander off in despair, and get eaten by a coyote. What then?"

Leanne grits her teeth, back to wrestling with the tent. "Then I can go home and sleep in my memory-foam bed and forget this stupid adventure. I can't *believe* my parents threw me under the bus and said I could do this on a school night. The nerve."

So this is where we find ourselves, Nova and me, on what we both would like to think of as the start of our last week together but really isn't. The together part, at least.

Because it's homecoming week, and even though the powers that be always ensure we play someone easy, you *do not want to lose homecoming.* It's bad for team morale, town morale, and especially bad-looking for coaches hoping to renew their contracts for another year. Since this is the one game *everyone* is sure to turn out for, they want it to be a good one, want the daily newspaper to say something nice the next day.

So they run us into the ground all week, reminding us it's about the game, not the dance or the mums and garters, *the game.*

They say it in italics, too, *the game.* Like it's this super sacred, living thing we have to cater to. Which I guess we kind of do, bringing offerings of sweat and Gatorade to its holy alter.

Fuck, I hate it.

I've never hated it more since realizing it's the thing that will keep me from soaking up every last second with Nova until we both have to return to our normal lives, whatever those are.

I say as much to her when, thirty minutes after Leanne and Fox managed to actually set the tent up in our backyard, we pile into my truck. I drive like I'm in a school zone the whole way to the nature preserve because Leanne and Fox are in the truck bed giggling like second graders with every bump. Not to mention I'm with Nova in the cab in the dark and I want it to last.

"This week is going to suck," I tell her.

"Homecoming," she says. "I know."

"You don't, though," I say. "It's like a weeklong festival here. There's stuff to do every day, and the football guys have to help with pep rally skits, and there's extra practices and team dinners and—"

"Sammy, I know," Nova interrupts. She doesn't sound mad or pitiful. Just matter-of-fact. "Really. It's okay. You don't have to explain that we aren't actually going to hang out this week. I get it."

And even though that's exactly what I'm trying to do, I argue with her.

"No, it's not that. I'll still see you—"

"In passing," Nova interrupts again. "I've been to high schools obsessed with homecoming before. I know it's not going to be much. I knew it when we said it."

The sound of Fox and Leanne laughing—periodically broken up by either kissing or shouting when we hit potholes—fills the cab as I search around for what to say, what to do.

"It's okay," Nova says, like she can read my thoughts. "We have tonight. We had today. We . . ." She takes a deep breath. "We have our memories with the crowns and the snails and all that. It's all good."

"A good goodbye," I say, not quite believing it myself.

"Question," Nova says. "Is a bad goodbye worth a good hello?"

She says it staring straight out the window, so I answer the same way. Maybe it's because we're not looking at each other, that she phrased it like the damned quiz that brought all of this back centerfield, but I'm honest. Brutally. Plainly.

"Always," I say.

Nova doesn't reply.

* * *

Nova

It's the best of bad goodbyes.

Sam tries to get us all to hunt for southern flannel moths and has brought along a headlamp for the occasion, but Fox is not interested in scholarly pursuits tonight. He keeps flicking off Sam's lamp and making loud kissing noises in Leanne's vicinity while she swears she's going to find another date to homecoming.

It quickly devolves into a game that is half freeze tag, half Marco Polo. When we get tired—and Fox declares himself the ultimate winner—it's back into the truck and to the Jordan house with the tent in the backyard for curfew.

We take turns changing into pajamas in the downstairs bathroom, all thanking Dawn enthusiastically for the mugs of "cold cocoa" she's made—which Sam whispers are just chocolate smoothies—as we pile into the tent.

It's a massive tent. One that even Leanne says is *overdone for a family that's gone camping exactly twice and both times ended in ticks and poison ivy.* There are four little individual "rooms" that radiate from the circle at the middle of the tent, which Leanne refers to as the *common area*, as if the space is more than like five square feet.

"No limbs in the common area," she reminds us as we hunker down in our sleeping bags. "Or you will get stepped on when somebody gets up to use the restroom."

Sam's and my goodbye is prolonged by exactly this when, at around two in the morning, I get up to pee and step directly on Sam's arm.

"Um, *ow*," he whispers as I unzip the tent.

"Your own fault," I whisper back. "This was foretold."

I think that's the end of it, that he'll roll over and go back to sleep, but it's not. Every time I believe we're at the end of it—our time together, our final-we-swear goodbye—it's not.

Sam follows me out of the tent before I can zip it back, comically folding himself nearly in half to exit.

"I'm coming with you," he says, still whispering.

"To the bathroom? I think I can manage myself, thanks."

Sam clicks on the headlamp I now see dangling from his hand.

"For protection," he says. "And light."

"Protection from what?" I ask. We're already crossing the back porch and he's still fumbling with the light. "Racoons?"

"There are coyotes around here," he whispers when I open the door. "You never know with these things."

"Well, I'm safe now," I say. "Your services are no longer needed."

Sam is disturbingly alert for someone who was woken up by excessive arm pressure at two in the morning. When I go to leave him standing in the doorway, his hand juts out lightning fast, grabbing me by my elbow to keep me from turning.

"But you would tell me," he says. "If you needed me or"—he pauses and blushes—"my services?"

The way he says it, *how* he says it, standing above me all imposing and brooding with sleep still tingeing the edges of his mouth, his eyes, his voice . . .

It's enough to make me want to throw both our futures—his so carefully planned, mine nebulous and uncertain—out the window and make a new one.

I blame it on the sleep—or lack thereof—how I stand on tiptoe when he puts his hand around my waist, how I put my hand on the back of his neck in answer. And though I don't pull him down, I also don't stop him when he lowers, lowers, lowers his lips toward mine and his eyes half close and mine follow suit.

Until light floods the kitchen, Sam's dad standing in the beam of the open fridge with his back turned to us.

"Nice night for camping," he tells the milk, the cheese, the leftover casserole, and cold cocoa. "Would be a shame for it to go to waste."

Sam and I don't say a word as we scramble back out the door and into the tent, his headlamp and my need to use the restroom completely forgotten.

* * *

We don't say a word for the rest of the week, beyond a mumbled *hey* when we pass in the hallway of his house or when he comes into his room to grab an animal-print shirt for the Wednesday homecoming spirit theme, a pirate hat for the high-seas theme for Thursday, an extra pair of socks for after the team's big win on Friday.

We don't say a word when Mom and I start placing boxes into the rented trailer outside our still-fried rental home, most of them barely touched.

We don't say a word when I feign exhaustion Friday and don't accompany Mom and Dawn and Keith to the home-coming game.

And we don't say a word when Saturday, the day of the dance, rolls around and I find myself coming down with something.

I tell my Mom it's a cold, but I know it's regret.

Chapter Twenty

Nova

At first, I think the knock at the door that comes just after the hullabaloo of everyone leaving in the limo outside is Mom coming to check on me.

But Mom wouldn't knock.

"Come in?"

It's Dawn, so *a* mom, but not mine. Her eyes have that misty *Crying, who me?* look to them that all moms seem to have when their kids do anything "big," and she must barely be keeping it together after seeing Sam in his homecoming finery.

I *might* have peeked, just once, from the window.

"Hey, kiddo, wanted to check in on you. Can I get you anything? Maybe some tea? A smoothie?"

"I'm fine, Mrs. Jordan," I say.

"*Dawn*, honey. We talked about this."

I don't remind her that in less than forty-eight hours, I won't call her anything ever again. I'll be gone, a tumbleweed blowing to the next town, the next school, the next place that I pray to any god listening is a pattern holder and not a pattern breaker like this town has been.

"Sorry," I say instead. "But thanks. I'm good."

When she doesn't leave immediately, I sit up higher in bed, trying my best to look convincingly sick while I do.

"Um, do you know where my mom is?"

I ask this mostly to see if it'll make her leave my room—well, *Sam's* room—so I can mope in peace, but she doesn't. Instead, she comes to sit on the edge of the bed.

"She went for a walk with Keith. They've both been biting at the bit since breakfast to go enjoy the cooler weather." Dawn smiles at me when she adds, "They're kindred spirits in that way."

"Mom loves being outside," I say. "She always says she picked the worst job in the world because she's looking at walls all the time. It's why she tries to schedule conference calls back-to-back, so she can take her iPad and walk for a couple hours."

Dawn nods. "Keith is the same exact way. I had to explain to him that Sam wouldn't appreciate him crashing your tent party the other night, but in exchange I had to promise him a family camping trip over Sam's fall break."

She's talking to me like we're family, like she's my aunt and we're talking about people we both know in the same way. Her tone says she expects I probably know all of this about Sam's dad.

"I made promises to Sam, too," she says, her tone conversational. "Lots of them since he came to live with us, but one most *interesting* promise just this morning."

Dawn stands up and walks into the hallway, returning shortly with a dark plastic box. It's cold to the touch when she hands it to me.

"Open it," she urges. "Go ahead. It won't bite."

When I do, I lose my breath so rapidly that I wonder if I actually *am* coming down with something.

A corsage. A beautiful, light golden tuft of flowers attached to a white band covered in twinkling stars.

"He insisted on the snail charm when we ordered it," Dawn says.

I turn the corsage round and round to find the smallest snail nestled in the petals of a rose with a thin ribbon.

"He said you would like it," Dawn says. "Do you?"

When I look up at her, she's smiling that knowing-parent smile. She knows the answer. She just wants to hear me say it.

I won't.

I can't.

"I'm sick," I remind her instead.

"We're all sick of something," Dawn says, her smile broadening. "Let's hope for you it's not a sickness of courage."

* * *

Sam

There's not much to getting ready for dances for me. The suit or tux or shirt or whatever is always ready ahead of time—thanks, Mom—and it's not like I can do much differently with my hair when it's this short.

All the same, it feels wrong to spend less than fifteen minutes in front of the mirror when I know that somewhere Abigail is in the final quarter of a *long* day of preparation.

The knock on my bedroom door is welcome, really. Gives me something to do other than stare at my sock drawer and try to pick between my two pairs of dress socks.

"Come in."

Dad steps into my room, a bemused smile on his face.

"You look . . ."

"Dweeby?"

Dad shakes his head. For once, there's not a hint of joking in his tone when he says, "No, you look handsome, son. But you also look . . ."

Again, he pauses, like he can't come up with the word. He shakes his head like it's lost forever, instead stepping forward to peer into my sock drawer along with me before extracting a pair with blue and white checkers in the corner I didn't even remember I had.

"For some pizazz," he tells me. "A good rule for life: If you can make it zany, make it zany."

"That's a lot of *z*'s," I say.

He watches me as I sit on the edge of my bed to put on the socks and shoes.

"Are you looking forward to the dance?"

I tighten my laces. It gives me an excuse to not look at him when I say, "Of course. Why wouldn't I?"

"You seem a little agitated. A bit cross, maybe."

"I'm not cross," I say. "I'm just waiting for the limo. How am I being cross?"

It's unusual for Dad to be this sincere.

It's also unusual for him to not have sage words of advice lined up neatly ready to go.

And right now he looks lost, like he's trying to tell me something but isn't sure how to do it.

"I'm worried about you," he says.

That's plain enough.

"Nothing to worry about." I smile. "Stop being weird."

"You've been acting unusual for a few weeks now. Your mom has noticed, too. I would hazard to say a lot of people have noticed."

"My coaches haven't said a word," I say. "And isn't that what's important?"

I'm proud of myself for keeping the bitter out of my tone, and yet Dad doesn't look fooled.

"Sam, you can talk to me, you know. Your mom and I only want what's best for you, but if you don't talk to us, we can't—"

"There's nothing to talk about," I say, and this time it is a *struggle* to keep my voice light, but I do. I clap Dad on the shoulder, use my brightest smile. "Everything is *fine*. Stop being weird and help me keep Mom from being too sappy about taking pictures, okay?"

Dad turns to leave. I can tell he isn't happy with how this conversation has gone, but I'm shutting the proverbial door. I'll shut the literal one if he keeps going. Where is this coming from? Have I done something wrong? Something to tip him and Mom off to me being anything but grateful and happy and good?

"We always told you that you could be anything," Dad says, his hand on the door. "I hope the anything you pick is happy."

He looks at me then, and I look back but I don't move a muscle. If I do, I'll crumble, I'll tell him everything—*ruin* everything—and I can't do that to him, to Mom, to Abigail.

Dad nods once, an end to our stare-down.

"See you downstairs," he says.

* * *

Abigail is objectively radiant.

A green dress matching her green eyes, a skirt that is long enough to pass inspection by our principal, who stands at the door ready with his ruler, but short enough to show off her very tan, cheerleader-perfect legs, and she's done something to her hair that makes it smooth in the front and twisty in the back with loose long pieces that fall all around her face.

At the beginning of the summer, I might have thought she looked like an elven princess. I still think that, I guess, but it's a follow-up to the much louder thought screaming in my brain: *I am drowning*.

Part of me meant what I said when I told Nova the night of the storm, that it would have been better if she hadn't come here. Because, looking back before her arrival, wasn't I happy? Or something close to it?

But now it feels closer to misery, like all the things I told myself I was excited for are chains instead of wings.

I remind myself again and again and again that I could be in the bad part of the before, that I could still be hiding beneath my bed in a house with grimy corners and parents who don't act like parents should. I could still be—my brain balks at the word even as it says it—*abused*.

My life now is so much better. Immeasurably better. But having Nova here the last few weeks, I see how it could go beyond better, how maybe it could go to *actually happy*.

But it's impossible. And not because of my plans and her plans, but because I know deep in my bones that if I were to let myself even think of loving her, I would never stop.

Ever. No matter what.

Even if she didn't love me. Even if she thought it wasn't a good idea. If I let myself get too close to her in the way that even I can acknowledge I've wanted to since seeing her name next to the 99 percent, then I know—

"*Sammy*," Abigail squeals. "Smile! This is going to be my new profile pic."

We're beneath a balloon arch. The DJ, who probably graduated from this school twenty years ago, is on the decorated stage. There is a little table next to his setup holding the homecoming crowns for the king and queen. The gaudy purple pillow they sit upon is almost as shiny as the crowns themselves.

I smile my bathroom-mirror smile. It makes my cheeks hurt.

Fox is by my side as soon as the camera flash fades, Leanneless. A quick scan of the room and I find her with a group of band kids. One of them is shaking his head at the DJ like he's personally disappointed by his music choices. He probably is.

"Sam the man, you look *fantastic*."

Abigail's giggle is higher than usual. She's excited and her most bubbly. She's looking at the crowns, too, but pretending she's not.

"Fox, you already told him that six times in the limo."

"He deserves to hear it again," Fox says, clapping me on the back. "I mean, look at the man. A tie *and* dress shoes. You've got yourself a real keeper, Abby."

Leanne joins us then, casting a skeptical glance down to Fox's old brandless sneakers that he claims used to be white, but it's hard to believe.

"Beats the alternative," she says dryly.

Fox leans in and gives her a peck on the cheek. "You said you loved my shoes."

Leanne makes a show of rolling her eyes, but she looks grossly besotted with him when she pokes her own sneakers—new stark-white Reeboks—out from her floor-length dress.

"I love *you*," she says. "So here we are."

I forget they're a couple sometimes, Fox and Leanne. Usually they hang out alone, or just me and Fox chill together, or we double-date with Abigail so it feels like a big group more than two individual couples.

But I can't help but notice the past couple weeks since Nova arrived that they've changed, too, come into sharper focus, like when I take my helmet off at the end of a game and get my peripheral vision back fully.

They've always said they want to go their separate ways after graduation, that they want to explore the world and not feel like they have to answer to somebody this young.

Fox doesn't look young when he looks up from Leanne's shoes, though. When their eyes meet, it looks like the old kind of love you hear about in country songs, the kind that ends with front porch swings and grandkids and photo albums bursting at the seams.

Maybe they haven't changed, though. Maybe I've just noticed because Nova and I feel like we're totally opposite: saying we want to stay together—even if we don't say it out loud—but knowing we'll part.

Leanne stops mooning at my friend long enough to look over to me and Abigail and smile.

"We should dance before the brass section slips the DJ money to play show tunes that heavily feature horn. They're over there pooling resources as we speak."

"You can *bribe* the DJ?" I ask.

But nobody hears me. Leanne pulls Fox, and Abigail pulls me, and then we're dancing in a group that dissolves into a blob in my vision, which I hate. Abigail's best friend, Catherine, bumps into me with a too-loud laugh and breath that makes me think she pregamed for homecoming. Did I mention I hate this? I hate this.

For once it's not totally because I'm an ass who isn't grateful for his life. I just *hate* dancing. Especially this kind, the kind that feels like it should be this big landmark event— because a guy should look forward to his senior homecoming dance, right?—but instead feels like forced excitement, which everyone knows is the worst kind. The one time I haven't, and even then it was barely tolerable, was the Sinatra Christmas dance with Nova.

It's so much touching, and it's not like football, where you *know* which way to go and what to do. You're just supposed to intuitively move your arms and legs and hips to the beat, all while knowing everyone is watching everyone else to see how ridiculous we look.

Embarrassing. And surprisingly exhausting. And surprisingly quick. I thought it would drag on and on, but the DJ fades the show tune to nothing as our principal takes the stage and the band kids—I'm guessing the ones who paid for said show tune—boo loudly.

"Enough of that, enough of that," Mr. Pérez says, tapping the mic he's brought onto the stage. "I know you want to get back to dancing, but first, there's some business to attend to."

Beside me, Abigail squeezes my hand.

"This is it," she whispers. "Catherine says she overheard some of the teacher chaperones talking about it when she went to the bathroom and—"

"Our homecoming queen and king . . ." A dramatic pause. "Abigail Shepherd and Finnigan O'Conner!"

Nobody is surprised, least of all Abigail and Fox, but we all cheer anyway, our shouts mixed with chants of "Fox! Fox! Fox!" like the world needs to be reminded of Finnigan's *true name*.

Even I can't help but laugh when they take the stage, my perfect girlfriend and my idiot genius of a best friend. They make a big show of it, their first dance, breaking at the very end so that Abigail can come to me and Fox to Leanne.

There's lots of cheers, lots of applause for the king and queen, and then they are carted off to some other room in the school to have their pictures taken. Leanne goes back to the band bunch, and I find myself standing alone at the side of the dance floor—which turns out to be the perfect spot to see Nova Evans step through the balloon arch entryway wearing a galaxy of stars.

Chapter Twenty-One

Nova

The whole car ride to the school, Mom said over and over how pretty I look, how grown-up, how she can't believe I'm already a junior and where did the time go, and as soon as we get to the new place she's unpacking the baby pictures and we're looking at every single one of them.

Dawn and Keith took pictures of Mom and me together before we piled into the Jordans' car. The star dress I went back for the very next day because it fit too well to leave behind—wonky zipper and all—pooling over my seat belt. I learned a long time ago that if I like something, best to buy it right then because it—or me—might not be there next time.

But even though I told myself this dress was nothing more than a pretty outfit to have in my closet, I wonder if I knew I'd be wearing it with Sam's corsage on my wrist.

Whatever nerve I have for this whole endeavor fades when I step through the high school doors to a world transformed into dark corners, a dance floor crawling with dresses in every color of the rainbow, and a DJ I can barely make out on the stage.

This was a terrible idea.

I can't tell if it becomes more or less terrible when Sam—who is standing just to my right, his back against a curtained wall—seems to sense that I'm here and looks my way.

Because of course.

This is how it always is with us.

I'm suddenly terribly self-conscious of everything: the dress, the corsage, my makeup that doesn't look nearly as glam as it would if I had been given more than ten minutes to do it.

But Sam is looking at me like he's Sammy and I'm Nova and I've just brought new toys for Snailopolis.

When he moves from his spot on the wall, I think it's toward me, but it's not. Instead, he skirts the edges of the room, making his way past tables littered with clutches and snacks and abandoned plastic cups of lemonade to the DJ. Said DJ looks more than a little irritated when Sam motions for him to lean down, motions to something on his phone, and then heads back toward me.

"What did you say to him?" I ask when he comes to stand beside me. As good "first words" as any since the incident after the night with the tent.

Sam doesn't answer.

He doesn't have to, because as the dance song fades, what comes next is answer enough.

"All righttttt, y'all. We've got another donation to DJ Tommy's kids' college fund up here, which means that our next hit is brought to you by one of your fellow partiers. Everyone throw their hands up and let's all rage to"—he pauses and closes his eyes like he is physically pained— "Frankie Sinatra's holiday classic, 'Have Yourself a Merry Little Christmas.'"

Apparently I'm so late to the dance that I bypassed everyone else's self-conscious period and went straight to late-night delirium and sugar high, because instead of the groans and sounds of confusion I expect to hear, someone yells, "CHRISTMAS SLOW DANCE!" and everyone runs onto the dance floor with their partners like it's the song they've been waiting for all evening.

Sam doesn't take me to the dance floor, though. Instead, he pulls me deeper into the corner, our arms stretched out between us like a tether.

"What about Abigail?" I ask as Sam returns my hands to his neck like the days between the tent and now didn't exist.

"Pictures," he says. "For the homecoming court."

And then we're swaying, our feet hardly moving. But somehow it feels like we're flying.

It feels like a bookend, dancing to this song. Like we started and will end swaying to Frank Sinatra crooning about how our troubles will be out of sight.

Maybe it's that Sam is so handsome in the twinkling lights, how his jaw seems sharper above his pressed shirt, how his arms look tense and lovely with the sleeves rolled to his elbows and his jacket forgotten on a chair.

It feels grown up, the way he smiles but not quite as he gives me a little spin, the way my dress flutters from my legs to wrap around his in a swirl of stars.

We could be dancing anywhere—beside a fence, in the kitchen, at a wedding—and it would feel just like this: Warm and safe and like a house of the most solid brick. One that's built on a sinkhole.

I forget the sinkhole bit when he leans down and whispers in my ear, "You look like a queen."

"Of Snailopolis," I whisper-laugh back.

"No," Sam says. "Of the universe."

When the song ends and we should split apart, Sam pulls me impossibly closer, my chest against his, our hands clasped together. He holds on to me like I'm a buoy in the open ocean.

"One more," he whispers. "I paid for it and everything."

Sinatra fades, and I think it's going to be another slow dance, another song where we can stay pressed together in the corner, spending more time on the best of bad goodbyes.

But then the dulcet tones of "Grandma Got Run Over

by a Reindeer" blare over the speakers, and I can't help but laugh, the kind of full-bodied, stomach-clenching laugh that almost, *almost* makes me forget that we're not here together, that Sammy is Sam and he is dating Abigail pattern-breaker Shepherd, the homecoming queen. His *real* queen.

Sam laughs, too.

And our faces are close again, just like in the kitchen.

But this time his dad isn't here to stop us as we lean.

And lean.

And lean.

*   *   *

Sam

Kissing Nova is not like anything, at least nothing I can describe.

In the early days of therapy, when I couldn't put names to all the things I was supposed to talk about, I remember telling Dad how frustrated it made me. He suggested I try identifying emotions and events by what they are *not*. Dad said it was an art concept, one he learned from his favorite teacher in high school.

He said, "Son, sometimes drawing an object outright is too difficult, but we can trick our brains into the same result by drawing the space around an object. You can do the same with your emotions. You can list all the things you're not feeling and sometimes that's the best way to get to the bottom of it. Do you understand?"

I did. Sort of. But now I totally get it.

Because kissing Nova is not painful.

Kissing Nova is not all tongues and teeth and lips like I thought it would be. (Instead, it's soft and warm and gentle.)

Kissing Nova—really kissing her—for the first time does not happen to the tinkling sounds of harps or a romantic slow song like in the movies. Instead, it happens as Christmas singers talk about Grandpa watching football after his wife gets involved in a reindeer hit-and-run. Not exactly a Hallmark-card moment, but it feels even better, more fitting.

Kissing Nova does not fix everything. I don't suddenly have this crystal clear clarity about how to fix all my problems in life. I can't even pinpoint which problems should be addressed first thanks to the spell she weaves with just her lips. (But her lips *are* magic. How are they so soft and textured at the same time, like the smoothest grained wood?)

But maybe most important, kissing Nova does not stop time, even if it feels like it.

I know this because even as I force myself to let go of my fistful of stars at her side and her hand slides from my neck to my chest, time keeps ticking, dancers keep dancing.

And because clocks don't stop for good things—even the very best of things—Fox and Abigail return, crowns atop their heads, smiles on their faces as they come from within the curtains directly beside Nova and me, close enough that I can watch every emotion flicker across Abigail's face as she takes us in.

We're not kissing anymore, but it's clear Abigail thinks maybe we *did*. We're still leaning toward each other, around each other like we're trying to fit as closely together as possible, like *I* am trying to get lost in the Nova galaxy.

Whatever she knows, *she knows*.

In a stupid, detached part of my brain, I want to know what she's thinking. What *does* she see? Because Nova and I have spent weeks ignoring it, renaming it, reframing it, and I'm still not sure what exactly is between us.

Love seems both too loaded and too small a word. It's not big enough for what we share, but it's also too fine a point. Friendship is something Fox and I have, and it's not that with Nova. So what is it that Abigail sees?

Whatever it is, it makes her take the crown off her head and—in a surprising show of force—she throws it straight down onto the hard ground. The wire and the rest of it make a disappointing *thud*, but the fake crystals explode and skitter across the floor, radiating out from where the four of us stand like a star exploded and we're all at the mercy of the shrapnel.

Which, I guess we are.

Abigail is off like a shot, her green dress that matches my tie trailing behind her as she leaves the way she came, crownless and crying.

Something about her leaving, about her frantic footfalls as she runs away makes something snap in me.

"I'll be . . . ," I say to Nova, my words not coming. Fox stands to the side of us, his mouth still open in a cartoonish O.

I face him head-on, gesturing to Nova. "Take care of her."

And then I'm off, running out of the dance, down the hallway, listening for the sounds of Abigail crying. Somehow I know she's not outside, and I'm rewarded for following my gut when instead of tears, I hear music.

Classical music.

She's sitting against her locker in the senior hallway. Her phone is beside her, blaring something angry and violent-sounding with lots of strings and a low, repetitive note over and over. Her back is pressed ramrod straight, her legs sprawled in front of her like a little kid.

I wonder what she was like as a little kid. I wonder if she would have liked being part of Snailopolis. I wonder if I would feel differently about her if we had known each other when we were younger.

"Go away, Sam," she says.

I don't know what to do with my hands, so I put them in my pockets. I find a large piece of lint and roll it between my fingers.

"I want to talk."

"*Go. Away.* If you wanted to talk, we could have talked in the limo or at dinner or during the pep rally or after the football game or after football practices or over the summer or . . . or . . ."

Abigail's voice breaks. She turns her head away from me to dab at her face with a part of her dress.

I take the chance of her not looking directly at me to sit down beside her, not touching, but close enough she could take a good swipe at me if she wanted to.

I'd deserve a slap. Because she's right. There were so many times before now—both before Nova and after Nova coming here—that we could have talked.

But I never did.

The music suddenly shifts to something almost romantic-sounding, and this seems to displease Abigail, because she angrily stabs at her phone screen to pause it.

"What is it?" I ask.

Abigail doesn't look at me. "What is what?"

"That music."

She raises her eyes to mine. And instead of looking furious and accusatory, they just look sad.

"*Romeo and Juliet*," she says.

This is *so* not important right now, but it's the only thing my voice can latch on to, so I say, "I thought that was a book."

"Play," she corrects. "It's a play." She sighs, like she's also glad to have something to talk about that is not what we should be talking about. "It got turned into a ballet in the thirties. This is a Russian composer's score for it."

"What part of the play is this?"

The world's tiniest smile—maybe it's a grimace—turns one corner of her lips upward.

"The part where the Montagues and the Capulets meet onstage."

"Oh," I say. "Makes sense. It sounds angry."

"That's because it is."

Without Abigail's phone, we can hear the low thump of the definitely not Christmas music coming from the dance. I wait to hear the swinging open of the heavy metal doors, the thud as they bounce from their stoppers. *Someone* must be following us: Fox or Catherine or Nova.

But no. We're alone, Abigail and me, and I'm suddenly feeling very, very frightened that it will be for the last time.

"We can't break up," I tell her.

She snaps her head toward me.

"Why the fuck not?" she asks.

"Because," I say. "Because."

Abigail widens her eyes in an *I'm waiting* kind of way. When I don't add anything else, she makes an exasperated sound and lightly bangs her head against the lockers.

"That's all you've got?" she asks. "That's *it*? You seriously can't come up with anything better than 'because'?"

"I'm nervous," I tell her, my voice rising a little. "I'm . . . I don't do well with conflict."

She snorts. "Well, that's obvious."

"I . . ." I stop, take a deep breath. "I had a shitty childhood, okay? I don't want to go into it, but—"

Abigail gets up on her knees, any bit of sadness gone on her face leaving only red-eyed fury.

"No," she says. "No, you do *not* get to blame your shitty behavior on a shitty childhood. Maybe if you had *talked* to me about it during the millions of times I asked about what you did when you were younger. Maybe if you had let me *in* instead of always keeping me at arm's length, but no. I am worth more than that, Sam. *You*—despite your douchebaggery—are worth more than that. Don't try to scapegoat this, too."

"I'm not trying to scapegoat," I argue. "I'm trying to explain."

"You're trying to get out of this and still feel good about yourself," she says. "You're trying to justify everything. It's not my job to fix that for you."

She sits back on her legs and straightens her dress around her.

"I know it's not," I say. "I'm not asking you to. I just want to explain."

"Explain *what*?" she asks. "How you were kissing the new girl? How you've been acting *so weird* for weeks? Not returning my calls or texts. Like, I know you're not the most communicative guy ever. I'm not stupid. I knew that when we started dating. But you used to at least pretend to be interested in going places with me and coming to have dinner at my house and seeing me at football games. Now you just . . ." She trails off with a shrug. "I don't even know."

"I wasn't kissing her," I say, an impulse. A lie. I don't give Abigail a chance to refute it before I hang my head and whisper, "Well, I was. But it's never going to be more than that, Abigail. I swear it."

Her sigh sounds tired, not angry or sad. She's not crying when she answers, "And neither will we, Sammy. You know that, right? You've *known* that."

A huge part of me wants to beg her to stay, to beg her to give us another chance. I can *almost* see it, Nova's leaving and my recommittal to Abigail, to us, to the cheerleader-football-player dynamic, to *really* trying.

But something Nova said sticks in my brain, how we—Abigail and me—owe each other more than that, how we deserve more than that.

And we do.

"I know that," I tell her. "But I swear I haven't known. Not really. I wouldn't . . ." I stop, and cover my eyes. "Why is this so hard?"

Abigail's laugh is tinged with sarcasm, but she smiles to offset it. "Probably because we're actually *talking* for once, Samuel."

I wince. "Oof. Samuel. Not Sammy?"

I used to hate it when she called me that, but I'd love to hear it now.

"No," she says, leaning forward to jokingly slap my wrist like it's a punishment. "You don't get a pet name when we're friends instead of boyfriend-girlfriend."

That surprises me.

"We're still friends?" I ask. "Really?"

She really is beautiful. I notice it in how her hands seem to move with graceful purpose when she brings them to her face and smooths the hair back from her forehead.

But mostly I notice how beautiful it is that she is still sitting here beside me when she has every right to leave.

She inhales deeply, looking at the ceiling instead of me when she says, "Yes, Sam. We're friends. We could have always been friends, you know. *You* were the one who asked *me* out, remember? I was perfectly happy just being with you, just being . . ." She trails off.

"That's my fault," I admit. My zany socks are peeking out from beneath my pants, and I run my finger over their checkered print. "I thought it was what you wanted and . . . I liked you, Abigail. I still do."

"It *is* what I wanted," Abigail says. "But not that way. Not if you were having to . . . to make yourself want it, too."

There's a good answer to that somewhere, but I don't have it, so I give her the best one I've got, the truest one.

"I really am sorry," I say.

Abigail's sigh is long and low. "Me too," she says. "I knew something was wrong and I should have pushed harder, should have *made you* talk to me or broken things off myself but . . . I thought it could last, you know? At least until graduation."

"You don't need to apologize," I say, and it's true. "It's on me. All of it."

Abigail is quiet for a minute.

"Hey, Sam?"

"Yeah?"

"Can you promise me something?"

I pause at that. Because promises are big things. Because I've prioritized some over others when really I shouldn't have made them in the first place.

"Depends what it is," I say.

Abigail's smile is small and sad.

"If you're going to date Nova . . . don't. At least not yet."

"We're not going to—"

"You might," she interrupts. "And maybe you should, but not now. You need to figure out your shit and let her figure out hers, first. That way neither of you gets hurt because of rushing something that needs time to brew."

"I'm sorry, Abigail," I say again.

Abigail stands, offering her hand to pull me up behind her.

"Don't be sorry," she says. "Do better."

Chapter Twenty-Two

Nova

I know in the grand scheme of things the earth is billions of years old—like dinosaurs and Sistine Chapels and redwoods and whatever else old—but it's hard not to feel like this is the worst thing that has ever happened.

Which is patently ridiculous because I am standing next to an outdoor water fountain and in a dress that costs more than four individual college application fees, but still.

When Mom comes to my SOS-text rescue, I expect her to be in an Uber or maybe on the bike we cart from place to place but rarely use. But instead Mom is in the front passenger seat beside Keith, and I die a little that she hitched a ride from Sam's dad to come get me.

He lets Mom out at the curb in front of where I'm leaning against a low stone wall and gives her a look before smiling at me and saying, "I'm going to park in the student lot. No rush. Text me when you're ready for a pickup, 'kay?"

"Thanks, Keith," Mom says as she closes the door behind her. "I'll let you know."

She doesn't come straight toward me. She's doing that thing where parents think if they stare at us hard enough and long enough, they can see through our skin to the cogs and wheels of our brains.

Mom does not have this superpower. If she did, we probably wouldn't be here in the first place. If she knew me better than I know myself, she would have caught how confused I am, how lost. Right?

My stomach is still full of butterflies from watching Sam run after Abigail, my nervous system still on high alert, and it makes me angry. It makes me unreasonable, but I'm powerless to stop it.

"Why did you bring Keith?" I ask.

Mom looks startled at my tone, hard and narrow like a thorny stick, but she keeps hers even, Mom-like.

"You said you needed me," she says simply. "That was the fastest option."

"I don't want him here," I say. "I don't want *any* of the Jordans here."

I wish Mom looked confused at this, but she doesn't. She looks a little sad.

"Because of your feelings for Sam?" She phrases it like a question, but it isn't one. "Because something happened tonight and it confused you?"

It's like a slap, a hard one right across the cheek. I actually bring my hand up to my face to try to stop the stinging red in my cheeks, the deep red blush.

"No," I lie. "No, I'm just sick of it."

"Sick of what, honey?"

Her voice is so calm, and it snaps the leash on any shred of rationality. Mom and I are not the fighting mother-daughter type. We have always been on the same page with curfews and boyfriends and the stuff we're supposed to argue over. We're a team, a well-oiled machine.

Not whatever this melodramatic scene is playing out to be.

"I'm sick of moving," I say, my hands clenching into fists atop the wall between us. "I'm sick of feeling like I don't know who I am because I am never unpacked enough or settled enough or *established* enough to figure it out."

Now Mom *does* look stunned. "I thought you liked—"

"I don't know," I interrupt her. "I don't know if I did or if I just *told* myself I did because there wasn't another option. I don't know what I like or who I like or what *I'm* like because I don't ever have a chance to try staying in one place, one house, one school for more than a few months."

The tears come hot and angry without my permission. I wipe them away with the back of my hand, not caring that it's going to smear my makeup and make me look like a splotchy raccoon.

"And now it's messed up everything here because I don't *want* to go, but I have to because he has a whole life here and a girlfriend and . . . and . . ."

"And you don't want to leave because you love him more than anything," Mom finishes for me, her voice eerie calm. "Always have since you were kids, since you played in the yard after school and snuck out the window to see him sometimes when you worried."

Now it's my turn to be stunned. I never knew what it meant to be floored, not really, until this moment, but I am. I literally have to sit down, stepping back from the wall and turning around so I can brace myself against it, drawing my knees up to my chest.

The grass makes dull crunchy sounds as Mom walks around the wall to stand beside me. She stays there for a moment, looking down at me and trying to see through my head—which I'm starting to wonder if she can actually do—before sitting down and pulling her knees up to mirror my own.

"How do you know that?" I ask her, my voice quiet. "About Sam?"

She doesn't answer at first, her head tilted back, looking at the sky you can barely see because of the lights outside the school. Then she scoots closer to me so that our elbows are touching.

"Mom?" I ask when she doesn't say anything.

She sighs. Her voice even but slow like a confession when she says, "I knew Sam's dad when we were kids."

I blink, glad I'm already sitting down or else I might've fallen over.

"Um, what?"

"We were friends," she says, still looking up. "All through middle and high school. We lived next door to each other, if you can believe it."

My mind is whirling, both listening and not.

"Wait, Sam's dad-dad or his actual dad, Mr. Jordan?"

"Well, they're technically both Mr. Jordan, since they're brothers," Mom says, "but I mean his current dad. The one who *used* to be his uncle."

I breathe a sigh of relief, not sure what I would have thought if Mom was friends with the man who harmed Sam instead of the one who saved him.

"Why didn't you say anything?" I asked. "Did you know his brother lived next door to us when Sam and I were kids? How—"

"I didn't realize it was Brad Jordan until the day Keith came to take Sam home to live with him and Dawn. I didn't know Brad very well, other than he was a couple of years older than us and a bit of a troublemaker in high school, so I never recognized him. And I didn't have a reason to meet Sam's parents, since you never went to his house, never asked to."

She sighs again. "And then they were gone—Sam and Keith—and it didn't matter anymore. You were far too young for me to tell you the whole gory story after I realized the connection."

"But you didn't say anything even when Sam was over here that morning before Nature Club, either," I argue. "Why wouldn't you mention if you grew up with his dad? It doesn't make any sense."

Mom's eyes look like they're trying to tell me something.

"I didn't recognize him, and I hadn't seen his parents yet. I didn't know he was Keith and Dawn's boy. I hadn't spoken to them in years and years, not since they got married, I think. Unless you count the day they came to collect Sam and I saw them through the window."

"You were at their *wedding*?"

"Yes," Mom says. "For a time, Keith and I were friends. Very good friends."

"Like dating?"

Mom doesn't snort very often, but she does, now. "Not exactly. Something more than that, I think. Or maybe less. But something different."

She's still looking at me in that weird way, so I ask, "What are you actually trying to say? Why are you being so weird about knowing one of my friend's parents from way back when?"

Mom sighs. "Because Sam's biological father and his adopted dad—both Brad and Keith—grew up in an abusive home like Sam did."

"How did you know Sam was abused?" I ask. "I never told you that."

"You did," Mom says simply. "You were little, Nova. You didn't know that's what it was, not fully, but you talked about playing with Sam and the way he hid his 'boo-boos,' and I knew."

"And you let me play with him?" I ask. "I mean, don't get me wrong, I'm glad you did, but I'm . . ."

"Surprised?" Mom asks. "Once I realized what was going on, I did my best to help where I could, how I could, and I was *always* watching you. Always. Even if I didn't know about Sam's troubles at home, I would have watched you. I saw you two play every day from your window. I used to take my laptop and phone into your room so I could look out your window and keep an eye on you both."

It's like my memories are rewriting themselves, even though nothing has changed. I run through them like playing cards in my hand, shuffling from palm kiss to dance to car race to Snailopolis ceremony, knowing that we weren't alone beneath the shade of the tree like we thought. Mom was always there, hovering out of sight in the background I didn't know existed.

"I guess you had to," I say finally.

Mom nods. "It's my job to keep you safe."

"Did you think about telling me I couldn't play with him?"

"I did," Mom says. "But . . . I remembered Keith. I remembered how, when we got older, he said I was sometimes the only thing good about his day, a bright spot. He used to call me Sunshine when we were younger."

"Sunshine," I echo. My tears have stopped, and I am grasping at the new information whizzing by me, my anger momentarily forgotten. "Why haven't I heard about Keith before now? Did you not stay friends after his wedding? Was his wife jealous?"

Mom laughs. "Dawn doesn't have a jealous bone in her body," she says. "No, Keith and I went our separate ways after college. We kept in touch through undergrad, but the last time I saw him was their wedding."

"But *why*, though?"

Mom shoots me a look that says my tone is whiny, but I don't care. I'm whiny with curiosity.

"It just happens. Sometimes people and things from your past are better kept there than dragged into the present. Sometimes people are in your life for a period of time, and then that period ends and it's time to go on."

"But something must have happened," I argue. "You can't be *that* close and be somebody's sunshine and then . . . just . . . not."

I wonder if I said something wrong, because Mom's eyes look wet all of a sudden.

"It happens all the time," Mom says. "And sometimes it's on purpose, sometimes it's on accident, and sometimes it's in between. Sometimes it's what's best, even if it makes you sad to let go."

I open my mouth to say something, but Mom isn't done. She turns toward me, unbending her knees so she can sit up and hold my racoon-eyed face in her hands.

"And, Nova? I am so, *so* very sorry if you feel you've had to leave more behind than you should have because of my job."

She's full-on crying, now, and it occurs to me how absurd we must look sitting beside a wall as dance music rages from behind the double-door entrance to the school, Mom in her usual leggings, me in my star dress. We've never been very traditional, Mom and me, but this takes the cake.

"I should have said something sooner," I tell her. "After Seattle, after the Liam debacle and—"

"No, I should have noticed," Mom says. "It's my *job* to notice."

"But you can't do that if I hid it from you on purpose," I say. "It's not your job to be a mind reader and I wanted . . . I wanted it to keep being okay. Because I didn't *always* hate moving. But I feel like all of a sudden I'm looking at college applications and I'm supposed to be able to plan the rest of my life, and I don't know what I want that to look like."

Mom smiles. "Have I ever told you about my favorite teacher? Mrs. Mann in high school? She was an art teacher. It was a class Keith and I took together, actually. She would say if you were struggling to sketch something, you should try drawing the negative space around it. She used to say all the time, 'What isn't there is just as important as what is. Narrow in the space you know you don't need, and you're left with what it is you want.'"

I think about that for a second. "I don't really care for long-distance running," I tell her.

Mom's laugh is wet and bright. "That's a start, Nova."

We're both quiet for a minute. Inside, the music has changed enough to catch my attention, and I wonder if somewhere in the school, Sam and Abigail are making up, if they are explaining and healing and redefining their own negative spaces.

I don't know what I want, but I know I *don't* want Sam being sad and lonely when I'm gone just for the sake of feeling like what we shared—as kids and in the past couple of weeks—meant something.

"I want him to be happy," I whisper aloud, not totally meaning to, but Mom nods like she understands. And maybe—now that I know about her and Keith and their weird parallel universe to me and Sam—she does.

"And if he's half the boy his dad is and was, that's all Sam wants for you, too, my love. It's up to you to decide if he is part of the negative space or the drawing going forward."

Chapter Twenty-Three

Sam

My careful life with my careful choices unravels in the span
of two hours. One minute I'm listening to grandparents being trampled by reindeer, the next an aggressive Shakespeare
ballet, and then, finally, the oldies station playing over fuzzy
speakers in Braum's.

I can't count the number of times we've sat like this, Mom,
Dad, and me. Them sitting side by side at the booth across
from me, always with their cups of ice water and the straw-
berry shake they split between them, me with my soda and

the chocolate shake I'm never able to finish because I eat too many fries.

But usually this seating arrangement comes after football games through the years or the season I tried basketball or for lunch on Sundays the few times a year Mom forces us to go to church as a family.

Never after a homecoming dance.

Never after I've wrecked everything.

I called Dad after Fox found Abigail and me still sitting at the lockers. She went to find Catherine after giving me her parting gift for my months of less-than-stellar boyfriendhood—a kiss on the cheek.

Abigail Shepherd is more than I deserved.

And now, listening to Elvis sing about hotels of heartbreak because apparently *everything* is going to be achingly ironic tonight, I have to admit the unraveling to my parents. More than that, I have to take the rest of it down, too.

I know my parents love me. I know they want me to be happy. But I'm so far in, so deep into our plans for the future, I'm *terrified* they're going to tell me I'm making a mistake.

Because I probably am.

"Sam, eat your food," Mom says.

I decide to start with an easy question.

"Um, how is Nova going to get home from the dance if y'all are both here and her mom is trapped with no car?"

"Nova and Mara are already back at the house," Dad says.

He glances at Mom and they do that silent-exchange thing

where they have a whole conversation without me catching a word.

"Speaking of which," Mom says, her voice slow like she's waiting for Dad to stop her, "there are a few things we need to discuss."

My anxiety inexplicably lessens at this. Maybe if I'm not the only one sharing Big Things my things will seem less big.

"Like what?" I ask.

Mom and Dad give each other one more long look, Dad takes another sip of the shake, and Mom takes his hand when he starts to speak.

It's impossible, what he says. He talks about how when he and my father were kids, they used to be afraid of coming home after school because they were never sure what kind of dad *they* would find. They spent most of their time outside, avoiding the house until the last possible minute, which—Dad says—sometimes backfired because their dad would get angry at them for being "late for dinner" on nights where he brought home stale sandwiches from the supermarket he worked at.

This is not the impossible part. I know most of this from years of hearing bits and pieces of Dad's childhood, how he survived, how he understands what I'm going through, how I'm safe and he knows it's hard to believe, but I am.

The impossible part is what comes after a shuttering breath from him, a pat on the back from Mom.

"I met Mara when we were in seventh grade," he says. "Her family moved into the house next to ours, and one day when I was hiding out in the little abandoned park that bordered our fences, we ran into each other. Literally. She was going one way, I was going the other, and we were both lost in our own worlds, both running from our thoughts."

I can't keep up, can't comprehend what it is he's saying.

"You knew Nova's mom?"

"I did," he says. "She was . . ."

He looks over at Mom, who smiles as she picks up where he left off.

"Mara was your Dad's sunshine," she says. "That's what he called her: Sunshine. And they were very, very good friends."

I keep looking at Mom's face, trying to find jealousy or anger that isn't there as Dad says how he and Mara stayed friends through high school, kept in touch in college, how she came to his and Mom's *wedding*, and then . . .

"So that's it, then?" I ask. "You just lost touch?"

Dad nods. "Your mother suggested I reach out to her not too long ago, but Mara and I have had an understanding for years that we will always be friends, just maybe not close ones. I didn't want to intrude on her life when it wasn't my place."

It's not a tidal wave, exactly, the overwhelming amount of information. I don't feel like I'm drowning, but it does feel like I'm doggy-paddling in circles.

"But why are you telling me this *now*?" I ask. "Why didn't you tell me when you realized the rest of it?"

Dad takes over. "Because Nova told us what happened at the homecoming dance with Abigail, and it's time you knew. You're grown enough—have been for some time—to make your own choices about your relationships, son."

I lean my head on the table. "It's too much to take in," I say.

Mom's hand combs through my hair.

"Was there something else you wanted to tell us?" she asks. "While we're spilling our guts at Braum's?"

My head stays on the table, so Mom doesn't hear my mumbling.

"What was that?" she asks.

I mumble it again, trying the words out on my tongue where my parents can't hear to see if they feel right, the final unraveling.

Because isn't it enough to break up with your girlfriend in a high-drama situation like homecoming? Isn't it enough to find out that you are another link in the chain of history repeating itself, maybe for the last time because—again—you lucked out with the best parents in the world, you lucky son of a bitch, and shouldn't that be enough? For tonight, for this booth at Braum's, for a lifetime?

Dad tries this time. "Sam, whatever you have to say, there's no safer place to say it than here."

Somewhere deep down, I drag everything up, all the uncertainty and the way the tidal waves lash over and over again at every practice, every game, and I make myself say what I've been thinking for *months* out loud.

"I don't think I like football," I say.

I say it with my head up, my eyes staring straight at my parents so I can watch them crumble, watch them as their faces fall in disappointment and despair as they realize all the practice hours and the private-coaching instruction and money they've sunk into this was for an ungrateful, clueless, idiot of a kid.

My stomach aches with nerves as they process what I've just said, their eyes darting as always to each other before coming back to me.

They say nothing.

Maybe they didn't hear me.

Maybe they don't understand.

I take a deep breath.

"I don't want to go to college on a football scholarship," I say. And then, because I'm already in it, I keep going. "Maybe I don't want to go to college at all? I don't know. But I know I don't want to play football for four more years. Not like that."

They look at each other again, and their lack of response is *killing* me.

"Please say something."

One more glance, and finally, Mom looks at me, her face contorted in the confusion I was expecting. The outrage surely can't be far behind.

"Is that it?"

Now it's my turn to second-guess what I've heard.

"What?"

Dad tries, dipping a fry in ketchup and saying, "You don't want to play ball anymore, right? Is there something else you wanted to tell us?"

He's eating the fry like this is a normal conversation, like it's every day that his kid changes his entire life plans over the course of a few hours. Mom is, too, fighting with Dad for ownership of the little paper tub of ketchup like there isn't a whole container of it on the counter behind them.

"Um, no. That's it. I thought you guys would be disappointed."

If they were different kinds of parents, there might be hugging, maybe some more tearful confessions, some assurances that they just want me to be happy and that I should have told them sooner.

But this isn't that kind of family. This is *my* family. So instead, Mom shrugs and says, "Does this mean I can clear out all those free baseball caps that have been collecting on the mantel for the past two months?"

I blink. "I guess so."

Dad for the first time all night looks upset.

"Those are *licensed products*, Dawn. They are at least forty bucks a piece. You're not just throwing those in a bag to collect dust."

"I will if it gets them off my mantel," Mom argues. "The minute the calendar says it's November first, my Christmas decorations have to go up there."

I'm too tired to be anything but relieved that they spend the rest of the meal arguing over what is considered an appropriate amount of holiday decor.

* * *

Nova

The text lights up my phone screen on my last night in Sam's bed.

Need some company?

We didn't talk at all yesterday. Sam's parents decided to go and spend the day at a nearby state park "to reset as a family," something Mom and I were invited to join in on but declined. They also invited us to dinner, but we bowed out of that, too.

Mom and I did our own version of a hard reset, which involved Mom confessing she'd been thinking about starting her own company so that she could work remotely and no longer need to travel around. She could make her own schedule, set her own rules, and she was sure to mention that once the choice was made, we could *buy* a house. Not rent. Not have a temporary lease. *Buy.*

We could stay.

We're going to do this one last assignment, but then we're going to settle down, buy a welcome mat, and—Mom looks dubious about this, but I make her promise—get a cat.

I'm looking at adoptable cats online when Sam's text comes through.

Sure, I say.

His knock still startles me, though. Probably because it's nearly midnight and the last handful of weeks make my soul feel like it's been put through an old-fashioned clothes wringer and then ironed and then worn and then washed again.

"Come in," I whisper, my heart still racing in my chest.

Seeing him walk in and close the door behind him does little to stop the heart thing. He's all boy, all Sam now and Sammy then rolled into one.

And like so many areas of my life, I don't know what it is I want to do, what my answer will be to the question I know he is going to ask.

"This wasn't covered on the quiz," he says.

He doesn't sit on the bed like I expect him to, but instead kneels beside where I was lying before he came in, forcing me to lie back down to be face-to-face with him.

"What wasn't?"

He licks his lips. "How to say goodbye and what to do about it."

"I know," I say. "I kinda wish it had been, because at least we would have multiple choices to choose from, right?"

Sam leans a little closer. I can feel his breath when he talks.

"Well, the way I see it, we can either (a) say goodbye forever, (b) say goodbye for now, or (c) make another promise, promise."

"What *kind* of promise, promise?"

Sam shrugs. "Don't know. I was hoping you'd have an idea."

I have *so* many ideas, but the prevalent one is the one that is hardest to say, the hardest to believe.

But I make myself say it anyway.

"I think . . . ," I say slowly. "I think we have to just . . . let it happen."

He scrunches his forehead. "Let what happen?"

"All of it," I say. "The me-and-you thing, the life thing. I think we just . . . let our planets keep orbiting the sun and let everything take its course like it's meant to. I don't know who I am, Sammy."

"You're Nova," he says, like it's simple.

And maybe it is or will be, but it's not to me, not yet. "It's not fair to you or to me to make promises we don't know if we can keep," I say. "You're figuring out who you are, I'm figuring out who I am. Maybe we need to become whoever we are becoming first and then we can circle back later."

Sam is crying, but I can tell it's not the depressed kind of crying or the angry kind of crying. It's the kind of crying from a good goodbye.

"But what was this all for?" he asks. "Aren't we being stupid? Breaking the promise, promise?"

"No," I say, burrowing a little deeper into the pillow so I can use the corner of the pillowcase to wipe his eyes. "No, it's brave. It's us admitting we don't have all the negative space around us yet, so it's not right to try to include each other in the final frame, you know?"

Sam laughs at that even as fresh tears fall. "Mrs. Mann's wisdom is truly for the ages."

I chuckle. "Truly."

He stands then, going back to the door to leave, but he pauses with his hand on the knob.

"Nova?"

"Yes, Sammy?"

"One last good night kiss? Before you leave?"

I think he's asking for a kiss like homecoming, one where we got lost in each other's lips, and I'm so worried that if we do I'll take it all back. I'll beg him to text me, to call me, to FaceTime me and come visit me. I'll screw the fact that I don't know myself half as well as I want to and let it be that we morph slowly into each other instead.

Which isn't the right answer, I know, but for a blink of an eye, I can see it: us making promise after promise, promise to each other into perpetuity, never stopping to wonder if we're doing it out of habit or love or both.

But I say, "Yes, of course," and promise, promise myself I can be strong. I can stop myself from folding under the weight of Sammy Jordan's kiss.

I close my eyes, roll my lips from the pillow, and for a brief moment, I'm suspended on his bed like Snow White waiting for Prince Charming's kiss.

But this isn't a fairy tale. This is the story of the king and queen of Snailopolis, and we make our own patterns.

My eyes flutter open when Sam kisses my hand in a long, lingering caress.

"It goes where it needs to go," he whispers. "Just like us."

And for a moment, that is enough.

"Like us," I echo.

The End

All stories end. After the lore has run its course, the middle beasts have been chased to ground, and the last page is turned, the story must come to a rest, including this one.

Yes, even the tale of the girl and the boy beneath the giant oak tree and the teenagers beside the fragrant gardenias will fade. The book will shut. The fire will be put out, the teller will sleep as the moon wakes.

But the stories still matter, even after the telling. Even after the end.

The little girl and the little boy will always matter. They'll live on in the minds of those who hear their story, but they'll also live on in each other even as they are once more scattered to the mercies of space and time and colleges and lives that they will live independently of each other.

They—like you—will carry bits of the before into their nows and thens and whens and all that comes in between.

And that is enough. It has to be, because that's all that's left.

Unless

Unless lightning strikes twice. Unless the tale begins anew, same players, different stage.

Unless you are very, very lucky, and then sometimes, you get a peek. A glimpse. The Greek word that means "words tacked onto the end."

Sometimes, dear friends, you get an epilogue.

Epilogue

Sam

There are lots of reasons I should not play on the green today.

First of all, my hands are *shot*. Between traversing the length of campus at least five times a day in the cold, dry Texas air—because of course my art classes are on the *opposite side* of campus from my science classes—and the usual scrapes and cracks from staying up too late working in the shop, I shouldn't even consider staying outside longer than necessary. What I *should* be doing is driving the twenty minutes back home to dump my hands in the tub of Vaseline Mom bought and placed on the entry table I made for her—my first actually decent project from freshman year—with a pointed look last semester.

She eventually gave up on being subtle and started calling me Sandpaper Hands halfway through sophomore year.

Second of all, this is my *second* super-senior year, thanks to the whole couldn't-decide-and-panic-double-majored thing. Which actually worked out pretty well, because it turns out there are lots of jobs that like it when you have a wildlife management degree and can also make just about anything you want at your workbench.

Anyway, next year I'll be *making* money instead of having it sucked out of me each semester, and it can't come soon enough, but it's not going to come at all if I don't finish this stupid final project for my hand craftsmanship studio.

Sinking an hour into a pickup flag football game on the green isn't going to help.

But I ignore my stinging hands and head there anyway. Because as it turns out, when I'm not trying to make it my entire identity, I still enjoy aspects of playing football. My final project can wait another hour or two.

Josh and Zada are there, two pickup game repeats I see in nearly all my science classes even though we have different majors, and I recognize a handful of the others milling around in clusters.

Zada lights up when she sees me, running over to shove the ball into my hands like it's made of fire.

"Thank god," she says. "I'm not being team captain again.

Too much pressure, especially since a bunch of them are un-known variables."

"Huh?" I ask.

"The psychology students? They're here for that confer-ence. A bunch of them saw us and came over and asked to play. One of them is wearing *heels*. I don't know how she expects to make that work, so maybe try not to choose her for our team, 'kay? Because you *will* pick me for your team."

"Roger that," I say, saluting her.

Josh comes to take the ball from me, thumping his hand against it like a tambourine.

"All right, all right, all right, y'all. Let's get some teams go-ing! Psych kids? I don't know how you do things in . . . Where is it you came from?"

"Chicago," one of them yells helpfully.

"Chicago, right. So I don't know how y'all do things in Chicago, but in Texas we fight fair. House rules are three flags with one on each side and one on back, 'kay? None of this trying to put them in creative spots."

He's still going on down the long list of rules I'm pretty sure he adds to every time—because unlike me, Josh *desper-ately* wanted to play football but didn't have the knack, so he settles for being lord of the flags—when, like lightning, she blazes onto the green.

"Sorry!" she says, waving to the girl in heels. "God, I thought it was supposed to be *hot* here. Last time I was here, I practically fried, and now I'm worried I didn't pack enough sweaters."

She throws a pair of shoes at the girl in heels followed in

quick succession by a puffy jacket, a scarf, and—placing the last one on her own head—a beanie with a poof ball atop its peak.

Around the brim are knit snails, neat little rows of them, all wearing crowns.

"Nova," I whisper.

I can't help it. It's pulled from me. Like a curse, or a prayer.

I hate to admit that I folded, but I've seen her on the internet. A couple weeks ago, when my final project made me say enough shitty words that Mom would have made me gargle a whole Bath & Body Works if she'd heard, I took a break to skim mindlessly through my phone, through social media. And like always, I thought of Nova. But this time, I decided to indulge.

I made my own promise, promise to myself after we said goodbye, that I wouldn't become one of those creepers obsessed with a girl I had zero chance of ever seeing again. And except for once during my freshman year—when she was, according to Instagram, graduating from a high school in the Midwest—and a fruitless glimpse last month that only produced a single tagged photo of her with some guy on a beach . . . I hadn't checked.

Twice in five years is not a terrible track record.

And maybe it's *because* of the final project that she's here. Like I summoned her by drawing it, designing it, and then— where no one would know but me—burning a rudimentary snail into the underside of the lid by my signature.

Whether it was because I was weak and tried to find her socials or the stupid burned snail, it must have put whatever god or force it is in charge of the Nova-Sam-Snailopolis timeline on high alert, because she's *here*. Right in front of me.

Straightening her snail hat and laughing with friends. Psychology major friends.

She figured out her thing. And she looks *happy*.

I'm panicking, thinking about if I should approach her or just leave. Maybe it's best to keep some things in the past.

But even as I think it, my mind is unraveling into a future that, if you asked me, I could truthfully say I hadn't imagined until this moment. One of those Hallmark-movie futures with Christmas trees stuffed with presents and my mom making us smoothies and hers making instant coffee because she never did learn how to sit still. And there, in the corner, behind mountains of presents, is Dad holding a kid who looks a bit like her, a bit like me, and a whole lot happy.

In the golden imagined future, Nova turns from where she's thanking Mom for the smoothie and she shoots me a knowing look, the kind that says she's going to drink carefully in case of stems.

And then all of it—the after imagined future, the before of the October of my senior year of high school, and the before of our childhoods—melts away and leaves Nova Evans looking at me in the now, the same knowing smirk still on her face.

Like she could see it, too, the sliver of future.

Like she wants it, too.

"Sammy Jordan." She grins up at me. Her voice is unchanged, perfect. "What *are* the chances?"

She laughs when I pull her forward out of the line of pickup players, her hands coming to my chest to steady herself.

"I'd say about ninety-nine percent," I say.

Acknowledgments

It's my fourth time writing acknowledgments, which means it's also the fourth time that I've considered hiring a skywriter, renting a billboard, or reserving a host of singing telegrams to thank all the lovely humans who have made publishing my stories such a joy.

First and always foremost, the incomparable Thao Le. If publishing is the sea, you are the best of anchors no matter the vessel. THANK YOU for spotting flying whales in the sky with me five years ago and all the strange adventures since. I can't wait for the even weirder ones ahead!

Secondly, to Vicki Lame and Vanessa Aguirre for their editorial expertise and their forbearance in the face of many emoji-filled emails. THANK YOU also for your extreme generosity in extending the deadline for this book when I panic messaged, "I think London Bridge is falling!" and promptly took a week off to watch Queen Elizabeth II's funeral coverage. I owe y'all a lot of Whataburgers of gratitude. Long live my editorial queens, and long may you reign!

Team Wednesday is going to call for a *lot* of singing telegrams because there are so many people to thank: Sara Goodman, Eileen Rothschild, Eric Meyer, Cassie Gutman, Diane Dilluvio, Devan Norman, Lexi Neuville, Brant Janeway, Zoë Miller, Kelly South, and John Karle. Thank y'all for your endless wrangling and kindness. Extra special thanks to Kerri Resnick and Giuditta Bertoni for the most perfectly romantic (with a side of secret snail) cover ever.

To my family and friends. What a gift that there are too many of you to list. I'm so grateful we're out of the MySpace age because I'd rather write another entire novel than pick just eight of you. Thanks for making real life far more interesting than fiction. Thank you for giving me a reason to write and to not write.

And finally to Eddie and Henry, a category all your own. I love you more than Snoopy loves space, more than Buzz loves Woody, and more than all the books in the world. I'm pretty sure we're not coordinated enough to be the Three Musketeers, but whatever we are, it's the joy of my life.